Release the Virgins!

Release the Virgins!
Edited by Michael A. Ventrella

Fantastic Books
1380 East 17 Street, Suite 2233
Brooklyn, New York 11230
www.FantasticBooks.biz

Simultaneous hardcover/trade paperback publication.

Hardcover ISBN: 1-5154-2383-2 / 978-1-5154-2383-6
Trade Paperback ISBN: 1-5154-2384-0 / 978-1-5154-2384-3

First Edition

Table of Contents

Foreword
Ian Randal Strock, publisher

DID YOU EVER have one of those late-night conversations with a bunch of erudite friends, and one of them says something that sounds so incredibly clever that the rest of you start to build on it, and it turns into an idea that you all adopt as the next really big thing? Of course, in the morning when everybody wakes up (and sobers up), the idea turns out to be not really quite so wonderful.

Some background: we were sitting at a table in the bar; it was late on the third night of a four-day convention. Heidi caught a fruit fly and I said *Drosophila melanogaster*, its Latin name. Thomas translated that as dew-lover dark-belly.[1] That led him to reminisce about his time as a biology student, and at one point in the fruit fly's life cycle, he had to "release the virgins."

Michael said "I can turn that into an anthology." Thomas said "I can do that cover." And then I scratched my chin and said "I think I can publish that." Gail and Hildy seemed to come up with ideas for stories telepathically.

And now here we are.

---

1. The name drosophila comes from the Ancient Greek words *drosos* meaning dew, and *philos*—with a Latinate feminine ending as *phila*—meaning lover. The name melanogaster also comes from Ancient Greek, from the words *melas* meaning dark-colored, and *gaster* meaning belly.

Introduction
Michael A. Ventrella, editor

ALTHOUGH ENTHUSED BY the excitement of this project (as well as the great authors who said, "Sure, I'd love to do this!"), I was also worried that we would not get a large enough variety of stories to make this worthwhile.

"Every story must contain the phrase 'Release the Virgins' somewhere," I announced. I asked the invited authors to give a short sentence on how they would use the phrase, and was delighted when I received lots of different ideas.

I then opened the submissions process to anyone, but also required a short description beforehand, to assure we weren't receiving too many duplicate ideas. After a week, I amended the process with the admonition "No more unicorns!"

By the time I was ready to pick the few stories remaining for the space left, I had gone through over sixty submissions. So you're seeing the best of the best!

So now it's time to (everybody together now) *Release the Virgins*!

Valedictory
Lawrence Watt-Evans

LISBET LOOKED UP at the huntmaster's eyrie, towering above the wall of the reserve. She knew her father was up there, but she couldn't catch so much as a glimpse from this angle. She hoped she wasn't going to embarrass him—or herself. The unicorns couldn't *really* tell, could they? Not when it was just the one time. *Surely* they couldn't. That was merely a legend.

She knew a lot of girls wouldn't have risked showing up for the hunt afterward, but wonderful as her night with Kraddig had been, she was not about to give up her annual opportunity to see and touch a unicorn, to hear its musical whinny, and look into its eyes as it laid its head in her lap, just because of that one little slip.

Of course, she would only have the unicorn to herself for a moment; then the netsmen would swoop in and bind the unicorn up, holding it securely so that the surgeon could safely remove its horn, while Lisbet was pulled clear on her swing and hoisted clear of the animal's wild struggles.

Lisbet remembered how that felt, soaring safely up out of the enclosure as the netsmen secured their quarry—it was thrilling, but sad, too, knowing she would not see or touch a unicorn for another year.

The first time Lisbet had almost cried, feeling as if she had betrayed the beautiful animal, but her father had comforted her, assuring her that the unicorn would be released unharmed as soon as its horn had been removed, and that it would not hold the ruse against her—and sure enough, she was almost certain that it had been the same unicorn that followed her into the trap two years later, its horn regrown, her treachery forgiven.

Many people argued that the mere fact that the unicorns allowed themselves to be captured repeatedly, year after year, meant that they did not really mind. Some people thought that the beasts must consider it an elaborate game; others thought that perhaps they *wanted* to be rid of their horns, before they grew too inconveniently long. The scholars, though, said that the unicorns simply didn't remember, that as part of their magical purity they were incapable of recalling anything unpleasant. If that was true, then the unicorns would forget the whole thing the instant they were freed, so any suffering or sense of betrayal would be short-lived.

The girls' feelings were not so transient, but Lisbet had long since learned to live with hers. Seeing the miracles of healing made possible by the powdered horns easily outweighed any guilt over tricking the unicorns, and she had happily signed up year after year, eager to once again see one of the beautiful creatures up close, to feel the impossibly soft fur of its muzzle, to smell its sweet breath and look into the sparkling depths of its eyes.

She looked around at the other girls. Most of them were younger than she was. Oh, Tassa was still there this year—Lisbet thought Tassa intended to die still eligible, though the hunting committee did not allow any of the lures to participate after their thirtieth birthdays—but Lisbet was one of the half-dozen oldest. Most of the friends she had made in her six previous years in the hunt were gone now.

Sharan had said she would be here, but then she had met Orin and withdrawn her name. Lisbet couldn't blame her; Orin was an attractive man. Not as nice as Kraddig, but still charming.

Almost half of the girls were complete strangers, most of them here for the first time. The repeaters were eager, looking forward to seeing unicorns again, but many of the new ones looked nervous, or even scared. A few seemed downright terrified.

LISBET HAD ALWAYS considered herself a natural leader here because of her father's position, but now she had seniority, as well; she could only see three or four who had done this more often than she had. Lisbet could not resist giving a few words of encouragement.

"Don't worry," she said to them, speaking loudly. "No one wants you to get hurt—not the hunters, and not the unicorns. They're all trying to *protect* us. We haven't had an injured lure since I was a baby, when a silly twit named Filiana tripped over a root and broke her wrist." She smiled, and saw a few of the younger girls smile timidly back. "And the unicorns are so wonderful!" she continued. "You'll see. They're more beautiful than you can imagine, and you won't just *see* them, you'll touch them. You'll look into their eyes, and feel their…"

She had intended to say more, but before she could continue, her father's voice boomed out from the speakers, interrupting her. "*Are the locksmen ready?*"

Lisbet could not see the response, but she imagined it—she remembered watching from the eyrie when she was little, seeing the blue flags waving from the entrance of each trap.

"*Netsmen?*"

Those flags were orange, and there were half a dozen for each trap.

There wasn't time for any more encouraging speeches. "You all know your numbers?" Lisbet called. "You know where to lead your unicorn?"

Most of the girls nodded; she didn't worry about the ones who didn't. Most of them would manage just fine once they were out in the reserve, and any who didn't—well, most years saw a few traps remain empty, for one reason or another. In peacetime, forty or fifty horns should be enough to supply every healer in Berunia; they didn't need the full sixty-four the reserve could handle.

"*Release the virgins!*" her father cried.

Then the big doors swung open, and sunlight poured into the waiting area.

"All right, girls," Lisbet called. "Let's go lure!"

She had rather hoped for a cheer—most years at least *some* of the girls cheered—but this was a relatively somber bunch, and they surged out of the enclosure with only a little chatter and a nervous giggle or two. Eager to prove herself still able, Lisbet ran ahead of the others, scanning the forest for any signs of their quarry.

She didn't see any. Usually she spotted a flash of white or a silver sparkle almost immediately, but this time she saw nothing but trees and grass.

She had been assigned Trap #51, well around to the right; the entrance the girls used to enter the reserve was between #32 and #33, and those two traps always went to the youngest, least experienced girls, but the others were supposedly assigned at random. Lisbet glanced back to see the other girls spreading out along the wall, alternately watching for their own places and peering into the woods, looking for the unicorns.

Lisbet heard a rustle, and turned to see whether one of the unicorns was approaching her—while they could move through the forest silently if they chose, they didn't like to startle the virgins, and would usually allow a glimpse or make some small sound before drawing near.

She didn't see anything, but off to her left she heard someone exclaim, "Oh!"

Then another girl murmured, "So beautiful!" and a whole chorus of surprise and delight sounded around her as the unicorns emerged from the forest, driven by their inexplicable urge to place their heads upon virgins' laps.

But Lisbet didn't see any. She hurried into the trees, away from the wall. She imagined her father up in his eyrie, staring down, watching her failure, and she wanted to get out of his sight, under the canopy of leaves.

She could hear the other girls running on the grass, leading their prey toward the numbered traps. The cries of wonder had mostly died away, but there were still distant giggles and coos.

Then she heard the rumble and slam as the first trap closed, and the cheers of the locksmen at a successful capture. One unicorn had been boxed in, so that even its magical stealth could not save it from the ropes of the netsmen.

She looked back at the wall and saw Trap #51, the big door open and waiting for her. She saw a sunny little patch of grass beyond, with the swing for her to sit on, all surrounded by a ring of bushes where the netsmen were hiding.

A dozen yards away she saw a flash of color as a girl in a flowing sky-blue gown dashed by, and then the gate of #50 rolled into place, the locksmen quickly securing it. Another virgin had done her job, and would be hoisted out while the netsmen and surgeon did theirs.

More gates slammed; more men cheered.

And she had yet to see or hear anything of the unicorns themselves. She felt her face flush red. She had never before resorted to such a thing, but she called quietly, "Unicorn? I'm here!"

There was no response.

The horrified realization sank in that the unicorns really *could* tell, even if it was only once. She hadn't wanted to believe it, but there was no other explanation. And when she—the huntmaster's own daughter, an experienced lure who had never before, in her six years in the hunt, failed to attract and capture a unicorn—returned to the wall without having so much as glimpsed one of the elusive beasts, everyone else would know what she had done, as well. She had been a fool, signing up as a lure again this year.

But how *could* the unicorns tell? She wasn't any different, not really.

Magic, she supposed. Magic could do the impossible. That was rather the *point*.

#52 closed. The pace of traps being sprung slowed, though she could still hear the shouting of the netsmen struggling to corner their prey without harming them or being gored, and the excited squeals of girls being lifted from their traps.

And the gate of #51 still stood mockingly open, the little carefully cultivated glade beyond still empty, the locksmen and netsmen no doubt waiting impatiently. They were probably speculating on what was taking so long.

She looked up to see little Vivin from Green River being hoisted away on her swing, her face flushed with excitement and her pink skirts billowing. Lisbet thought she saw tears in her eyes, though, as she was carried away from the unicorn she had just been fondling.

Lisbet finally realized, as Vivin vanished over the outer wall, and as the shouts of the netsmen faded away as the last animal was bound, as she looked around at the woods and did not see any trace of hoof or hide or horn, that she was never going to see a unicorn up close again. She was too small to be a netsman or a locksman; those were always big men, not petite women.

And she had disqualified herself as a lure.

Tears started in her own eyes, tears of frustration and loss and embarrassment. For a moment, she wanted to blame Kraddig, and say it was all his fault, that he had seduced her, but she knew that wasn't true. She had wanted it as much as he did. Blaming him wouldn't be fair.

But then she heard a rustle. She turned, peering deep into the woods of the reserve.

And there it was—a unicorn, a *big* one, watching her, but not approaching. Sunlight sparkled from its silver horn and dappled its pure white hide as it looked directly at her.

"Unicorn?" she whispered, her tears drying. She took a step toward it.

It backed away a step and shook its head, its mane fluttering like a cloud.

She understood. She was not going to capture it. She was not allowed to touch it. But it was giving her one last look, a chance to say goodbye.

"Thank you," she said. In a moment of inspiration, she blew it a kiss.

It nodded its head, and then in a blur of white and silver it was gone, vanished among the trees.

She stared after it for a few seconds, then let her shoulders slump. That was it, then; it was over. She would never touch another unicorn, never smell one's sweet breath again. She turned, and began walking toward Trap #51.

As she approached the door, she waved to the locksman. "It's not coming," she said. "It's just me." Her eyes were welling up again, and her voice shook, but she knew she had to own up to the truth. The men might tease her, might make bawdy jokes, but it would surely be worse if she tried to pretend.

No one said anything as she walked to the swing and sat down. She beckoned to the netsmen. "We're done here," she said. "Send me up." Her throat tightened, and she was barely able to add, "I'm sorry I wasted your time."

No one answered; there were none of the crude remarks she had expected. She closed her eyes as the netsmen emerged and began coiling their ropes; she held on as the swing began to ascend.

And then, as she cleared the top of the wall, she opened her eyes and saw two men waiting for her on the platform—her father and Kraddig. She swallowed, barely able to keep from bawling.

When she stepped off the swing onto the platform she could barely stand, and for a moment she thought she might fall at her father's feet, but Kraddig rushed forward to catch her. She was startled to find herself wrapped in his strong arms, his cheek warm against hers, as he murmured words of comfort.

Looking over his shoulder, she found herself meeting her father's gaze.

"Kraddig told me what happened," he said. Even in her state of abject misery, she was dimly aware that he did not sound angry, which puzzled her.

"I'm sorry, Daddy," she said, her voice muffled against Kraddig's tunic. "I didn't believe they could really tell."

"Oh, of course they can tell! You've known that since you were a baby! How could you not believe it?"

"I don't know, I thought... I don't know," she sobbed.

"You didn't *want* to believe it," Kraddig suggested.

"I didn't," she admitted. She snuffled, and tried to stop crying. Rather to her surprise, she mostly managed it.

"Well, now you know," her father said. "You can have the unicorns once a year, or you can have Kraddig, but you can't have both."

"Well, it's too late now," Lisbet said. "I don't have a choice anymore."

"No," her father agreed, his voice gentler. "You don't."

Kraddig said, "I may not be as wonderful as a unicorn, but at least I'm here a lot more than once a year."

She managed a weak smile at that, and pressed herself more tightly against him. He *was* there all the time, and while he might not be as beautiful as a unicorn, he had uses they did not. He didn't just want to rest his head in her lap.

"He's a good man," her father said. "When he realized you were really going through with it, he came to warn me. He talked his way past the guards, and told me he would take all the responsibility and I shouldn't blame you."

"Oh, that's not right!" Lisbet said, pulling out of Kraddig's embrace. "It's very generous, but it isn't true. I'm sorry to disappoint you, Daddy, but it was as much my doing as his."

"I'm not disappointed. I thought it might be," her father said. "You've always gotten your own way."

"I didn't today. The unicorns wouldn't have me."

"But *I* will," Kraddig said, pulling her close again. She raised her lips to his, and kissed him.

That kiss lingered until at last her father cleared his throat.

"So," he said, "with that settled, is it too soon to talk about grandchildren?"

Sidekicked

Hildy Silverman

"A.L.S!" PROFESSIONAL VILLAIN Teen Devil pronounced the acronym *Alice.* "It is time to release the vir—hold up." She planted her hands on her hips and glared accusingly at the corpse dangling from the elaborate netting slung from the conveniently isolated warehouse's ceiling. "What in the biff-bam-pow happened to you?"

The corpse in question neither said nor did a thing to defend his actions. He simply dangled by the strands of unbreakable, rope-thick spider silk wrapped around his purple neck, bulging eyes fixed emptily in opposing directions, mouth hanging open to reveal a swollen tongue.

"A.L.S?" Teen Devil turned to her android assistant and jabbed her forefinger at the offending body. "What the hell went wrong?"

"Nothing, O mistress of mayhem." A.L.S. 2.0, a/k/a Annoying Little Sister (not to be mistaken for the original Alice, may she rest in peace), raised one shiny red finger. "I contacted Sidecar and conducted three weeks of text exchanges via the Right-O Valentine app." She raised a second finger. "Believing he was going to, as you fleshies say, *get some* from a fan, I lured him to this location." A.L.S. raise a third finger. "Following the pre-recorded cry for help from his anticipated lover, he climbed up into the rafters." A fourth finger rose. "Soon, he was hopelessly tangled in the Web of Death Model 169-C, where as you can see," a fifth finger completed the set, "he remains trapped as planned."

"He is not just trapped." Teen Devil pinched the bridge of her nose just beneath the red, horn-tipped mask covering the entire upper portion of her face except her blue eyes, which were heavily lined in black. "He is dead!"

"Well, it *is* called the Web of Death, my sister in the satanic."

Lord, she needs an intellect upgrade! Teen Devil glared at her mechanical minion. Enunciating each word precisely, she said, "Yes, I know that." She sighed. "Check your programming. What does it say about actually killing a Heroic sidekick?"

A.L.S. paused, wide blue eyes whirling for a few seconds. "Ah. I understand your consternation now, my lady of—"

"Enough with the… the…" Teen Devil waved her hand rapidly, searching for the right descriptor. "Fawning."

"Shall I turn off my flattery subroutine?" A.L.S. tilted her head to one side.

"Ye… well, not entirely. Just dial it back by half, m'kay?"

"Will do. You bitch."

"That's not… ugh!" She slapped her hands against the sides of her head and stomped in a circle. "Never mind, that's so far from the *ish* right now. The point is, we murdered Supercycle's sidekick! The Architect of All is going to dismantle us both."

A.L.S.'s black lips dipped down in a frown. "Technically, we did not kill Sidecar. My scan of this scene reveals that he must have slipped and fallen while attempting escape. His subsequent wriggling to regain his footing caused the rope to wrap around his neck, resulting in additional panicked thrashing, which led to—"

"His strangling his own stupid self to death. Yeah, I figured that out."

"Therefore, we are innocent of murder."

"I somehow don't think the Architect will see it that way. After all, we put him in this apparently poorly inspected trap in the first place." She wondered if she could sue EMCA, Inc., for selling her a trap that clearly wasn't up to code, safety-wise. Or maybe she would just blow up their CEO's house. She wished she could blow *him* up, but no. Then she'd have to negotiate her way out of two murders.

Being a villain became complex once the godlike Architect arrived from a world far, far away and reset the rules by which her planet was permitted to continue functioning. The Architect was willing to accept that their new world was divided into Heroics and Villains, with a smattering of ordinary folks available to save or torment.

However, the Architect refused to allow them to continue bumping each other off in pursuit of good or evil goals. Anyone who broke the One Rule—no murder—was subject to summary dismantling; a very unpleasant punishment that all newly minted Heroics and Villains were forced to observe via recordings from the early days after the Architect's takeover. The Architect observed their own rule, so the condemned didn't just die—they spent the rest of their natural lifespans dismembered hovering in a zero-gravity prison cell watching their own limbs drift past while howling in torment.

It was incentive enough to obey.

"I've been so careful." Teen Devil gazed heavenward. "I've stolen. I've vandalized. I've ransomed more sidekicks back to their Heroics since I donned Mamma's mantle than Villains three times my age."

"You are a wünderkind of woe." A.L.S. nodded approvingly.

"Damned right, sister, and I'm *not* about to go down so soon in my career over this suicidally stupid shithead!" She spun to glare into the android's gleaming red face. "So, what are we going to do about this?"

The android regarded her implacably. "We could attempt to cover up the error. Cut down the body, dissolve it in acid, and burn all evidence of the Web and our ever having been here to ashes."

Teen Devil liked that option, but then reconsidered. "Supercycle won't stop looking for his sidekick, like, ever. He'll go whining to the Architect if necessary, and then—hold up. You hear that?"

A grumble just outside the warehouse doors rapidly surged to a roar, which was soon followed by an explosion and the shriek of steel blowing apart. Teen Devil instinctively hopped in front of A.L.S. and projected a shield from her right gauntlet to protect them from the fiery tornado of flying debris that followed.

"Sidecar, my partner in propriety!" A very large, gleaming chrome motorcycle with a man's ruggedly handsome face just beneath the handlebars skidded to a stop. "I have come to set you free!"

"Fuck me," muttered Teen Devil. Her gaze darted around as she sought an escape option. The remains dangling above caught her eye, and her heart skipped a tiny, hopeful beat.

The motorcycle tilted back onto its rear tire, which split and elongated into two thickly muscled legs in chrome-colored tights. The center of the cycle retracted into an impressive six-pack of abs, while the handlebars seemed to melt and flow into a mustache framing the pouty lips of a now full-sized face. "Teen Devil. I should have known you were behind this." The human Supercycle form's voice was impressively stentorian.

As it should be, what with all the money he spent on Mamma's Diction and Intonation for Heroics and Villains class. Her mother, who previously wore the devil's mask (using the moniker D'evlin D'etails) had gone into teaching at the local community college after hanging it up.

Former Villains didn't exactly have retirement accounts to fall back on—
*especially ones abandoned by husbands who blame them for their
youngest child's death.*

"Unfortunately for your plans, I made sure *my* sidekick had a tracking
chip embedded in his flesh." Supercycle folded thick arms over his broad
chest and flashed the chrome-grilled grin that sent many of Teen Devil's
so-called peers into heart palpitations.

She nodded in a show of respect. "That was an act of genius, right there."

"Thank you." He sounded both surprised and smug.

"Almost as ingenious as charbroiling your own sidekick." She rocked
back on her heels and stared up intently.

Supercycle followed her gaze. His grin vanished. "Wha… wait. No.
No. No, no, oh, no!"

"'fraid so, Shiny Knight." She sighed theatrically. "You had me dead
to rights on kidnapping. Would have rescued Sidecar from my trap, gotten
a great photo op of you marching me off to jail in every media outlet, if
you'd just come in here like a human instead of—how did you blow open
those doors anyway? Grenade?"

"Tailpipe blast." Supercycle absently waved at his posterior. His gaze
never left the charred remains of the dangling Sidecar, an expression of
utter horror contorting his otherwise perfect features.

"So, you basically blew up everything, including that poor putz up
there, with a giant *fart*?" Teen Devil tried to suppress a giggle, although
not very hard.

"Oh, by all that's fast and furious!" Supercycle sank to his knees and
covered his face. His head shook slowly back and forth.

Teen Devil looked over at A.L.S. and winked. Seemed this was their
lucky day. They might have inadvertently killed a sidekick, but thanks to
her shield causing Supercycle's ass-blast to ricochet upward and fry
Sidecar's corpse beyond recognition, no one would ever know they were
sort-of responsible for his death in the first place.

She returned her attention to Supercycle, all hunched over and pathetic
in his grief, and the small part of her that still felt a thing or two for others
sent a twinge through her insides. *The poor, careless dope.* He probably
really liked Sidecar. Possibly raised him, at least in part, and taught him
everything he knew about being Heroic. *Maybe even considered him a kid
brother…*

She approached him cautiously. "Hey there, Big Wheel. I know it's tough to lose someone and all, but, um, you know. It was an accident. Life goes on, and all that happy horseshit."

"Do you think anyone will believe that?" Supercycle clamped two ginormous hands over her own much smaller appendage and clung as if to life itself. "Do you think the *Architect* will?"

"I mean." She tried to free her hand to no avail. "Maybe? But c'mon, you're a Heroic. It's not like—"

"Exactly!" Supercycle released her and clamped his hands against either side of his head. "It would be one thing if a Villain killed him. Their punishment would be harsh enough."

"*Indeed.*" A.L.S. managed to imbue the single word with tremendous meaning. Teen Devil shot her a dirty look.

Fortunately, none of their exchange penetrated Supercycle's self-absorbed funk. "A Heroic killing someone, even if I could prove it was a hundred percent unintentional? I'll not only be dismantled; my entire legacy will be eradicated from world history. It will be like I… like I… I cannot even bear to say it."

"Like you never existed? Entire life rendered utterly meaningless and worthless?" Teen Devil couldn't resist twisting the knife.

"Ah, you understand." Supercycle rose to his impressively full height, and regarded her eagerly.

His eyes aren't even red, she noted. *There goes my brotherly love theory.* "Um, I understand what exactly?"

"Why we have to keep this all under wraps. Hide the, ah, evidence," he pointed up, "and make sure *no one*, especially the Architect, ever discovers what happened." Supercycle nodded in agreement with himself.

"What in the actual—" A.L.S. began.

Teen Devil quickly cut her off. "Of course, because, your legacy, right? Too important to have it wiped out because of a simple mistake." *Holy shitballs, this is working out better than I could have dreamed!* "Don't worry, Rolling Thunder, I got you."

"Excellent!" Supercycle stuck out his hand to shake, but hesitated. "You do understand that I'm very sad about my old chum dying, right?"

"Clearly."

"And that this isn't about me, personally, securing my place in history as one of the greatest Heroics of all time." He spun a large chrome ring worn on his right ring finger with his thumb.

"Certainly not." She struggled to maintain a straight face.

"Because the world needs me, to believe in all that I stand for, lest they lose faith in good and succumb to—"

"Me?" She rather liked that idea.

"Well, evil in general, but I suppose if the cute li'l devil's mask fits." He tweaked one of her horns and winked.

It took everything Teen Devil had not to lodge one of her curb-stomping boots firmly in his explosive rectum. Managing to retain her composure, she replied, "Since we're all on the same page, what do you propose we do?"

"Surely you have cleaners to tidy up and remove evidence of your misdeeds."

She glanced meaningfully at A.L.S. The android regarded her blankly for a moment before releasing a robotic sigh. "I will get right on that, my boss of bosses. However, you are both failing to consider an important detail."

"Which is?" Teen Devil and Supercycle asked in unison.

"How will you explain where Sidecar is? He has been omnipresent during your crime-fighting capers, Supercycle. The press and the public will have questions if he is never seen or mentioned again."

Good point. Teen Devil rubbed her chin with a forefinger. Ideas swirled around her mind that she instantly analyzed and rejected until one showed promise. She allowed it to coalesce.

"Your mechanical minion isn't wrong." Supercycle's massive shoulders slumped.

"She rarely is." Teen Devil grinned. "I assume that, like any good Heroic, you and your sidekick maintain alter egos when you're not on duty, right?"

"Correct," he said slowly.

"And you've taken care never to let the paparazzi photograph you without masks and costumes on?"

"Well, it's not really a costume in my case," he spun the ring again, "but you've got the gist." He looked puzzled. "What are you suggesting?"

"Simple, Chrome Dome." She slapped the center of his broad back. "We're gonna find you a replacement Sidecar!"

"TIME TO RELEASE the virgins!" Teen Devil cried.

Supercycle cocked an eyebrow at her, and she shrugged. "What? I mean, they're all auditioning as fresh meat. Brand-new sidekicks. Besides, I'm willing to bet that at least half of them *are* actually—"

"Can we get on with this, please?"

"Fine." She snapped her fingers. "A.L.S., let the first one in."

The entire day, would-be after wannabe sidled, sprang, shuffled, and strutted into the office space she'd rented under a false Heroic identity, and demonstrated their abilities. Or, in many cases, a sorry lack thereof.

Maybe it was because they'd had to advertise the auditions in such a way as to not raise anyone's suspicions as to whose sidekick the tryouts were really for. Plus, they had to phrase the open call so that only young men who roughly matched the original Sidecar's height and weight applied. Or maybe it was Supercycle's insistence that the position be offered in exchange for *exposure* instead of cold, hard cash.

Whatever the reasons, after three long days, they had to acknowledge they'd not exactly attracted the cream of the aspiring Heroic crop.

"By my shiny pith helmet, how many more?" Supercycle moaned. He was in human form, dressed in plain clothes, so as not to be recognized. Teen Devil sat next to him wearing an angelic Heroic disguise, white mask obscuring her features. *He might not care if I recognize him out of uniform after our temporary truce ends, the smug bastard, but I sure as hell do.*

"There are only ten remaining candidates." A.L.S. ran a fingertip down the holographic pad projected in her palm. "Today."

"*Ugh.*" Supercycle dropped his face into his hands.

"Buck up, Free Wheelie." Teen Devil punched him in the shoulder. "One of these bozos must be sidekick material."

"Really? Which one, huh?" He flung a hand toward the one-way mirror behind which the candidates milled in a waiting room like veal in a slaughterhouse holding pen. "That kid, whose superpower is sprouting zits on every square inch of exposed flesh? Or the genius who spelled *sidekick* wrong on his application?"

"He really did think it was sidequick, didn't he?" She giggled. "Wowzers."

Supercycle glared. "This is *not* working. And neither am I, sitting in here day after day, wasting time trying to find another Sidecar. Crime isn't going to fight itself, you know."

She rolled her eyes. "There's got to be a nugget of gold among all these turds. Besides, what choice do you have? You need a Sidecar." She gestured toward one of the candidates leaning against the wall, watching the rest contemptuously. "What about that dude… A.L.S., what was his name again?"

A.L.S. glanced down at her checklist. "Q Fortier."

"Yeah, that's right. He knows Krab Maggot, or was it Crave Manga?"

"Krav Maga."

"Whatever. One of those kicky-punchy fighting styles. Plus, he's self-righteous and good looking."

"A little *too* good looking." Supercycle scowled. "That one's after more than a sidekick gig. Pass."

"Hm." She licked her lips, and reluctantly returned her attention to the task at hand. "Well, maybe the next one will fit the mask."

He leaned back in the folding chair that creaked threateningly under his shifting weight. "Right. Okay, who's up?"

They ran through the remaining ten disappointments. "No one?" Teen Devil asked after the door closed on the last one. "Not even the guy who could run really fast?"

"He wasn't bad." Supercycle frowned. "But no. None of them have that *je ne sais quoi*."

"Crime on a cracker. Okay, send 'em all home, A.L.S." Teen Devil tugged on the sides of her uncomfortable mask. "I think you've got to be a little less judgy. You're not going to find an exact replica of original recipe Sidecar."

"I know, but come on." Supercycle rose and paced in front of their desk. "There's got to be an option remotely in the ballpark!"

He twisted the large, intricately carved ring on his right hand. It glinted in the light, and now that she was up close, she saw it bore the Supercycle symbol she'd seen emblazoned on the covers of so many Heroic fan magazines and online ads.

Interesting.

"Tell us a little more about Sidecar." She nodded toward A.L.S. "Maybe that will help us choose more likely candidates, weed out the wastes of time."

"Well, let's see." Supercycle leaned against the desk and rubbed his square jaw. "He was a little older than I guess you are. Twenty, twenty-one, something like that. Short brown hair, blue eyes."

"Yeah, that's not news, Tire Fire. I did see him when I kidnapped him, remember?" She stood up and leaned across the desk. "I mean, what made him sidekick material?"

"Oh. Sure, let's see." He scrunched his features as if struggling to remember. Then he snapped his fingers. "He thought I was great. Told me all the time how he strived to become half the Heroic I am someday. He tried to come up with solutions to crimes, but was always just wrong enough that I could show him up in front of the cops. He never got upset about that." Supercycle's features softened into an affectionate grin. "Instead, he'd proclaim he was so stupid or slow, and thanked goodness for my wisdom while I patted him on the head."

"*Wow.*" Teen Devil looked over at A.L.S. and widened her eyes. The android met her gaze, and shook her head slowly.

"I know, right? Boy, I do miss his adulation." He sniffled.

Teen Devil returned her attention to Supercycle, or more accurately, his ring. "What about his abilities? Could he fight?"

"Eh, decently. He could take on most villainous minions and hold his own. He struck the right balance of helpful without hogging the limelight by winning singlehandedly."

"Gosh, he sounds pretty… yeah."

"Yeah." Supercycle nodded. "You see why he's so hard to replace."

She took a calculated risk. "So. Could he transform into an actual sidecar? Or, like, a moped?"

"What?" Supercycle laughed heartily. "No, no, of course not." He tapped the ring on his finger. "The power to become the Cycle is mine alone."

Very interesting.

She affected a humble posture. "I think I might know someone who could be your new Sidecar."

Supercycle tilted his head to one side. "Really? Who?"

She tapped the center of her chest. "Me."

Supercycle stared at her as though she'd transformed into a sentient motor vehicle. "Ummmm, what now?"

"Me." She spread her arms wide. "We've got a pretty good rapport going, plus I can brawl with the best of them… but not better than you, of course." She nearly choked on the last bit, but maintained a straight face.

"But you're a—"

"Don't say girl." She leaned in close, and all but hissed in his face. "Especially don't say it like it disqualifies me."

He raised both hands in a placating gesture. "I was going to say *villain*. You're a Villain. And, well, the girl thing is kind of significant, since Sidecar was a guy."

She settled back into her chair and propped her booted feet on the desk. "Fair enough. But I've been wanting to get out of Villainy for a while. Let's face it, crime just isn't that much fun when you're severely limited in the mayhem you're allowed to inflict. Plus…" She debated revealing so much about herself, but decided that some truth was needed to make her pitch sound authentic. "Look, I kind of fell into the Teen Devil thing because of my mother. She, well, she was really good at Villainy, until she screwed up and got followed from a bank job by a Heroic."

Teen Devil swallowed hard. "She changed into her plain clothes and went to pick up my little sister, Alice, from school. The Heroic, Lightning Lass, came flying after her. Mamma panicked and sped through a red light, and this truck just… it T-boned the passenger side."

A.L.S. squeezed her shoulder lightly. Teen Devil brushed the back of her hand across her eyes before continuing. "Anyway, that was the end of Alice, and of Mamma's career as a Villain."

"And yet you followed in her dark footsteps." Supercycle frowned.

"Believe me, my mother is *so-o-o* pissed about it. Says I'm just rebelling to get back at her because I don't… because I can't forgive her for screwing up so monumentally. Like Dad couldn't… and so I'm showing her up. By doing wrong—right."

She had to pause and swallow the lump making her voice squeaky. "But I know how this will all end." She locked gazes with Supercycle. "In prison or responsible for killing someone I love, or maybe winding up dead myself. Because even with the Architect's rules, accidents still happen."

Supercycle regarded her for several beats. "Those same accidents can happen to Heroics," he said quietly. "As I've proven."

She sniffled, and shrugged off A.L.S.'s hand. *Enough wallowing. Focus!* "Be that as it may, at least I'd be doing something good when that happened. And isn't that what you Heroics are all about? Do-gooding?"

"You really want to switch sides?" He looked skeptical. "As a Villain, you're used to leading. This is a sidekick position. Won't you miss being in charge?"

She let out a harsh laugh. "In charge of what, exactly? An android version of my dead sister? No offense, A.L.S."

"None taken."

Teen Devil rose, walked around the table, and stood before Supercycle. Grasping his thick forearms, she pleaded, "Take this chance on me. I'll wear Sidecar's mask and garb—with all the protective padding no one can tell I'm a girl. Besides, he was on the skinny side. We have a similar body type."

"You kind of do." Supercycle studied her as if seeing her for the first time. "Actually, you're about the same height, too. Similar blue eyes."

She plucked a few hairs free of her headpiece and waggled them. "Brown hair, too. Almost like it was meant to be, right?" She grinned as brightly as she was capable. "Go on, give me a chance. If it doesn't work, we can go back to the auditions."

He shuddered visibly at the notion. "A test run then? No commitment... okay, why not?"

"You mean—" She clasped her hands.

"Sure, let's try it out. Ride along with me on a Heroic jaunt tomorrow, and we'll see how it goes." As she started to bounce, he held up a hand. "I'm not promising anything yet."

"No need. I'll show you what I'm made of, you Heroic slab of metallic man meat!" She hugged him, hoping that wasn't taking it too far.

Supercycle chuckled and patted her head. "We'll work on your fawning, Sidecar."

SHE PUNCHED OUT Atomic Wedgie's second-to-last minion, then stood aside dutifully while Supercycle got the last rev in by driving directly into the Wedgie himself and launching him into the branches of a tree. The Villain screamed all the way up and then again on the way down until he landed with a *whoof* wrapped around a thick branch ten feet off the ground. He dangled and wheezed as Supercycle shifted into human form and stood manfully grinning up at his foe. "Now who's the biggest bully on the playground, eh?"

What does that even mean? She looked around at the applauding bystanders. *Geez, guess Mamma's right—say any nonsense in the right tone of voice, and everyone'll think it's brilliant.*

She realized Supercycle was staring down at her. *Oops, it's my line!* She dutifully gazed up at him, and spoke in a tone modulated to a somewhat lower register than her own natural speaking voice. "Gosh, Supercycle, you were amazing! Do you think I'll ever be as powerful as you?"

He chuckled, and patted her like a good puppy. "Maybe someday, chum, if you study hard and follow my lead."

She beamed outwardly while seething inside. She couldn't take much more of the bowing and scraping she'd endured over the past three months. *Almost at the finish line,* she soothed herself. *Just play along a little longer.*

By the time firefighters got Atomic Wedgie out of the tree and turned over along with his minions to the cops, Supercycle and temp-Sidecar were already back at his headquarters. Supercycle raised a hand to snap for his butler (*because of course he has a freaking butler. Heroism does pay*). Teen Devil/Sidecar hopped to her feet. "Hey, let me get it for you. Least I can do what with all you've done for me over the past months."

He lowered his hand and smiled. "Sure, kiddo. Vodka and tonic, with—"

"A splash of WD-40. I've been studying more than your fighting style." She hurried over to the bar just out of his eyeline across the huge living room, and began pouring and mixing.

"I have to say, I'm impressed by how quickly you've adapted to sidekicking."

"Well, I have a great teacher." She returned and handed him the drink, then took a step back, folded her hands primly, and waited.

He took a sip. "Mm." He cocked his right eyebrow. "Maybe a little heavy on the motor oil." Her heart skipped a beat. "But good." The next beat came right on time as she watched him gulp down the rest.

She held out her hand for the glass. "So, I think it's just about time we finalize our arrangement."

"Agreed." He handed it over and started to rise. Hesitated. "Uh, so, Sidecar worked in exchange for room and board here at the mansion, plus exposure of course. It's a high-profile gig, could lead to... to... bigger. Stuff." He shook his head.

"You okay, Motor Breath?"

"I think I might've drunk a little too fast. Feel... funky." His words slurred.

"No worries. I'll ask Quentin to get you some pink bismuth." She snapped her fingers.

"That... would be... ssssswellll." His chin sank to his chest. A moment or two later, he started to snore.

"Supercycle? Oh, Supercycle?" She tentatively snapped her fingers a few times under his nose. No response.

"Miss? Is there something you desire?" Supercycle's butler appeared behind her.

She rose slowly. Then she whirled around to face him. "Yeah, baby. World domination." Hopping into his waiting arms, she added, "And you."

They kissed passionately until she pulled back. Breathlessly, she said, "Okay, let's get moving, Q. That drug I slipped him only lasts about an hour."

Quentin—or Q, as he preferred—nodded. "No worries, sweetheart. We got this."

He helped her haul Supercycle's inert form to the secret basement garage, where they locked him up in the even-more-secret holding cell where he interrogated particularly recalcitrant Villains. She slipped off Supercycle's ring and stepped out.

Q pressed a button, and a steel, soundproof door slid into place. "There," Q muttered. "That's what you get for not choosing me to be your new sidekick." He glared at the cell. "Asshole didn't even recognize me when I came to audition. I've worked for him for five friggin' years... didn't even know my last name!"

She patted Q on the shoulder. "He did have one point. You are *def* meant to be a full-fledged Heroic." She caressed his firm bicep and licked her lips.

Q grinned and cupped her face. "This is gonna be amazeballs, babe. You'n'me, Heroic and sidekick—at least on the surface. Are we gonna clean up!"

She smiled, and slid the Supercycle ring onto his right finger, then took a step back. "You sure you know how to work it?"

"Do I. When you're just the butler you might be invisible, but you see everything." He spun the ring right three times, then left twice, and right two more times. An aura flared around him as the aura of the Supercycle surrounded him, melding his body into its huge, gleaming chrome form. "Vroom, vroom," he said from beneath the handlebars.

She clapped. "Awesome!"

"Hop on, let's take a ride." He leered at her.

"You got it." She started forward, then paused. "Tell you what. Why don't you take your new Heroic self out alone first? You know, get a real feel for being the Cycle. I've got some details to address in the meantime."

He conveyed a shrug by tilting forward slightly. "Suit yourself, babe. Back in a few." He revved his engine, attempted and failed to pop a wheelie, swore, and peeled out for the open road.

As the garage door auto-shut behind him, A.L.S. came out and met her in front of the cell. "Did all go as planned, o daughter of deception?"

"Sure did. Hot Stuff is the new Supercycle—and just as observant and bitter as I expected." She mentally patted herself on the back for having had A.L.S. run thorough background checks on all the sidekick applicants, thus uncovering the fact that Q Fortier was none other than Quentin, seemingly devoted but actually long-suffering butler to Supercycle. It hadn't taken much effort once she became a frequent visitor to the mansion to seduce him into supporting her plot to overthrow Supercycle and replace him with someone whose self-interests more closely aligned with her own.

Teen Devil smiled warmly at her companion. "It's actually almost a shame that I'll have to lock Q up, too. He is awfully..." She shuddered and hugged herself. "*Yeah.*"

"Then why not let him remain Supercycle? He makes an effective ally."

She dropped her arms back to her sides. "No. Q will make a fine consort—eventually, once he realizes his only choice is that or living in the cell next to ex-Supercycle's for life—but he doesn't have the stones for what I have planned."

"Revenge." The android regarded her with what would likely have been the mature version of her lost, lamented little sister's features. "It is a risky endeavor, my demonic diva."

Teen Devil balled her hands into fists. "Now that I know how to become the Supercycle, and once I have Q work out all the operational bugs, I *will* track down Lightning Lass. Hell, it'll be easy—I can roll right up to her during the next Heroic team-up, and she won't expect a thing." She smiled widely, feeling the pleasure conveyed in such an expression for the first time since Alice died. "And then I will leave tread marks up and down her crushed corpse!"

"And the Architect?" A.L.S. asked. "They will hunt you to the ends of this world to punish you."

"Let them try. Even gods have weaknesses." Her smile faded. "And highly motivated devils have their ways of finding them."

Command Decision
Steve Miller

"DALTREY'S STILL WAITING in holding orbit. Wants to know why we haven't solved this yet! If the CMEs clear up, he figures they can be down in thirty hours or so."

The intel officer, Lizardi, spoke low, just in case someone had a mic working nearby. She and her companion leaned against a rail fence at the top of steep slope, observing.

Bjarni, the ad hoc planetary specialist—by dint of being the only member of the unit to have been on world before—nodded.

"I had a note, too. Says Righteous Bispham's making noises re contract specs. Daltrey still wants to be there to turn the Nameless over to the Bispham, and the Bispham wants to Name them before they act. Silly damn—"

"Local custom," she said, with more than a little asperity.

After a pause, "You know, I think Daltrey's hoping to get out. If he gave me terms, I'd buy him out. I think we could keep it together just fine."

The specialist nodded. Everyone always says they want a chance to be the boss...

"Any luck?" she asked after a moment of silence.

Bjarni took a deep breath, recalled his mission. His sensitive nose alert tried, but disappointed.

The planet smelled green when it didn't stink of sulfur from the open wounds of the tectonics. The seacoasts and islands smelled green with the giant seasonal rafts of seaweed spicing the tricky winds, the brief plains had smelled green with the waves of grasses... and now the mountains smelled green of the great bristling tar-spotted pine analogues and the moss-walled rocks of the upswept basalt.

Years since he'd first smelled it as a traveling student. This time—he'd had a sunny tour so far instead of a war, landing ships aground and mired in swamp after taking damage from the stellar storms that had grounded both sides as far as the mercenary units went. They'd managed to get their hovercraft out of the landing ship, but were on the wrong side of the mountain when those comms went haywire and some of them crisped, grounding them the second time.

Elsewhere around the planet, the green scent might be over-ridden with the scent of blood, of burning fields, of weapons cobbled out of machines meant for peace, the ozone of overworked electronics and overlay. This mountain had none of those, being as comfortably rural as a rustic guided tour.

The scent he really sought, the one that had intoxicated him on his private visit to InAJam as a youthful wandering philosophy student, was the cusp of green fungi. He'd been entranced by InAJam; he had some of the language and loved it, and more, he loved the food and admired the people. He even dreamed about the place. The most frequent dream was about the ripple he'd seen, when the fragrance of the carpet growths intensified and the colors changed as the spores of one generation fell on the neighboring growths from another, changing them.

"I smell something," Major Lizardi said, but her nose still had a hard time separating the wood flavoring from the aroma of over-cooked meat, as she'd seen at dinner the night before. She blamed that on growing up on Surebleak, and if she survived long enough, she'd eventually get a taste for finer things, but she'd likely not be able to smell a ripple in action.

He pointed then to the small sandpile, and said "Cat!"

She wrinkled her nose then, and said "Not that!"

Bjarni's nose tried again, and he turned to his companion, shaking his head Terran-style, adding the laconic "No," emphasized with a sigh, "not that either. Not from this direction, anyway."

"They're out there somewhere! They can't let this ripple go unnamed!"

She, of course, had never seen a ripple, and while his experience was slight, hers was from training vid and poorly prepared sleep learning. On the other hand, she was right—the New Decade was to be declared within the next three days, and the local beliefs required any ripple coinciding with a new year to be celebrated and named and feted.

The politics of that new decade had brought the mercs into play; but who expected the centerpiece of the event to be stolen away so that the planet might be without their most important export for years? He grimaced, thinking of the loss to the gastronomes of the galaxy if the untouched initiates didn't come together somewhere by the appointed time.

One of the things Daltrey did right was letting the officers chance the food—their local cooks fed him very well and the others enough. While Lizardi tried the fungi, she wasn't a fan like he was. He'd tried to introduce some of the others, explaining that they were not in fact eating cat, as numerous as *they* were around, but a variation of shroom with touches of this and that protein and… and it wasn't proper meat from hoof or vat, and they grumped it, going with bar rations and instant soups. Bjarni reveled in all of InAJam, especially the food.

Which was why Bjarni was out beyond the lines on an alien mountainside with the intel officer, sniffing the winds of morning, hoping to sense a sign of the missing religionists or their rogue captors. That was what *she* was searching for. Something to tell Daltrey, some hint of how they'd win this thing, after all.

They stared down the greensides a while longer on this, the sacred side of the hill, looking toward the most distant and all but invisible sea, before turning toward the awkward pod camp in the lee of their downed hovercraft craft beside the idyllic lake.

THE OTHER SIDE of the mountain felt crowded. Soldiers guarded busily, as if they were able to do something real while waiting to be rescued, a rescue depending on one side or the other winning so that they might be either ransomed or lifted from this place by a working ship. Too, there were pilgrims, wandering through, offering food and oddities on their way up the mountain.

Bjarni smiled at a couple trying to sell him a carved bird, touching hand to forehead and speaking the local language, telling them "I have too many already. How would I feed more?"

They laughed, touched hands to foreheads in response, a real smile coming back.…

"The locals act like they know you," Lizardi said before they parted. "Are these regulars?"

Shake of the head. "They may be—there are a few I've seen before—but I think there's a special smile, almost a family expression, you get after you've sat at meals here, when you speak the language."

She shrugged. "Might be it. It feels like they all recognize you."

He shrugged back. "I feel at home here, Major. I guess it shows."

The continent they were on was basically flat, with three folds of hills that rose to these mountains—the central high point of the continent where most of the people loved the flat lands.

Here was the lake, on a high plateau with one last taller hill swathed in vines and berry brambles behind it, overlooking their camp site. That last hill also held a religious refuge, a temple occupied by a few fanatics who could sometimes be seen standing, watching the plants grow, else soothing them with water and fish-meal. Pilgrims came and went, bringing food for the most pious and taking away whatever they might learn on the hillside.

The pilgrims were also anticipating the High Ripple—something that came once every fifty standards or so, and which coincided this time with the Decade. The signs had been good that this was the year the six variants would all prove good to spore and mix...

Below their plateau, which was occupied by the few ground-side forces of Daltrey's Daggers, was another reached by a barely tended road, home of a small town. From that town was a spiderweb of paths and rough roads leading in all directions, and below that were a series of hills and lakes leading to a plain. The daily pilgrims came that way, past the soldiers, and up into the sacred.

What exactly the sacred was for the locals, Bjarni wasn't sure. To him it was the whole of the planet—a single month roaming about as a student on memtrek between course years had convinced him that he wanted to retire here. The war so far hadn't unconvinced him.

He'd written papers about his student experience. He'd mentioned the ripple, standing on a deck and watching the ground cover slowly go from one shade of green to another over a few hours as seasons changed, as the dominant fungi's spores spread themselves into the mat of greenery underlying all. When his home ship's fortunes waned and it was auctioned away from the family—they really should have listened to him!—he'd ended up destitute rather than a student, stuck on the other side of the galaxy, saved by a merc recruiter's happy offer of employment.

To this day, a dozen years plus on active duty and another three between calls, he thought of himself as exactly what he was—an administrator par excellence, a logistical technician making the force able to fight when it wanted to, with records impeccable and practical to keep everything in order, who happened to work as a merc. Intel Major Lizardi had ferreted out his connections and brought him on board for this tour.

In his pod, Bjarni went over the latest news, of which there wasn't much: The mercs on either side hadn't got permission to put the action on hold while the fighting infrastructure got put back together. Instead, Daltrey's orbital office sent multiple instances of the same command with the hopes that someone would pay attention, and the Bandoliers did the same for their side. Neither side knew the whereabouts of a certain important group of people, and neither side wanted to give too much information the other side could use. No one even knew what they looked like!

"The young people" was the phrase that kept being used, The Nameless!

Bjarni'd watched the wording of communiques, watched what weather reports they could get, and handled the ongoing inventorying and replenishment lists—not much else to do!—and waited for dinner. He wasn't sorry when he left his databases for the day, trudging down to dinner in the makeshift mess hall, with the late dusk skies already colored with the twisty bands of reds and yellows, purples and greens, as the auroras flared anew—or judging by the comm techs, continued to flare. He'd picked up a small parade of cats along the way, as he so often did here, and they walked him delicately to the mess hall, and were still there in the full dark to walk him back to his pod under the intricate flowing colors of the night.

HE HADN'T LET any cats in, but something woke him from his vague dream of shrouded faces, piercing eyes, and the sounds of local rhythms. A sound? An aroma?

Bjarni sniffed, catching nothing but ordinary scents, but he knew he had sensed something! The dream? Could he have been smelling this in his sleep? Could something have leaked in from outdoors?

He walked to the door, glanced into the night, to see the aurora, muted to slight shimmers.

He sniffed once, hard.

No joy. No joy. He'd know, of that he was sure. He'd smell when the ripple came through, know that the initiates had done the deed and melded the newest food, or failed. He'd also recall those eyes!

* * *

IN THE LATE afternoon next day, Bjarni broke from his logistical and admin duties, and walking away from the busyness, unsurprised to find the sharp-faced Lizardi out as well, standing by her pod as if waiting for him. The planet felt good to be on, even if there was war and destruction elsewhere, and being out in it a necessity turned pleasure.

Bjarni nodded at the major, and she back, and they proceeded wordlessly.

They passed by the guards on the well trodden path leading toward the temple. The rules were clear—they were not to approach the temple without invite—and none from that structure had bothered even to survey the medical camp or its denizens. Other locals had come and from the town below, seen that the strangers were settled well, and gone, some to the temple and some back down, in what was a constant stream of locals.

It had taken the guards a while to get used to the prohibition on detaining all the pilgrims who wandered through camp: it was a given that someone dressed for pilgrimage was indeed a pilgrim. It was written: pilgrims do not engage in warfare.

The compromise Daltrey had reached with his counterparts in the local forces and the other side was that people—the pilgrims themselves—need not be searched. Could not be searched.

The baskets and packs they had might be searched, but not individuals; and for that matter, standing orders said no shooting of wildlife, and especially no shooting, eating, or killing of cats. The cat thing didn't bother him, and the good behavior of the unarmed pilgrims made them as much curiosity as problem.

It was a confused war, far from Daltrey's Daggers' finest hour. They'd signed on to help defend one side's Decadal Ritual from interruption, only to discover that this wasn't a simple binary argument, but a long-brewing fight among a dozen different groups, most showing changeable allegiance. And that Decadal Ritual? If it was a failure, there'd be crop shortages or worse, and the rulers would have to find new jobs—or new heads.

This time, instead of looking down, they looked up. There were birdish creatures hovering and swooping, among which a dozen drones might have hidden had not rules demanded that no such be flown. The temple was a stark white structure with red lines painted randomly across walls; in the lowering afternoon light it was quite beautiful.

A bustle behind them then, steps nearby. Bjarni felt a twinge in one nostril. Fine spice, fine shroom somewhere close.

Alert now, Bjarni twisted where he stood. He recognized the sounds and the style of a walking caravan of people from the flatlands. This particular caravan was swathed each in voluminous robes quilted from the robes of ancestors, which had been quilted from robes of ancestors, which had been quilted before them.

They carried baskets, all sixteen of them, and they were roped together as proper pilgrims were, basket to basket as one line and person to person as another, walking—here at least—with a low chant. Cats walked with them purposefully, staying close, it appeared, to particular pilgrims, and careful not to impede the march.

Along with the chant there came another twinge. His nostrils flared, and then he realized it was probably the aromas of the pilgrim's breakfast or lunch. The song got louder as he moved in their direction—not because he was closer, but as if they were gaining in volume as they closed in on their temple above.

Bjarni finally heard some of the words, which were a hymn to the sky with its star that brought the rain. Of course it did—such things were as basic as the aggregation of mass into hydrogen and into stars, thence gravity leading to spheres collecting hydrogen and thus to atmosphere, atmosphere and solar energies to weather, weather, gravity, and energy leading to life....

As the pilgrims closed on the pair, the steady upslope breeze broke, so now a dozen scents mingled, all of food worthy of the gods. The locals, poor by galactic standards, ate as well as CEOs and potentates elsewhere. It was an easy world to live on, epicurean food literally underfoot much of the year. This caravan carried a fortune in fragile food.

The leader was a woman of middle years, as tall as he or the intel officer, carrying a basket. Bjarni had seen her the day before, and he thought, days before that as they skirted the enclave, she often the last of them, stopping from time to time to sweep the trail this way or that, or attend to a branch needing repair from their passing. In a real war zone, you'd have thought she was looking for sensors!

Today the woman was in front, and she eyed Bjarni with care. He had the visible weapon, after all, even if he didn't offer the same demeanor as the camp guards. The middle of the line of travel drew his attention. They moved at a different gait and rhythm—their own and not the leader's, despite the pilgrim ties. Their baskets were smaller than the other travelers'.

Also, the air was full now of the scent of shroom, from somewhere, the breeze muddling the source.

Bjarni stood as if rooted, watching, caught a glance from that group—"Inspect!"

Surprised, he looked to Lizardi, who had a palm up, indicating the group should stop.

"Spotted something?"

"Not me," she said, "but you're all aquiver!"

"Inspect, now!" This time she raised her voice, placing herself in front of them with both hands raised for emphasis.

Her peremptory demand acknowledged, came a ritual lining up of the group; one by one men and women alike opened their hand-woven baskets and stood back six paces from the potential contagion of the foreigners. The cats, however, stayed each and every one behind the baskets they'd walked with, and the chant went on—not by all of the walkers but by a group in the center of the pack—the most devout, perhaps.

The major raised a hand, and from the camp came several sentries on a dead run.

Inspection of the locals wasn't usually his job; his job was compliance with an astounding number of rules and regulations. He was in charge of the proper on-time filing of notices, invoices, analyses, and reports as generated by a mercenary unit working on a fringe planet, barely a hundred years this side of being interdicted for Problematic Practices.

In the center of the line, the singers were six youngsters, not farmhands by his guess. They tried to hide in the cowls of their robes as they stood away from their baskets, but they did no good job of it. Still, they kept up their chant, with at least two dozen cats arrayed among them.

Lizardi gestured in their direction, and looked at him pointedly as the fluent expert among them. The caravan leader stirred a little, as did several of the others. In an antagonistic population, he might have been concerned.

The chant continued. His nose caught nuance of fungi, cooked and uncooked, and he felt a rising awareness, almost an arousal as might happen with the very finest of the fungi-concentrates.

He closed with that section of line, and the volume went up again, though they turned somewhat away from him, at least five of them did. The sixth sang something different in the song, something he couldn't quite make out as the robes' hoods muffled words as well as faces.

Walking between the people and their burdens, he saw these baskets each had what he'd now expected, fungi being carried to the mountain. These were not piled high like the other baskets, but were mere handfuls, redolent of the highest quality.

Bjarni mimed throwing hoods back, saying in the dialect— "You may show your faces to the sun, may you not?"

Around him, a rush of the cats, flawlessly groomed, crowding him as he was nearly an arm's length from the shortest singer. He waded through carefully and—they'd not listened yet.

While the other five singers sang the chant louder, this one sang softer. He looked into the face and saw the eyes of blue-green, his breath catching. He thought, too, that the robed visage was as startled as he. Now he mimed with more force the throwing back of hoods.

As one, they did, revealing beauty. Strong faces, unlined, alert, singing—he was within touching distance now, the song loud, this one with intense eyes singing off-key a little—no, singing special words to him!

"We knew you would be here, we knew it was you, we knew you would find us, we knew that you could. We are we... we grasp the ĉampinjono!"

There was a commotion at the end of the line. A sentry stood in front of the leader, not holding her but standing between her and these six. The cats still milled about.

The six sang on, loosening further the travel robes, showing exquisite garments beneath—

The singing stopped.

Looking in his face the beauty in front of him said, "We have the husks, we have a duty. The day should be the day, friend, this day should start the ripple!"

"You will do this for us all. You have the touch! I saw your face in a vision, I knew it!"

Bjarni whirled, raised his voice.

"Major, this group. This—*force*—they walked through our lines in the guise of mere pilgrims. These six must be freed! They must get to the temple now!"

It took her a moment to comprehend the bright colored outfits beneath the robes—and the sentries bore down upon the others with professional interest.

"Mud and blood," she said without heat, seeing those arrayed before her. "Mud and blood times fifty!"

The beautiful one looked into his face and tugged at the ceremonial ropes attaching all together. "These have a magic about them. We cannot fight—if they ran we would have to run with them! We need these bindings taken off!"

Bjarni looked to the major, waved at the initiates. "We must get them to their temple—they tell us it is today. They must have their ritual today!"

He dared to hold the hand of the initiate with the amazing eyes, and showed the rope with an extra metallic thread within to Lizardi.

"We have to get this off of them!"

"I don't know the language, Bjarni. You tell them."

Bjarni turned toward the woman who had been leader, now disarmed.

"*Liberigi La Virgulojn!*" he said, repeating it in trade for all to hear. "Release the virgins!"

"ARE YOU COMING?"

Lizardi shook her head, waving at the barely controlled confusion about them.

"I can't. I'm going to organize this"—here she laughed— "and then, I have to tell Daltrey he and his friend will have to miss the party. I'm on the spot—command decision and all that."

That quickly he'd been led by the freed virgins and two keepers up the mountainside to the blindingly white buildings where several dozen acolytes cheered their appearance and rushed to preparation. The chant resumed, and grew steadily in volume as passing pilgrims collected to add their voices.

Bjarni was given over-robes to wear, and brought to a thin stone seat, where a pair of attendants appeared, bringing him a bowl of water from a stone pool shimmering in the afternoon light, that he might wash his hands in preparation to witness… what?

He sat running over his reading in his head—obviously parts of the rituals were not usually shared with commoners and strangers.

He'd not been expecting the disrobing of initiates, nor the use of the pool as a kind of game of ritual cleansing while their bags and cats sat nearby.

The clean and naked virgins leapt from the waters of the sacred pool with no hesitation, charging among the cats to grab handfuls of the colorful fungus from their baskets. And then, full of excitement, rushed to their bower, holding hands and chattering as they flung themselves within.

The coreligionists outside began to sing louder, and two found drums.

Laughter rose from the bower and became passionate, and more such laughter rang out over the mountainside, nearly smothered by the chants.

The drumming and singing went on until there was yet another burst of passion. The shadows on the long lawn lengthened, and now the inside of the bower lit up as column after column collected the setting sun's rays and directed them within.

There was singing from within, a shout of cheer. Shortly after the six initiates emerged, one robed in red, one in yellow, one in green, one in blue, one in orange, and the last in purple, each collecting their baskets and the escort of cats.

They came as a group to Bjarni, and he stood.

"We, we get to stay here tonight," the one in purple said. "We are not done yet!"

The others laughed in agreement, quick glances stolen among themselves.

"The other part is not done yet, either. We need to collate these ĉampinjono, and we wish you, Bjarni, to help. Walk with us…"

Walking was not easy—the cats were back, weaving between feet, prancing with tails held high, as if they too were part of the secrets here.

They walked to the small apron of green beside the temple—from here they looked down the mountainsides that led to the hills that led to the flat lands, the camp and town behind the temple, unseen.

"Hold your hands together, thus!"

The one in purple made a wide bowl of his hands.

Bjarni followed suit, watching as the youths suppressed smiles, the solemnity growing on every face.

"Hold as that. We shall each place ĉampinjono upon your hands. These are not poison!"

Bjarni smiled. Yes, many of the mercs had been warned not to eat random plants from this place—but these, these he could smell already!

The virgins—or perhaps the not-virgins—crowded around, discussing in quiet voices, each taking two of the stringy fungi from their baskets and holding them above Bjarni's hands. It was hard for him to not snatch one, to bury his face in one, to eat it raw. Overpowering—

"When we drop these in your hands, you must squeeze your hands together, squeeze tightly, and hold them. It may be a moment, it may be ten. Warm them, but do not look. When they sing, you may open your hands and free them. Do you understand?"

He looked from face to face, all beautiful in their own way, all serious, all eager.

He nodded.

That was the moment they rushed to him. Treasure fell into his hands, the ĉampinjono, that was the moment he closed his eyes and squeezed. The fungi moved within his hands, as if they lived—but of course they lived! His hands did feel warm and warmer. Sing?

He opened his eyes, seeking direction. The initiates crowded each other, repeating for each other what they'd done for him.

Now his hands felt more movement, and a vibration, heat. From within his grasped hands came a weird sighing, and then a clear, birdlike sing-song, heard through the chanting still going on. He closed his eyes, sure he could smell the most wonderful smell in the universe—the chirping increased!

Startled, he opened his hands to find not birds but flat rust-golden flakes, vibrating, expanding until they filled his hands to overflowing.

"You may blow them away now, Bjarni. Release The Virgins!"

He did that, and saw that each of the initiates was doing the same—opening hands and releasing these…

As the flakes hit the carpet of green, a great sighing went up. The green turned gold here and there, the spot at his feet and in front of him sighed louder. The rusty gold spread, and a hand-width, two, three, five, the length of his body… the green appearing to flee before it now, the sigh getting louder until the lawn was singing and the colors rushed out into the world, rushing down mountainside at breakneck speed, the world full of the undercurrent of sound, the familiar aroma fascinating, exactly that from his dream.

The six approached then, each rubbing their hands across his, smiling together at the slight gold shimmer of spoor-stuff that all seven now shared finger tip to wrist.

There was an awkward moment then, as the initiates looked one from another.

The one with the intense eyes looked at him, perhaps sternly.

"This ripple is Bjarni's Ripple, now and forever. By morning, it will be so around the world. You have freed us to revivify the ĉampinjono—and we will remember always the lesson you brought! It will be said for every ripple. Release the Virgins!"

Are You There, Cthulhu? It's Me, Judy
Beth W. Patterson

"THEY WERE BRED in Australia, you know." Roxy's nostrils flared in self-righteousness, spreading her freckles like a drop of detergent in a grease pan. "That's why they can jump on their hind legs. They're trained to scare away the kangaroos." She imperiously tossed her mane of black curls out of her eyes.

Faustine and I exchanged furtive glances before returning our attention to the stocky beast: a wingless Pegasus intent on gobbling up every bit of vegetation in sight. This morning was shaping up to be like an unheralded Christmas. We had expected to do the usual routine of feeding the horses, and we'd found this miracle on four legs having seemingly materialized overnight. Eighth graders like us were prone to wild flights of imagination, but we couldn't figure out what a horse this special was doing at Camp Gunigugu. Even for our equestrian group, this creature seemed out of our league.

Our unit counselor, a kindly corn-fed woman who went by the name of Stitch, had briefed us on our new arrival, but had broken the bad news that riding him was out of the question. We three had theories, having read Marguerite Henry's *White Stallion of Lipizza*. Until now, the only real excitement had been a visit from the blacksmith, who had demonstrated how to reset a horse's shoes. This might have been only mildly interesting had he not displayed a full four inches of butt crack every time he bent over. But now we were witnessing something magical.

I knew I was going to lose the bet with Faustine by correcting Roxy's crackpot facts first. Underestimating my patient ginger-haired friend had been a mistake. But after three weeks of listening to Roxy shoot off her wiseacre attitude with completely erroneous minutiae, I couldn't stand it anymore.

I licked my lips. "Austria, not Australia," I muttered. "Lipizzan horses are from Austria. You know, Europe. They are considered to be national treasures." I was no expert on the breed, but I was pretty sure that at least that much was accurate.

"If Slipper's really a Lipizzan, would anyone even notice?" Faustine wondered aloud. She had a point. We attendees had chosen this program because we didn't have horses of our own and were just starved for saddles and soft noses to pet, not caring if the animals had three legs. At this point, it was easy to conveniently perceive a grade horse as an Arabian.

At age thirteen, I still believed that all things were possible, but decided I'd rather get some answers than speculate. "Busey would know," I murmured.

"You just want another chance to talk to him!" jeered Roxy, sticking her tongue out at me. The riding counselor's camp name was Bucephalus, but his moniker had to be immediately compromised for the youngest campers to pronounce. A scholarly cowboy, Busey could rope a steer as easily as he could regale us with every Greek myth corresponding to the constellations overhead. He was also devastatingly handsome, and I had made up my mind that I was going to marry him someday.

Faustine saved me by chiming in, "It just doesn't seem fair. Why keep this horse here if we can't ride him?"

I couldn't resist a challenge what I saw one. I held my tongue, but my mental cogwheels were in motion as Stitch led us all to the common meeting hall, Lame Deer Lodge, for lunch. Along the rust-red dirt path lined with pine trees, by the time we'd trod the half-mile, I already had dreams of flight.

THE CABIN I shared with Faustine and Roxy was sacrosanct during our post-lunchtime leisure hour, and Faustine often found excuses to get Roxy out of there during that time. On principle, I had resolved that would never lose my temper at Roxy. As one of the tallest girls in my school, I championed my classmates who were often bullied. My blonde hair made me appear to be more of an innocuous buffer (even with a permanent bright green streak down my temple, which I pretended was a mark of the Great Old Ones, even though it really came from my addiction to the over-chlorinated swimming pool).

Whenever the other two would leave the cabin together, I'd try doing my pectoral exercises in private, in hopes of expediting my development into womanhood. Bending my arms, I'd swing my elbows in and out, chanting under my breath, "Get back, get back, I must increase my rack!" But of course I'd inevitably start to feel silly and switch to pushups, whispering, *"Ph'nglui mglw'nafh Cthulhu R'lyeh wgah'nagl fhtagn."*

That afternoon I worked extra hard, thoughts of riding Slipper dancing in my head. I even managed to have a silent word with my master before afternoon riding class.

Are you there, Cthulhu? It's me, Judy. I know you must be awfully busy in the mighty city of R'lyeh, and might not hear my thoughts with you being dead and all. But my friends don't understand me, and I really think that I could ride Slipper if the counselors would only give me a chance. People say that you will be ready for resurrection when the stars are ready. Don't you think the stars are ready for me too, Cthulhu?

My friends don't know that I actually talk to Cthulhu. I don't want them to think that I'm some sort of goody-two-shoes. On day five, Roxy had overheard me mumbling his name to myself, so I'd lied and said that I wished I could visit Honolulu, and how awesome Hawaii must be. She snorted, "Why would you want to leave the country?" I'd bitten the inside of my cheek and said nothing.

HAVING EATEN, RESTED, and communicated with my tentacled master, I felt invincible in the riding ring.

"Y'all try cantering 'em now!" Busey's wish was my command. I clapped my heels against my mount, Booker, a one-eyed sable gelding with a white star. He eased into the smooth, rolling gait along with the other horses. Around and around the ring we went, while my ancient iPod offered faint background mood music through the small speakers on the light posts. I'd loaded some of my favorite music: Ani DiFranco, The Virgins, Blue Öyster Cult, and the Lovecraft-inspired The Darkest of the Hillside Thickets. Booker's gently rocking canter was perfectly in time with The Virgins' "One Week of Danger." Between this low-level flying and fleeting glances at Busey, I wanted this to last forever.

The crunch of boots on gravel marred my slice of heaven. "Youse know there's no riding tomorrow, dontcha?" said a new voice. The tiny weasel-faced man who was arts and crafts director chose to interrupt this slice of perfection by animatedly approaching the ring, causing a few of the horses to shy. I remembered that his camp name was

Rimbaud, like the painter, but his ham-fisted demeanor led everyone to think it was Rambo. Busey scowled, called for a halt, and met Rambo at the gate.

"Total solar eclipse, and all activities are canceled," sneered Rambo. "Aren't you concerned that the horses will act funny?"

"Eclipses don't bother horses," Busey replied, unperturbed. "They confuse chickens, and songbirds go quiet for the few minutes that the light is dim. But horses don't need sunlight to stay active."

"You know the campers are going to want to see it," Rambo cajoled. "Once in a lifetime kinda thing." He grinned at us ingratiatingly. "Not that you'd care about eclipses, Busey. You'd probably rather shovel…" he checked himself, "…hay."

Our fearless leader smirked, and I went weak in the saddle. "Eclipses have been significant throughout history," he replied. "The Ancient Greeks believed that they were a sign of angry gods and the beginning of destruction."

Rambo was no match for Busey's intellect, and even being taken down in front of an audience of young girls appeared to emasculate him. "I hope you *love crafts,* Busey," he fumed, "because we're about to get us some extra glue!"

Love crafts! And a total eclipse! It was a mystical sign from Cthulhu! But the tension was still rising between the two men, so I kicked Booker in his sides and pulled back on the reins, muttering "Up!" under my breath. My horse reared halfheartedly with a frustrated snort, forcing both counselors to drop the subject and focus on me. Busey took another step toward Rambo, saying, "Now, why don't you leave me to my young riders and stop spooking the horses? Liability is a terrible thing." Rambo stormed off onto the trail, leaving us with our hero.

We had loads of questions, and hurried to brush and cool off our horses, the sooner to corner Busey in the tack room before Stitch was to herd us away to the lodge for dinner.

"A LIPIZZAN? YOU girls are pretty observant." The scent of the tack room was already intoxicating with the mixed smells of leather, saddle soap, and fly wipe, and Busey's drawling approval made me a little dizzy. We sat at his feet on the tack room floor, the cool cement floor a welcome anodyne for the dusty summer heat.

"So it's an *Austrian* breed, then?" I pressed, hoping that my casual elbow to Roxy's thigh would appear accidental.

His gray eyes twinkled in amusement. "Yes and no. They are associated with the Spanish Riding School of Vienna, Austria. However, the breed was developed in Slovenia."

"Ooo, like where the vampires come from!" Roxy gabbled.

He chuckled. "No, my young friend, I believe you're thinking of Romania. Anyway, they are often trained to do things that no other breed can do. They can *courbette,* which is the jump on their hind legs. There's also the *capriole,* which is when all four hooves leave the ground. These were all tactics to scare an enemy in battle."

"So Slipper is a warhorse," I marveled. "Why in Cth—I mean, why in God's name is he here at a girls' summer camp?"

Busey sighed, suddenly reminding me that he was a grown man with responsibilities I might not be ready for. "I know his owner. The guy got himself into heaps of trouble with the law, and I agreed to take Slipper off his hands until he could get himself sorted out. Let's just say his owner won't be able to ride for a while, so this big fellow needs some company."

Are you there, Cthulhu? It's me, Judy. I think I'm ready to do this, to ride a Lipizzan! And if it's not too much to ask for, I want to do something that makes Busey really notice me, Great Old One! Someday I will be old enough for him, and I need to do something really special to get his attention.

EVEN WITH THE nickering of the horses at dawn, I just couldn't focus on their morning feeding and watering with an impending natural phenomenon. Everything seemed perfectly aligned with my destiny.

I could contain my idea no longer, gathering my cabin mates into a conspiratorial huddle. "Look, we already know how to saddle and bridle by ourselves. What if we snuck out of our cabins late tonight, borrowed Slipper, and tried to see what it was like to courbette?" The thought gave me a delicious shiver. "No one would see us if we led him all the way to the land at the edge of the camp property by the fire tower."

"The land by the fire tower?" queried Faustine. "Isn't that where the cursed Indian burial mound is also supposed to be? Don't you think that might be risky?" I sometimes resented my clever vulpine-faced friend for having so much sense.

"We won't get to ride today," I cajoled. "There's going to be a total eclipse, remember? It's bad for your eyes if you look directly at it."

"That's because it makes your pupils really small," chimed in Roxy. "And you can go blind because if you stare at something bright enough, your pupils close all the way and get stuck shut."

I was beyond caring about Roxy's overbearing attitude at this point. "It's a straight shot. The dirt road leads from our unit to the pastures, then the tack room by the hitching posts, and beyond that is the trail to the fire tower."

"I'm in," muttered Faustine, extending a hand. Roxy and I clasped our own over hers.

THE ECLIPSE WAS utterly Lovecraftian. I'd seen pictures in magazines and on the Internet, but none of these could have prepared me for witnessing total coverage. It appeared much more massive than I'd imagined, yet felt close enough for me to pluck it from the air like some alien sunflower, or a portal into realms normally reserved for the mind. It was a mating of the sun and the moon, a cosmic fertilized egg attaching itself to the walls of collective consciousness. And even better, as evening came, the whippoorwills were exceptionally noisy, as if waiting to catch fleeing souls leaving a body, just like in "The Dunwich Horror." My heart was a-flutter, and I pep talked my companions into a fervent *esprit de corps* after bedtime.

Nobody has the will power to stay awake like an eighth grader. We develop these skills through rigorous training at slumber parties. It typically took five minutes of yelling to wake one of the counselors, but we took no chances in our silent escape. We were hypersensitive to every creak and twig snap.

My black Miskatonic University shirt (which had sadly misled my parents into thinking that I had academic aspirations) was my best concealment. I tried to pretend that this was not an unattended stable we were facing, but a Cyclopean city dripping with green goo instead. The thought cheered me, and I led the trio.

With every step that took us away from our unit and closer to the stables, the absurdity of our mission increased in my mind. I could tell that the others silently shared my sentiment. Roxy's taciturnity was proof of that.

As the dirt trail curved toward the pasture, Slipper was easy to spot. His white coat shining in the moonlight, he was a vision of… lazy befuddlement. He raised his head at our approach, but when Faustine grabbed his halter, our prized equine simply lay back down, pulling my friend's tiny frame down with her. She let out a tiny squeal as she hit the ground, but was otherwise admirably silent. A couple of horses in the adjacent pasture whinnied their annoyance.

Once we had finally gotten him onto his feet, he sighed in resignation and followed us to the hitching posts outside of the tack room. Luckily, the horses' saddles and bridles were balanced on beams that bore their names, and our flashlights were sufficient for locating Slipper's tack.

We worked in silence. *Brush him down, check. Blanket, check. Hoist saddle on and cinch, check. Bridle, check. Knee Slipper in the belly to deflate his barrel, tighten the girth, check. Hey, we're doing it all by ourselves!* And before we knew it, we'd swung open the barn gate and were leading him down the trail to adventure.

It was actually a peaceful outing. The rhythmic plod of the horse's hooves on the dirt path made for a Zen-like mantra against our conspiratorial silence. All we had to do was keep our flashlights steady and occasionally yank Slipper's head away from the shrubs he intermittently tried to eat. We didn't dare try to ride him until we reached the clearing by the fire tower.

Now what?

Since it was my idea to pilfer him, I decided to take the initiative, and hiked my foot into his stirrup. Roxy gave me a leg up, and lo and behold, I was sitting astride a national treasure of Austria.

There was just one problem. He refused to budge an inch.

"Why won't he move?"

"I don't know! Most horses just walk when you kick their sides. Maybe Lipizzans are trained differently?" I tried wiggling my seatbones a little, and Slipper took a few steps forward.

"Let me grab his bridle and see if I can jog him a few paces." Roxy slipped a hand into Slipper's cheek piece, but the horse just shook his head, tempting a broken finger. He trotted ten feet, suddenly separating me from my companions. Then his body lurched to the right and began to lean and lean and lean. I slipped my feet out of the stirrups and launched myself off his back before he hit the ground with a groan. And there he lay, motionless.

"Is he… dead?" squeaked Faustine.

"Li'hee Cthulhu!" I swore.

Like sailors escaping R'lyeh, we fled the scene. We managed not to get caught as we snuck back into our cabin once more. Nobody made a sound, and I'm sure nobody slept.

SO OF COURSE at sunrise, when Slipper wasn't in his pasture, Busey tried not to panic. By the time we sat down to breakfast at Lame Deer Lodge, the entire camp was abuzz with news of Slipper's disappearance.

The walk back to the barn was just truly awful. I felt like I was awaiting the gallows, even though we hadn't been caught. Busey was standing by the pasture in a deep, serious discussion with the swimming instructor we all knew as Kelpie.

We scuttled off to the hedge that marked the edge of the woods, as far out of earshot as we could get.

"If you had only one wish," Faustine groaned, "would you make this all go away?"

"I don't know, Faustine!" I snapped. "I wish a lot of things! I wish that Busey would see me as more than a little kid. I wish that we hadn't taken Slipper out and that he was still alive. I wish I were developing. I wish that some label would release The Virgins as a box set…"

There was a shuffling noise coming from the woods, and a massive dirty white beast emerged from the trees. I was unable to fathom how a stunning white horse identical to the one we had just lost was coming to find us. *Maybe I can just pass this one off as Slipper,* was my brief hopeful thought, a split second before I took in his compact conformation and realized that this was indeed the horse we'd lost… returned from the dead.

And then the horse's jaw dropped, and I heard a voice in my mind: *You uttered the incantation.*

"Ph'nglui…?" I asked, confused.

No. "Release the virgins." It is our code for "Carry from the summoning place." You have freed us.

My heart began to slam against my ribcage like a mule kicking a barn door. "Are you a Great Old One like what Lovecraft wrote about?" Faustine seemed more aghast at my talking to Slipper than she was at his reappearance.

The equine rolled one ear back in uncertainty. *I do not understand the nature of this "Lovecraft." Is this a human?*

"How can you not know about Lovecraft?" I shrieked, and then realized I was screaming at a zombie horse about having not read something. I decided that I was perhaps a little stressed out, and took a deep breath. "I guess it doesn't matter. Let's see some action! Release the virgins, release the virgins!"

"Judy, who are you yelling at?" Roxy called out. "Hey, look, Slipper is alive!"

The crash coming out of the stables startled us all, and Busey took a step toward the action, placing himself between us and the three men emerging from the tack room in business suits, one of whom I recognized with a shock.

"Boss, what do we do now?" said the familiar weasel-faced Rambo. "We've been waiting since sunrise, but the horse ain't in the pasture." His eyes widened when he saw Slipper untethered. "This green-haired freak," he continued, indicating me, "gave the code 'Release the virgins,' but Armando the Arm isn't here with the truck!" His accomplice, who was a towering Frankenstein completely lacking a neck, grunted.

The third man was the obvious leader, a shaggy-haired man sporting a goatee and shades. He shrugged, saying, "We start shooting. I think Uncle Sugar could give us a pass if we convince the media that some hunters got outta control... mistook some of these girls for deer in season."

The shriek "Daddy!" pierced through the confusion.

The shaggy man peered over his shades. "Roxy, what are you doing here?"

Roxy's face crumpled. "If you only called now and then, you'd know I was here at camp!" She flung out her arms and grabbed Faustine and me around our necks. "This is my *real* family!" The sudden lump in my throat was only partly due to her grip.

There was no time for Roxy's dad to explain. For at that moment Slipper, a born warhorse, decided to slowly rise to his hind legs. The men barely had time to move before the Lipizzan sprang at them in a perfect courbette. He hopped forward twice more before launching himself into the air, all four feet leaving the ground in a breathtaking capriole, hind hooves lashing out with terrifying power. Rambo jumped backward into the Neckless Wonder, who lost his balance against Roxy's father. They toppled like a trio of dominos, knocking their heads against the barn and hitting the dirt with a solid thud.

Some of the other girls screamed, but we three stood in paralyzed shock. Kelpie went running toward the jumble of thugs. She held a finger under the nose of each one, then flashed us a thumbs-up.

Busey's smile was rueful. "They're not dead, only unconscious. Now, isn't it a lucky thing that Kelpie is also a cop? She'll have a team here within ten minutes."

We stalked away from the rest of the group. The erstwhile bossy member of our trio was understandably subdued. "Roxy, how could your dad not know that you're here at the camp?" I asked her as softly as I could.

Roxy hung her head. "Because I never see him. He couldn't care less if I'm at camp, in Europe, or on the moon."

I was suddenly very glad that I'd never lost my temper at Roxy. Faustine and I embraced her in an awkward but supportive hug.

"Hey, look, we saved the day. If your dad was doing anything wrong, at least he won't be hurting anyone again. And we saved Slipper!"

Roxy's gaze was a million miles away. "No," she mused. "Mafia guys might kill other people, but at least they don't do anything bad to horses!"

"SO THESE GANGSTERS... did you ever suspect they would find Slipper here?" I might have done anything to win over Busey, but I still had some questions. We three sat on the camp office's ancient couch, which was stupid-comfy. We'd answered police questions for the past two hours, and had been absolved of our sins in light of the fact that three grown men trespassing in a girls' camp was not going to go over well in court.

His jaw tightened and his temple flared, but his gray eyes were soft as ever. "Of course not," he replied without hesitation. "I love horses, but you girls are more important to me than a whole herd of Lipizzans. Even if *some of you...*" he gave a dramatic pause to clear his throat and glare at me, "...broke a million camp rules. Whatever your hare-brained stunt was going to be, you saved Slipper and got some bad guys locked up." His face suddenly looked stricken as his gaze fell on Roxy, but she batted a hand dismissively before he could issue an apology.

I paused to try to sort out my mixed emotions: flattered by his loyalty and annoyed at being one of a throng of children too young to be romantically viable. I tried to shove that weirdness into a far corner of my mind and ask one more question.

"That Indian burial mound... is it really cursed?"

"What do you mean?"

"We lost Slipper on that big hill by the fire tower. It's supposed to be haunted, and he fell over and stopped moving, and he must have come back to life, or his corpse got reanimated or something..." Even for as avid a reader as I was, I realized I was making an idiot of myself in front of this perfect man.

Busey buried his face in his hands, and his shoulders began to shake. I felt bad for making him cry, until I realized that the tears running down his face were from laughter. My face got hot.

He put his hand on my shoulder, steadying us both. "Sweetheart, I'm not laughing at you. Slipper must have decided he'd had enough of your adventure, and just gotten ornery and stubborn. It was a protest move."

"But he dropped on the burial mound."

"If that were a *Native American* burial mound," he gently corrected me, "it would have been protected by the state. It's actually..." for the first time, he actually looked sheepish, "...an ugly Christmas sweater dumping ground."

I must have made a strangled noise of confusion, because he continued to confess. "Every year, just after Christmas, all the staff have a reunion and bury the ugly sweaters that we're afraid to regift or donate to a thrift store."

"That can't be good for the environment," I chided.

He shrugged. "Only the sequins."

IT WAS WELL past bedtime when we finally walked past the pasture on our way back to the unit. I could make out Slipper's alabaster outline in the shadows, and I whispered, "Gallop faster, I hear mandolins." I no longer heard the voice in my head, but I was pretty sure that the responsive whinny back at me was our Lipizzan.

ARE YOU THERE, Cthulhu? It's me, Judy. Well, it looks as if my friends and I saved the day, and I kind of rode a Lipizzan, even if it was only a few steps. And now I know that Busey will never forget me, because I got him out of trouble! And when Slipper talked? I know that was really you. Thank you, Cthulhu. Thanks an awful lot....

Innocence Lost
Gail Z. Martin

I NEVER SAW him coming.

A relaxing walk on Hasell Street suddenly turned into a contact sport when the skinny guy in a hoodie slammed into me. I stumbled toward the street, and caught myself on a parked car. He staggered into the low bushes next to a parking lot, but never slowed down, turning the corner onto crowded Meeting Street before I could catch my breath.

"Are you all right?" The woman had a Midwestern accent, very noticeable here in Charleston, South Carolina. She might have been my mom's age, and she and her husband planted themselves on the sidewalk, so everyone had to go around us, giving me a chance to catch my breath.

"Yeah, I'm fine. Thanks," I said, pushing a strand of strawberry-blonde hair out of my eyes, more shaken than hurt. I'd gripped my small purse on reflex, but slung cross-body, nobody was going to get it without a fight. Funny, but the man who shoved me hadn't even tried to take it.

"Do you want us to call the police?" the man asked.

I shook my head. "No. Thank you. I didn't see his face, and he didn't take anything."

"You could have been hurt," the woman huffed.

She was right, but aside from perhaps a bruise where my hip hit the passenger door handle of the car I had smacked into, neither the car nor I was actually damaged. "Lucky for me, it's a soft car," I joked. I thanked the couple again for their help, and watched as they walked away toward the touristy parts of town. I stayed where I was, trying to get my bearings.

I felt the pull of magic, something old and strong that hadn't been present moments before. It took a moment before I collected my jangled nerves enough to focus. A few steps brought me to where the man had stumbled into the shrubbery when he bounced off me. The glint of gold caught my eye, lying beneath a short, slightly mangled boxwood.

When I bent down, I saw a small statue of the Virgin Mary, no larger than my hand. The gold leaf paint looked real, as did the small gems that glinted on her Queen-of-Heaven crown. I grabbed my scarf, and used it to pick up the statue without making skin contact, then I slipped it into my purse.

What was a guy who looked rough around the edges doing with an old statue that gave off strong magic vibes? "Stealing it" was the obvious answer, but why? Maybe I'd end up calling the police after all, but before then, I needed to check into the magic piece of the puzzle, and figure out what was really going on.

I'm Cassidy Kincaide, owner of Trifles and Folly, an antiques and curio store in historic, haunted Charleston. Most people think of the store as a great place to find estate jewelry or the perfect vintage accent piece, but the store—and I—have some pretty big secrets. I'm a psychometric, which means I can read the history and magic of objects by touching them—hence the careful handling of the statue. And the store, which has been around since the city was founded 350 years ago, is part of a secret coalition of mortals and immortals who keep Charleston—and the world—safe from supernatural threats. So when I decided to have a closer look at the stolen statue, I wasn't just whistling Dixie.

Even wrapped in my scarf and tucked into my purse, I could feel the buzz of the statue's magic as I power-walked back to the store on King Street. Maggie, our part-time helper, was busy with a customer. Today, Maggie wore a sari-silk broomstick skirt-of-many-colors with a matching strip of bright pink tied like a headband around her short, gray hair. Teag Logan, my best friend, assistant store manager, and sometime bodyguard, looked up when I walked in. With his chin-length, asymmetrically cut dark hair and whipcord build, Teag looks more like a skater boy than the Ph.D. drop-out he really is. Let's just say he found a higher calling in kicking supernatural ass than finishing his dissertation.

"Everything okay? It took you longer to get back than you expected." Teag automatically looked me over from head to toe, checking for injuries. I shook my head, and walked to the break room. "You're limping," he pointed out.

"Someone ran into me pretty hard on the sidewalk," I said. "My hip slammed into a parked car. Could have been worse." I glanced over at the customer, who was busy looking at beautiful old signet rings with Maggie, and Teag nodded, realizing there was more to the story.

"I'll be fine," I promised. "Let me put my purse in the office and grab some coffee, and I can come help up front." Mostly, I wanted to get away from the buzz of energy the statue put out, although I could use some java, too.

The store got busy then, and I didn't have a chance to talk to Teag for a couple of hours, as we matched shoppers to their ideal antiques. As I wrapped up a large, heavy silver tea set, I wondered how the purchaser— who told me excitedly about the bus tour she was on—intended to get it home. I mentioned shipping, but she said there was plenty of room under the bus. Hopefully, none of her fellow travelers decided to buy equally large souvenirs, or someone would be walking back to Toronto.

By mid-afternoon, the influx had slowed to a trickle. Maggie waved us off, promising to yell if she got swamped. Maggie knows what we really do at the store, and she's a godsend. Teag and I headed to the break room, and I sat down with a sigh.

"Spill," Teag ordered, giving me a worried glare.

"I was coming back from lunch, and a guy in a hoodie ran past and slammed me out of his way. When I got my bearings, I felt magic tug me from the parking lot—where he'd stumbled. And I found this." I pulled the scarf out of my purse and set it onto the table, where the small statue rolled free.

Teag leaned over for a closer look, but kept his hands behind his back. We've learned the hard way not to touch without sizing up the danger first. "Looks old, and authentic. Meaning I don't think it's a souvenir piece. Wanna bet it's stolen?"

"That's what I figured, but it seems like a weird thing for someone to steal," I said, shifting on my chair to ease the tender spot on my hip. "Easy to identify, hard to fence."

As an antique store owner, I have to be very conscious of where the items we buy for resale come from, and make sure the owner really owns them. That's aside from determining whether or not the pieces are cursed or haunted—which is true more often than people might think.

"Here." Teag went to the fridge and pulled out an ice pack, which he handed to me. Given the nature of what we really do—fighting off things that go bump in the night—the break room has an unusually robust first-aid kit. I pressed the cold compress against my sore hip, and sighed in relief.

"How about you sit with that ice while I see what I can pull up online?" Teag grabbed his laptop and went to work. He's got Weaver magic, which means he can weave spells into cloth and hidden data into information, making him a hell of a hacker. Moments later, he looked up in triumph.

"Looks like there's been a rash of break-ins at churches all over the Lowcountry," Teag said. "All of them Catholic, which isn't as common down here as it is us up North, so that's interesting right there."

Plenty of churches had valuable items, if a thief just wanted a quick buck. Silver items, antiques, artwork, even loose change in the donation box could be fair game for a grab-and-run. But the thief—or thieves—had concentrated on Catholic churches, which had to mean something.

"Can you tell what was stolen?" I asked, trying to figure out the connection.

"Give me a sec," Teag's fingers flew across the keyboard. After a short while, he sat back, stared at the screen, and chewed his lower lip, a tell that he was trying to make sense of what he found.

"Anything?"

"Yeah. In every case, all that was taken were statues—mostly of the Virgin Mary, but also of some saints. Not just the regular image of Mary, but some of the special ones like the Virgin of Guadalupe, the Virgin of Lourdes, Virgin of Montserrat. Most were old, some were said to contain relics, and—get this—several had reputations for miraculous healing or warding off evil."

Well, that explained the "magic" I'd sensed. Power—regardless of its source—calls to power. Miracle or magic, po-ta-toe, po-tah-toe.

"Which brings us to the million-dollar question—why?" I mused, taking a sip of my coffee.

"Could be a collector with specialized tastes," Teag speculated, still glaring at his laptop like it could be intimidated into giving up the missing information.

I shook my head. "I didn't get a look at the guy's face, but when he bumped me, I got a glimpse of his emotions. He was terrified—and I don't think it was of the cops."

"So maybe it's like the kid in that movie who could see dead people? You know, where he made a blanket fort and stole all the crucifixes to keep the ghosts away?"

"Yeah," I said as I weighed the statement and felt my intuition respond. "I don't know what he was scared of, but that would make sense."

"It must be pretty big if he's the one knocking over all those churches," Teag replied. "Because there've been at least twenty break-ins according to the report I hacked into."

I pulled out my phone and hit a number on speed dial. "This is Father Anne," came the greeting. "Hi, Cassidy!" Father Anne Burgett is an unorthodox Episcopalian priest who moonlights as a demon hunter. She's one of our allies when shit gets real, and she's also wicked with Cards Against Humanity.

"Hey there," I said, shifting again to keep the ice on my sore spot. "What do you know about the thefts of statues of the Virgin Mary and random saints?"

She was quiet for a moment. "Not much, other than the scuttlebutt I've picked up through the inter-faith meetings. Newsflash—clergy gossip. And when someone starts breaking into churches and stealing sacred objects, word travels fast."

"What are they saying?"

"Aside from telling everyone to lock their doors? Some people think it's an attack specifically on the Catholic faith, because it's only been their churches being targeted," Father Anne replied. "Others have pointed out that Catholic churches are more likely than others to have really old, really valuable objects. Protestants don't usually go for as much bling."

"Anyone talking about a supernatural cause?"

"Not out loud," she replied. "But I've heard some whispering inside the Society that the pattern could suggest the thief is either trying to summon something or ward it off—and neither of those options is good." "The Society" was the St. Expeditus Society, a secret organization of priests dedicated to eliminating supernatural threats.

"Thanks," I said. "Keep an ear to the ground for us, okay? We'll let you know what we find out, because I've got a feeling that whatever's up ties in to your area of expertise."

I ended the call and turned back to Teag, who was hunched over his laptop. "You look like a hound dog on a trail," I said with a chuckle. "Next thing, you'll be sniffing the computer."

Teag barely looked up. "None of the churches that were robbed had security cameras. But the corner where he ran into you did. I'm piecing together splices from the cameras along his route to see where he went."

"You're awesome. A little scary, but amazing," I replied. I went back up front to make sure Maggie didn't need help, but the afternoon tourist bump had already started to trickle off. By the time I came back to the break room, Teag greeted me with a Cheshire cat grin.

"I think I've got him," Teag said. I stood behind him and looked at the grainy footage of Hoodie Guy getting into an old, beat-up Toyota. The license plate was clearly visible, even though I still hadn't gotten a good look at his face.

"Let me hack the DMV, and we'll have an address," Teag said, making it sound like business as usual. Which it kinda was, for us.

A few more minutes at the keyboard turned up a name—Jason Durant—and an address. "Now all we have to do is figure out why he wants all the statues, and what to do about it," Teag said, sitting back and stretching.

"Once we close up, I'll take a look at the figurine and see what I read from it. Maybe it'll shed some light on why Jason was so afraid."

Maggie rang up our last sale of the day, checked in to see if we needed anything, then headed out, locking up the front as she went. Teag poured me a glass of sweet tea from the pitcher we always keep in the refrigerator, and sat down beside me at the table.

He held out one end of a thin strip of cloth, and I knew it was one he had woven himself, incorporating his magic into the fabric with every pass of the shuttlecock. We'd found through trial and error that if I held one end of the fabric and he kept hold of the other, he could see my vision when I tranced.

"Okay," I said, taking a deep breath and letting it out. "Let's see what's got him running scared."

I closed my hand around the statue, and found that it was painted wood, not carved stone as I had thought. I could sense its age—at least a century or two. The figure had a warm glow in my inner sight, a mix of serenity and worship and forgiveness that stilled my churning thoughts with an otherworldly peace.

But I could feel Jason's anxiety overlaying all of that like a stain. His terror felt like a punch in the gut, and my heart sped up as my breathing grew shallow. Nightmares. Terror. Voices in the dark. And beneath it all, the whiff of something evil, maybe even infernal.

"Cassidy!" Teag's voice urged me to break contact with the statue, and immediately the vision vanished. I slumped in my chair as I tried to get myself under control. Teag pressed the glass of very sugary sweet tea into my hand. "Drink."

We've done this so often, Teag and I have the routine pretty well rehearsed. Sweet tea grounds me, and the sugar rush re-sets my inner gyroscope. After a minute or two, I was back to normal.

"You felt it?" Sometimes I get images. Other times, just feelings. Tonight was less visual and more visceral.

"Jason's afraid something awful is waiting for him," Teag recapped, which was pretty much what I had gotten from the impressions. "But I didn't get the feeling it was a person, did you?"

"No. A ghost, maybe? Or a supernatural creature?" I took another long drink from the tea, and set the glass aside. "Why don't we take a drive past his house, and see what kind of vibes we pick up? Then we can figure out how to confront him."

"It might not just be confronting him," Teag pointed out. "We don't know if what he's afraid of is in his house, or if he thinks it's going to come after him."

"Yeah," I agreed. "And we need to figure out why he stole the statues, so we don't accidentally let something bad loose."

"Plus, if we can do it without starting the apocalypse, we need to get him to release the Virgins so they can go back to the churches where they belong," Teag added.

Even with the seriousness of the vision, I couldn't help but chuckle at Teag's comment.

WE LOCKED UP the shop and headed out to Teag's car. I sent a message to Father Anne about where we were going—safety precaution—since my boss, Sorren, was out of the country on business. Usually, he's our back-up, since he's a nearly 600-year-old vampire. Handy, that. But his work with the Alliance takes him all over the world, and tonight he was somewhere in Europe.

I wasn't familiar with the part of town where Jason lived. The houses were modest, and most looked in fairly good repair, although a few were boarded up or abandoned. As soon as we crossed into Jason's block, I felt a chill to the marrow, despite the warm Charleston evening. Psychic ooze leaked like an oil spill from an unremarkable yellow one-story house.

"There," I said, pointing.

"Yeah, I feel it, too," Teag agreed. Our gifts might take different forms, but dark, evil energy bled out from that little bungalow.

We kept on going, unwilling to let Jason or whatever entity he was hiding notice our interest or our abilities. "I think we need to bring Rowan in on this," I said, naming our favorite white magic witch. "Just in case it's more than Father Anne can handle alone."

"Agreed," Teag said as we drove back so I could pick up my car at the store. "You and I can be back-up, but whatever that was, it's not something we can fight outright."

Teag's martial arts training makes him pretty tough to beat, and I'm no slouch with my own set of magical weapons. We've both fought off enough ghoulies and ghosties and long-legged beasties to be able to throw down with the worst of them. But there's a difference between whacking the head off a zombie with a blessed machete and facing down something incorporeal—or possibly even infernal.

"Then let's call in the cavalry, and figure out our next moves," I replied. "Because I got the sense Jason's protections are at their breaking point, and I don't want to see whatever that is get loose."

THE NEXT NIGHT, we closed in like a supernatural SWAT team. Rowan rocked a Buffy look-alike vibe, with her blond hair up in a ponytail and wearing all black. Father Anne was her usual badass self, dark hair in a fade, clerical collar over a sleeveless black t-shirt that showed the colorful St. Expeditus tats on her shoulders and upper arms, jeans, and steel-toed Doc Martens.

Teag and I have both amassed a wardrobe of dark-colored clothing, because it helps us blend in when we're somewhere in the line of duty we're not technically supposed to be, or because it hides the blood and monster guts: always handy when you're running from a pile of creature corpses you've just torched.

Rowan set down a perimeter warding, to keep the evil from getting out in case something went wrong. It also carried a distraction spell, so unless we blew the place up—wouldn't be the first time—the spell would encourage the neighbors and the cops to look the other way.

Father Anne spoke a benediction, cleansing the area in her own way, making it naturally repellent to dark energies. Blessings and curses carry real power, more than most people give them credit for. I knew she also came prepared to do an exorcism, depending on what we found inside. While they did their thing, Teag and I set down a circle of salt and iron filings around the small yard, another layer of insurance.

We all wore protective charms—silver, onyx, agate—as well as religious medallions. Teag and I also carried Gris-Gris bags and jack-balls from a friend who's a powerful Hoodoo root worker, and some blessed Voudon *veves* on silver bracelets from another friend who's a kickass mambo. I'd found that protective energies tended to be more ecumenical than some of their ardent believers, and I knew the importance of taking good juju wherever I could find it.

As far as weapons—we were all carrying. I had my athame—my grandmother's old wooden spoon—that helped me channel my touch magic and concentrate it into a protective force. Just in case, I'd brought an antique walking stick whose resonance enabled me to shoot fire. Teag and I both had silver and iron knives—good against ghosts and other supernatural creatures—as well as a sawed-off shotgun with salt rounds and—just in case—a Glock with silver bullets. Rowan had her magic, and while Father Anne's faith was strong, her aim with a knife was downright wicked.

Time to roll. I felt a frisson of energy as I crossed the barriers, able to do so by the permission of their casters. Jason and the dark power would not be able to do the same. The closer I got to the house, the more I felt the taint of the entity or magic inside. Awful as it was, the power still felt muted, and I shuddered to think of what would happen if Jason hadn't stolen the blessed statues and called on their protection.

Rowan and I went for the front door; Teag and Father Anne circled around to the back. Rowan lifted a hand and blew it off the hinges. I heard a crack from the other side of the house, and figured our partners had kicked in the rear door.

"What the hell is that?" I recoiled at the sight of what lay before me. Where the living room should have been was a circle of saint's candles, most of them blackened and burned far down, as if they were lit 24/7. A row of unused candles sat to one side, and the soot-streaked empties supported my guess. In between the lit candles were the stolen statues of the Virgin Mary, facing inward, silent sentries to contain the evil Jason had loosed.

All around us, on every wall, someone had marked sigils and symbols of protection from every religion I could think of, and some I couldn't identify. They were spray painted, drawn with Sharpie, dug into the wallboard—and some looked to be written in blood. Little homemade shrines sat in each corner of the room: to Christ, Shiva, Buddha, and Papa Legba. The shrines held religious statues, candles, and offerings of food, coins, and liquor.

A thick haze of smoke drifted in the stale air—I couldn't tell immediately whether it was sage or weed—but it didn't completely cover the underlying stink of rot and sulfur. Because in the center of the candle circle, surrounded by a pentagram—good side up—and other protective symbols, was a small black hole that looked like it descended to the Abyss.

"It's a hell-mouth," Father Anne and Rowan said, nearly in unison.

Teag snorted. "Looks more like a hell-nostril to me." I knew he fell back on humor when he was scared, and his wide eyes told me he felt as terrified as the rest of us.

"Don't cross the circle!" Hoodie Guy—aka Jason Durant—lurched out from the hallway where he'd been hiding. "You don't understand—if that gets loose, we're all gonna die!"

"How did you open a hell-mouth?" Rowan turned her full attention on Jason, which made him wilt like the guilty teenager he was.

"I didn't mean to," he whined. "My grandmother was supposed to be some kind of witch, but my mama wouldn't let me study with her, because mama got religion and said magic was bad. Then grandma died. Only I found out I could do things that weren't normal—magic things—and I didn't dare let mama know. So I got some old books at a used bookstore and studied on my own. Except I screwed up, and that—" he pointed to the dark portal in the floor "—opened, and I don't know how to shut it. So I figured I'd put a fence around it and find out how to make it go away."

Jason didn't look like he'd been sleeping or eating, and he seemed contrite enough that I believed his story about accidental magic. We run into that a lot in our business, along with cursed heirlooms and haunted antiques. People mess around with powers they underestimate, and open up a highway to Hell.

"You're not going to turn me over to the police, are you?" Jason looked like he'd reached his breaking point. "I stole the statues, but I maybe saved the world a little. That counts, doesn't it?"

"If we all get out of this alive, we'll return the statues to the churches you took them from," Father Anne said sternly.

"And then you're going to apprentice with me, so this doesn't happen again," Rowan added, with a glare that could curdle milk.

Jason nodded miserably. "Anything. I swear, I'll do anything. Just… make it go away. I hear it screaming in my dreams."

That was our cue. Father Anne moved to the right; Rowan walked to the left. Teag and I fell back, unable to help actually dispel the darkness Jason had conjured, but ready to protect the two who could.

Father Anne began the exorcism rite, her voice strong and confident, rebuking the powers of evil. Rowan thrust out her right hand, palm forward, and blasted the hell-mouth with a torrent of white light that glared too bright to watch.

The portal shifted and writhed on its own, like a living thing, trying to twist away from the all-consuming energy. But it didn't vanish.

A blob of black ooze bubbled up from the small hole, and expanded into a horror of teeth and claws. Later, I'd find out we all saw it differently, that it played to our individual fears, but in that moment, I saw a creature somewhere between werewolf and demon. The stench of sulfur and rotting meat almost made me gag.

Teag didn't hesitate. He launched three silver throwing knives in quick succession, seconds before I raised my athame and sent a streak of cold, blue-white energy to strike the monster in the chest. It roared, a noise I'd hear forever in my nightmares, but it did not break the circle of candles. Dark blood seeped from where Teag's knives embedded, hilt-deep, in its ribs, and charred skin hung in ribbons where my strike had ripped into the body. Yet the were-demon still stood, teeth bared and claws unsheathed, promising bloody death to all of us if it ever got free.

Rowan and Father Anne's chants rose and fell, reinforcing each other. The creature stalked within the circle, glaring at us with a malevolence that made me shiver, and then it threw itself at the warding. A bright yellow light flared, rising from the saints' candles, and the monster fell back, howling.

"Look," I whispered to Teag. The symbols on the walls around us glowed with inner fire, shining as brightly as the boundary of light that rose above the sacred candles. Father Anne and Rowan spoke with authority, their voices growing louder, commanding the creature to be gone. Inside its prison, the were-demon shrieked, its body arching in agony. I watched, holding my breath, as its immense form was drawn back to the small black hole from whence it came, vanishing inch by impossible inch as the chants and liturgy continued.

I felt the struggle as the monster fought with all its power and the borrowed energy of hell itself, and I knew that Father Anne and Rowan had to be tiring. Teag and I didn't have the right magic to send the creature packing, and I hated feeling helpless. Then I spotted the woven and knotted cords on Teag's belt that he uses to store magic.

"Your cords," I hissed. "We'll be their extra batteries."

Teag loosed a cord, and we each held an end. I put my hand on Father Anne's shoulder, while Teag gripped Rowan tightly. I felt my gift flow through me and out to them, reinforcing and healing, renewing and energizing. Alone, the creature was too much for us to handle. Together, we were enough.

"*Benedictus Deus, Gloria Patri, Benedictus Dea, Matri Gloria!*" Father Anne shouted defiantly.

"So mote it be!" Rowan cried, sending another flare of white light at the luminous boundary that made it flash so brightly I had to look away.

When my vision cleared, all that remained was a blackened streak in the middle of the pentagram on the floor. No monster. No hell gate. Just Jason, on his knees, sobbing, and the four of us, gobsmacked to still be alive.

I shook myself to clear my mind, and loosened my hold on Father Anne's shoulder, fearing I'd gripped tightly enough to leave bruises. Teag let his hand fall as well. When we broke contact, both the priest and the witch staggered, as if the infusion of our energy was all that had been keeping them standing.

Father Anne rallied first and said an additional blessing to clear the space before she began to extinguish the candles and gather up the stolen Virgins. Rowan collected her wits a moment later, and strode over to Jason.

She squatted down, pulled him into her arms, and held him until he quieted. "Get your things," she ordered. "I'm not letting you out of my sight. Tomorrow, you start your training program."

"The police—" he began in a ragged voice.

"The police are the least of your worries," Rowan said in a stern voice. "You're now in the custody of my Coven, within the jurisdiction of the Society. And you will not be rid of us until you're properly trained and no longer pose a threat." The chill in her tone suggested that Jason didn't want to find out the alternative.

Her expression softened, just a little. "You'll get the training you need and the answers you deserve—and a group to have your back." She followed him as he went to pack a bag. It was obvious Jason was badly shaken by his mistakes, but I was confident Rowan and her coven's tough love would get him back on track.

"What about all this?" I asked, waving a hand to indicate the now-darkened sigils painted on the walls and the pentagram on the floor. "It's not going to help the resale value."

Father Anne looked grim. "I'll make a few calls. Between the Alliance and the Society, we've got people for that. I think we're covered."

I suddenly felt all of the night's work in every muscle and sinew, down to the marrow of my bones. I was drained and empty, starved and thirsty, and utterly exhausted.

"What about the statues?" Teag asked.

Father Anne shrugged. "The less said, the better. If they come back via a few well-placed 'friends' in the diocese, no one will ask awkward questions."

Rowan and Jason came back into the room. Father Anne tucked the holy figures into the small duffle she'd left by the door.

"Go home," Father Anne said, giving me a weary smile. "And… thanks."

Teag and I walked back out to my RAV4, as the others got into Father Anne's truck. "I don't know about you, but I've had all the excitement I can handle for today," I told him. Once again, we'd saved the world, and no one would ever know except us. "Time to call it a night."

How Mose Saved the Virgins of Old New York
Allen M. Steele

THROUGHOUT HISTORY, THERE are tales of men and women whose exploits cause them to stand tall above all those around them. Heroic figures, they're adventurers without peer, godlike but nonetheless human, capable of feats beyond those of mere mortals. Before the superheroes of comic books and movies, before Doc Savage and James Bond, there were Hercules and Gilgamesh, Prester John and Arthur Pendragon, Paul Bunyan and John Henry, and others, so many others: make your own list.

However, there are also those who, although once admired by their friends and feared by their foes, have become obscure today. Forgotten heroes, they've suffered the fate of legends who don't outlive their time, and thus disappeared into history's labyrinth… or became a different legend entirely.

This is a story about Mose. It may or may not be true.

LOWER MANHATTAN IN the early 1800s was just about the roughest place you could imagine. In the decades following the Revolutionary War and the founding of the United States, New York was on its way to becoming the city it is today, with sharp class divisions already emerging between its wealthy inhabitants and its poor. Nowhere was this more evident than in the lower east side. Waves of immigrants were crossing the ocean in hopes of making a fresh start in the new country. Impoverished, penniless, and frequently on the wrong side of the law, these migrants—mainly Irish and Italian—packed the tenements of Five Points.

The Five Points neighborhood got its name because it was where five major streets—Cross, Anthony, Little Water, Orange, and Mulberry—came together at Paradise Square. Five Points was dominated by street gangs, the predecessors to the Mafia and, later, the Crips and Bloods. Bearing names like the Native Americans, the Roach Guards, the Plug Uglies, the Black Birds, and the Forty Thieves, they engaged in every form of lawlessness you could name: street robbery, housebreaking, mugging, river piracy, prostitution, kidnapping, extortion, murder. Men and women alike joined these gangs, and even children were sometimes recruited. The police looked the other way—either they accepted bribes or, failing to do so, became marked men—and decent people such as you and I ventured into Five Points at the risk of their lives. Uptown visitors were sometimes found dead and stripped naked, their purses, jewelry, and even their clothes stolen from their bodies.

The largest of the Five Points gangs was the Bowery Boys. In the bloody street battles among rival gangs that could last for days and nights on end, the Bowery Boys usually came out on top by sheer force of numbers. It was estimated that, at its height, nearly 3,000 men and women were members. Like many New York gangs, they had a semi-legitimate standing as a volunteer fire company, Engine Number 28. When a fire broke out in a dwelling—as they often did; the whole damn city was a fire hazard—competing companies would race to the scene and fight one another for the distinction of putting out the conflagration, a service for which they would extort payment from the hapless occupants. Sometimes a house would burn to the ground before the firemen settled their differences and stopped trying to kill each other.

Like most gangs, the Bowery Boys went through a succession of leaders. The job didn't ensure longevity, and health insurance wasn't a company benefit. But among the gang's chieftains, one name rose above others: Mose.

Little is known about Mose today, or at least what could be safely regarded as factual truth. According to Luc Sante's history of old New York, *Low Life*, Mose's full name was Moses Humphrey, and when he wasn't running with the Bowery Boys, he had a day job as a printer at the *New York Sun*. According to *New York Night* by Mark Caldwell, Mose appeared in a contemporaneous Broadway show, *A Glance at New York*. He was also depicted in Herbert Asbury's authoritative *The Gangs of New York*, but he's noticeably absent from Martin Scorsese's movie of the same name. Mose's Wikipedia entry is little more than a reiteration of what's in the Sante and Asbury books, and a Google search turns up just a couple of contemporary lithographs that exaggerated his proportions. But not a single New Yorker whom I contacted for this story recognized his name or knew anything about him.

Mose has become forgotten, but in his time, he was a giant. Literally. He was said to stand eight feet all, with fists the size of hams and feet so big that he had to wear specially made boots, their soles studded with nails. His hair was fiery red, matching the vest, plaid trousers, and beaverskin stove-pipe hat that was the uniform of the Bowery Boys. When the gang went to war, Mose carried either a paving stone, which he used to crush an opponent's skull, or a butcher knife; during one street battle, he fought a hundred men on his own, and defeated every one of them. He could allegedly swim the length of the Hudson River in just two strokes and leap across the East River from Manhattan to Brooklyn; sometimes, just for the hell of it, he'd simply stand in the middle of one of these rivers and block riverboats from passing through. He could pick up Company 28's fire engine and carry it on his shoulder, its horses dangling helplessly from their harnesses. He smoked cigars two feet long, drank beer by the keg, and an entire cow had to be butchered for his dinner. Or so it was said.

For all of this, though, no one knows where he came from. Nowhere is it stated whether he was originally from Ireland, as many Bowery Boys were, or born on American soil. Maybe he came from… well, somewhere else. For all we know, there may be a farm pasture on the other side of the Hudson, some forgotten place in the Pine Barrens of New Jersey where, deep beneath the soil, there lies a craft from a faraway planet. America is a nation of immigrants, after all, so perhaps Moses Humphrey, aka Mose, traveled here from some unimaginably distant shore. If so, then his first name may have deliberately been given to him by Biblically minded adoptive parents.

In any case, it's clear that Mose was much more than a mere mortal. He was a superhuman. But even though he was leader of a fierce Five Points gang, he was also capable of acts of heroism.

Which is how one of the stories told about him involves the Bowery Boys' arch-enemies, the Dead Rabbits, and how Mose saved the virgins of old New York.

EATING, DRINKING, AND brawling were among Mose's favorite pastimes, but if the accounts of his exploits are true—and I'll leave it to readers to judge their veracity—then his favorite activity was firefighting. Indeed, it appears that the reason why Mose came to New York in the first place was to become a fireman, because no one had apparently heard of him before he joined Engine 28. The Bowery Boys were engaged in a lot of illegal stuff, but it doesn't look as if Mose was ever involved in any of it. Which is not to claim that Mose was any sort of saint, but simply that the most probable reason for his rapid ascent to the leadership of Five Points' largest gang was his ability as a firefighter.

Mose wasn't the only notable character among the early NYC street gangs. Asbury's *The Gangs of New York* (worth reading, by the way) tells of other Bowery Boys such as Bill Poole, aka Bill the Butcher, the basis for Daniel Day-Lewis's character in the Scorsese movie (which should have gotten the 2002 Best Picture Oscar), and Syksey, Mose's comparatively diminutive right-hand man. But lest you think I'm describing Robin Hood and his merry men, be reminded that these were the best of a lot of lifelong criminals, all of them cutthroats and thieves (except Mose, maybe).

Other Five Points gangs had notable members as well. One was a street brawler in the Dead Rabbits, Hell-Cat Annie. Asbury describes her as "an angular vixin... who is said to have filed her teeth to sharp points," and worn artificial nails on her fingers, made of brass and sharp as knives. In combat, she'd charge in with a screeching howl and throw herself straight at her opponents, gnawing off their ears as trophies. I doubt she was sexually harassed at the bar, but if she ever had been, I would've given a lot to have been there... on the other side of the room, preferably near the door.

Naturally, it was only inevitable that two such sterling characters should meet. So, one hot summer night in 1843, Mose and Annie and their respective gangs had it out.

When I learned about Mose from the Asbury book, I became interested enough to do some research of my own. Dig deep enough into history and you'll discover things that have never been published, which is why the story I'm about to tell you doesn't show up anywhere else. So I'm going to have to beg for a certain suspension of disbelief; I'm just reporting what I found. Or, to quote another New York criminal: believe me (and say what you will about Mose, but at least he was a nicer person than *him*).

As the story goes, there was a fire one night down on Water Street, which was just off Little Water, one of the five avenues that made up the Five Points. It was in one of the city's many tenements, the hulking, barn-like structures with low ceilings and few interior walls that were home to thousands of New York's poorest. Usually lit by torch, oil lamp, or candle, the tenements were immense, overcrowded firetraps. Forget sprinklers, CO_2 extinguishers, and fire-escape ladders: they didn't exist yet.

For whatever reason, once the building caught fire, it turned into an inferno very quickly. And since it was in their neighborhood, the volunteer engine companies arrived just as soon as news of the conflagration reached them. So the building hadn't been on fire but for a few minutes when Engine No. 28 came rattling down Water Street, accompanied by as many Bowery Boys as could be mustered on short notice.

Mose led the firefighters, trotting out front of the engine. The account I read claimed that he'd been dragging the engine himself—to give the horses a break, one supposes—but I choose to take that part of the story with a grain of salt. Even if you're skeptical about Mose's reputed size and strength, though, he must have been an impressive sight: a giant firemen in oilskins and brass helmet, leading his company into battle with the blazes, a demigod of first-responders.

Yet Engine 28 wasn't the only fire company to rush to the scene. Practically the same minute they showed up, another company entered from the opposite direction: the Dead Rabbits (the gang Leonardo DiCaprio belonged to in the movie). And at their head was Hell-Cat Annie.

Annie may or may not have been a firefighter, but if there was even a chance she might get to use her teeth, nails, and knives, she would've been there. She'd later become a drunk who'd die on the street, but in her prime, she'd been a she-devil of the highest order. And as a Dead Rabbit, she saw Mose not simply as a rival, but as the chieftain of her sworn enemies. So there was going to be no chance for a temporary truce between the Boys and the Rabbits.

Yet there was more to it than that. Like many of the Five Points gangs, one commercial enterprise in which the Dead Rabbits was engaged was prostitution, operated out of stalls—you couldn't really call them bedrooms, because some of them didn't have doors, walls, or even beds—in the tenement the Rabbits used as their headquarters. While there's no evidence to prove that the Rabbits forced underage girls into the oldest profession, it's entirely possible that they did. Even if they didn't, with slander as common then as it is now, gang members were likely to believe any lie that was told about a rival gang.

Mose had lately heard that the Dead Rabbits were forcing adolescent girls into sexual slavery. And he didn't like this, not one little bit. He might belong to a notorious gang, but there was something of a Boy Scout in him (yes, I know, the Boy Scouts weren't around yet; stop nit-picking, you're impressing no one). So the instant he saw Hell-Cat Annie coming down Water Street, the tenement fire was forgotten.

"Release the virgins!" According to the handwritten diary I found, this was what Mose shouted. There's no telling what his voice was like, but I bet it was as loud as a riverboat foghorn. No doubt it was clearly heard above the shouts of the firemen and the crackle of the flames, and that Hell-Cat knew what he meant.

"Ain't no virgins amongst the Dead Rabbits!" Annie yelled back, climbing atop a pile of bricks that had been a wall just moments earlier. "'Lessen ye talkin' 'bout yer own self, ya big galoot! No g'hal I ever met—" g'hal was the old Irish-American word for girl; gal comes from it "—kin say what they've ever hid yer pickle!"

This brought forth laughter from the Dead Rabbits. History doesn't record whether Mose had a girlfriend or what his sexual preferences may have been, but apparently it was a sore subject. Mose had a ready comeback, though.

"My pickle is just fine, Annie," he yelled back. "At least it's still there… I hear any man who lays down with you gets his bitten off and swallowed!"

Now it was the Bowery Boys' turn to have a laugh, and the last thing Hell-Cat would tolerate was a joke at her expense. "Then come over here an' show me yers!" she shouted back, raising an axe handle above her head. "I'll add it to my collection!"

No more words. Mose dropped the fire engine's yoke, Hell-Cat leaped at him from atop the brick-pile, and so began the battle between the Bowery Boys and the Dead Rabbits.

IN STREET COMBAT among Five Points gangs, rules were sometimes laid out in advance if their chieftains had a chance to sit down and parlay. For instance, it was often decided that guns would not be allowed, only knives. But when the battles were spontaneous, as this one was, there were no rules. So the fights were savage beyond belief, and lasted until one side lost so many people that it was all the survivors could do just to drag away the injured and the dead.

So it was that night.

As the tenement burned, its flames cast a ghastly red glare upon the battle between the Bowery Boys and the Dead Rabbits. Knives, brick-bats, shovels, fire axes… anything at hand became a weapon as the gang members forgot why they were there in the first place, and fell to fighting each other instead of the fire, which wasn't as much fun anyway.

No quarter, no surrender; they tore into one another as mortal enemies. Eyes were gouged, teeth were knocked out. Bones were broken, noses were pulped, throats were cut. Those who fell were killed on the spot if they didn't manage to crawl or be carried to safety. No ambulances were called; none would have responded anyway. The cobblestones were soon drenched with blood, and Water Street smelled of smoke and gore.

At the nucleus of the melee, Mose and Hell-Cat Annie fought.

It must have been an amazing thing to watch: a man and a woman— one superhuman, the other as crazy as an Irish pub on St. Patrick's Day— going at it as if they were in the gates of Hell. Mose had strength and size, but Annie was vicious and just plain nuts, and that made things equal. They fought barehanded, but neither of them needed weapons. Their hatred was enough.

Somehow, their fight left the street, and before either of them knew it, they were inside the nearby tenement, fighting within the furnace. Anyone with common sense would've called a truce at that point, but it's doubtful that they even realized where they were. The unnamed eyewitness who wrote the first-person account I read recalls catching a glimpse of the two of them, arms locked together as if in a homicidal waltz, the very walls burning around them.

There came a loud groan, like a giant rolling over in disturbed slumber. The groan grew in intensity, and then another noise could be heard, the creak of wooden boards under strain. Out in the street, combat came to an abrupt halt as firemen from the rival engine companies suddenly realized that they'd forgotten something important. Men on both sides dropped whatever they were holding or whoever they'd been trying to kill and belatedly began to pick up firehoses. By then, it was too late. Nothing could stop the tenement from destruction.

Most of the residents had already managed to escape, no thanks to the firemen who'd ostensibly come to save them. They stood on the other side of Water Street, watching as their home and belongings went up in fire and smoke. No longer locked in mortal combat, the Bowery Boys and the Dead Rabbits tried to do something about it, yet the water they pumped was no more effective than spit on a bonfire.

The roar became deafening, and then the roof began to cave in. Everyone on the street hurried to get out of the way as the roof beams collapsed. Both fire companies peered anxiously into the flames, trying to see what had become of Mose and Annie, but it was as if an opaque curtain of fire and smoke been had drawn across the hellish stage.

In the last few seconds before the walls fell in, a figure staggered through what was left of the front door: Hell-Cat Annie. Face and hands blackened by soot, hair half-burned away, she managed to lurch forth into the arms of her fellow Dead Rabbits as, with the bellow of a dying beast, the tenement collapsed into a fiery heap.

Mose was nowhere to be seen.

For the Bowery Boys, it was as if an impossible thing had happened. Until then, they'd believed that their chieftain was indomitable, unstoppable, perhaps even immortal. But it hadn't been Hell-Cat Annie who'd defeated him—she emerged from the flames without an ear or any other part of Mose's anatomy—but the fire itself. Mose had been a fireman second to none, but in the end, it was the fire that won.

So the Bowery Boys gathered their equipment and returned to the brewery that was their headquarters. No one spoke. When someone tried to eulogize Mose, Bill the Butcher pulled a knife and threatened to cut his tongue out; he wasn't in the mood for such things, however well-intended they may have been. As for Syksey, he mourned the loss of the man who was his hero. The Bowery Boys had lost their champion that night, and no one would ever replace him.

Then they walked into the brewery, and there at the bar sat Mose.

His face was as black as if he'd crawled out of a coal cellar. Most of his red hair was burned away, and he reeked off smoke and ash. Yet he was still among the living. The barkeep had broken out a keg of ale for him, and Mose picked it up now and then to take a drink from the spigot. His arms were singed, his skin red with superficial burns, but otherwise there wasn't a mark on him.

The Bowery Boys stared at him is disbelief. One of them even fainted. Then Syksey spoke.

"Yer still alive!" An understatement, of course.

"Yes, I am," Mose replied. A rather obvious remark as well.

"How did ye do it?"

"Well—" Mose seemed to think it over for a second, "—it wasn't easy."

That was the only explanation anyone ever received. Or at least the only one recorded in the diary I found.

MOSE DIDN'T DIE that day. In fact, history doesn't record his death at all.

For all intents and purposes, he simply disappears. There's nothing more written about him after a certain point. No graveyard in New York bears a tombstone with the name Moses Humphreys; no museum bears a fireman's helmet that was said to belong to him. Mose was once there, and then he vanished, and that's all there was to it.

But… maybe something else happened.

Legends don't die. Not completely, anyway. Sometimes the heroes of one era become heroes again, in another time and under a different name. If Mose was, indeed, a superhuman, then he may have had greater longevity as well. If so, he might have outlived Hell-Cat Annie and Syksey and Bill the Butcher and everyone else, and in time become someone else entirely. Another legend, and thus the source of other tales, tall or otherwise.

Although Mose has become all but forgotten in the early 21st century, stores about him and his feats would've still been known in the 1930s, when a couple of Cleveland teenagers named Jerry Siegel and Joe Schuster sat down to create a hero, one whose abilities are strikingly similar. Who can tell? It's all conjectural, anyway.

Yet it seems to me that we always have heroes of one sort or another. They're not always the creation of movie special effects; sometimes, they're closer than you think, perhaps even living among us. We often don't know who they are or where they come from, but nonetheless they're present, and every so often we hear about something they've done, some feat that's beyond those of mere mortals. But only for a short time, because soon they vanish again.

Mose is still here.

The Fires of Rome
Jody Lynn Nye

SENATOR AUGUSTUS AEMILIUS Caro glared sternly at the slender white robed priestess standing alone on the floor of the Roman Senate, dwarfed in the enormous amphitheater with its high, elegant pillars of white marble.

"Virgo Vestalis Maxima Caecilia Gaius Sempronius, you realize that if these charges of unchaste behavior are proven, then you will be removed from your office."

Caecilia never changed her expression, keeping her features a virtually theatrical mask. How dare that boar-haired, pock-faced brute accuse the chief priestess of Vesta of lying? Her testimony should be considered as if it came from the goddess herself. Fire roared in her belly, demanding that she avow her innocence.

But Aemilius didn't believe the charges any more than she did. She saw truth through the eyes of her goddess. Vesta, goddess of the hearth and protector of SPQR, the Senate, and the People of Rome, and she had been raised by her patrician parents to know the difference between true outrage and the screen of self-interest. Aemilius acted through the latter, and Caecilia had no intention of letting him succeed. "Removal from office" was a very polite way of saying that upon condemnation she would be taken to a place of punishment, stripped of her vestal robes and scourged, then led, with all due ceremony, to an underground chamber where awaited a bed, a chair, a table, a little food and, very soon thereafter, no air. Everyone would know her innocence, but no one would challenge the verdict, lest the displeasure of the Senate fall upon them, too.

Caecilia didn't intend to die or to lose the desirable estate in the Trastavere that Aemilius so very badly wanted to take from her. Vesta would protect her. At that moment, though, she felt very small and alone, a woman of short stature and small bones. She wrapped the shawl-like palla of her office closer around the all-enveloping white stola that clothed her from neck to heels.

All around her, the fifty members of the Senate, all high-born and wealthy male citizens of Rome, regarded her with amusement, speculation, suspicion, or confusion. Though every one of them had sent a servant or their wife to obtain fire to light and warm their households from Vesta's hearth, they were still wary of the mysteries that no male priests were permitted to perform. Caecilia also sensed jealousy.

"Let me be tried, then," she said, holding her head high. "The truth will be known. I have not broken my vows, and the gods themselves will so proclaim."

"So shall it be," intoned Marcus Junius Pera, tall, lean, and hawk-nosed. "And will you now return to your duties in the Temple of Vesta? Her protection for Rome is needed more than ever."

"I shall," Caecilia said, inclining her head majestically, making the *seni crines*, the seven ceremonial braids of her long, dark hair, bob under the white, ribbonlike vitta and modest veil. "Vesta will hold the city in her two cupped hands."

"I thank you and the other Vestals," Junius said. He bowed to her, prompting all the rest of the Senate except Aemilius to follow his example.

Rome stood as a republic, the first and greatest in the world. No Senator held higher office than any other, but Junius had been named temporary dictator by the Senate in the wake of the current crisis. Three years before, the Carthaginian general Hannibal Barca had broken the *pax romana* regarding borderlands in Iberia, forcing Rome to fly to the aid of the city of Saguntum. The Punic Senate had claimed that there was no *pax romana*, since no treaty had been verified proclaiming it, and in any case, the city lay south of the boundaries discussed, therefore Saguntum had only been liberated from the invading Romans. Ever since then, Hannibal, son of Hamilcar, had been a constant threat, appearing out of nowhere with gigantic armies including elephants—*elephants!*—and mowing down countless good Roman soldiers. Caecilia was scornful. Anyone who needed elephants to defeat Romans probably wasn't a very good general.

Caecilia knew perfectly well why Aemilius had made his move now. The mind of the Senate on the Palatine Hill lay to the southwest, in Cannae, and not there in the city. Unlike the Vestals, whose appointed mission it was to protect the city with their goddess-given magic, even in disaster greedy men like him saw only their own opportunities. She had to admire his cunning. If he wanted to gain an advantage no one would grant, a republic-wide crisis provided the perfect cover. It annoyed her that the Pontifex Maximus, chief over all temples in Rome, had not appeared to defend her in the Senate. Then she remembered that he was Aemilius's first cousin.

"The examination will be set for ten days from now," Junius said. His face told Caecilia that he had no taste for the subterfuge, but he had no choice. Aemilius was of the best families, and had significant influence, as well as almost endless wealth from his farms on Sicily. "Very well, then. Terrentius Ostracius, how goes the assembly of the new legions? Our scouts report that the Carthaginian faces our troops in Cannae. They will need relief as soon as the gods may grant."

Her situation handled, the Senate turned to the matters that they thought were actually important. Insulted, Caecilia spun and walked from the building. No man put out a hand to halt her. Her person remained sacred, despite the accusations. No one but the executioners, should it come to that, would lay a finger upon her. She would be led to her vault and made to climb down alone, without even a coal from Vesta's fire to comfort her. Caecilia had the sudden need to be before that fire.

With dignity, she mounted her covered, two-wheeled carpentum carriage for the descent to the Temple and Collegium of Vesta at the base of the Palatine Hill. Her lictor, Marcus, strode out onto the footpath.

"Make way for her august personage, the Chief Vestal Caecilia! Make way! Stand aside for Vesta's chosen!"

THE TEMPLE OF the goddess of the hearth had been built and ornamented with the same skill and pride as any of the other deity of Rome. Caecilia peered between the curtains shielding her from curious eyes as the bumping wheels moved from the common way onto the smooth flagstones of the temple precinct, admiring the high portico and the glorious white Carrera marble of the pillars that flanked the doorway. The porter, a short, fine-boned old man who had served the last four chief Vestals beginning when he was a child, rushed to offer aid as she descended. He extended his arm for her to steady herself.

"My lady, we were all worried about you," he said, the myriad wrinkles around his beady brown eyes contracting in concern. Timinius was a terrible gossip, a sin for which he ought to have been flogged, but his network of confidants had often been of use to Caecilia. In Rome, no amount of information was to be scorned.

"You are kind," she said, favoring him with a smile. "I will be all right."

"Oh, maybe not," Timinius said, shaking his head as he escorted her to the doorway of the collegium. "Senator Aemilius has called for the presence of two men he calls witnesses."

Caecilia was glad to hear him phrase the term so carefully; those were not witnesses, in the whispers around the city, but being called as witnesses to her alleged misbehavior.

"Indeed, they cannot be witnesses, for there was nothing for them to have witnessed," she said, taking her hand from his forearm.

"Of course there hasn't been!" Timinius said, in high dudgeon. For the first time all day, Caecilia felt like laughing, but she didn't.

"I thank you for your confidence. Go to your duties, as I must go to mine."

"Yes, my lady."

Timinius withdrew with alacrity, and stumped back to the entrance, his thin elbows pumping up and down as he walked. Caecilia regarded him with affection. His faith in her was unshaken. She knew that he would begin to gather information to impugn those who Aemilius intended to bear false witness against her. Would ten days be enough to find the wedge the perfidious senator had that would make a citizen lie under sacred oath? She felt a chill in her belly.

"Caecilia!" Doria, the next senior vestal, came fluttering from her dormitory nearest the entrance. "Vesta preserve us all! You are in time to lead the afternoon ritual. I was afraid I would have to. My spirit doesn't arouse the flames the way yours does."

Caecilia embraced her. "Come, let us ask the goddess for her blessing."

The Temple of Vesta, with its tall pillars, stood both awe-inspiring yet welcoming. The inhabitants of Rome, citizens as well as visitors, slaves, and children, never hesitated to enter the wide doors to the outer sanctuary. As her priestesses, the Vestal Virgins had the power to free a slave or spare a condemned prisoner with a single touch. Those who had been granted the mother goddess's clemency became generous with their donations to the temple thereafter. Even patricians of the highest status donated, if not from their hearts, then from self-interest.

In the robing room, Caecilia and her five sister priestesses bathed and garbed themselves in the ritual vestments of the day. Their simple headdresses and veils were removed so the temple slaves could rebraid their hair afresh in the seni crines, then the elaborate arrangement was crowned with infula and suffibulum, the white woolen fillet and veil edged with royal purple. The red and white ribbons beneath the latter signified their devotion to the goddess's task and their purity. They ranged in age from Doria's forty—she had been widowed and brought into the priesthood after her husband's death—to Ilonia's seven. The little fair-haired girl had been with them only a year, installed after the retirement of the last Vestal, Mariana. Caecilia prayed that she would live to see the girl fulfill the promise that had led the Pontifex Maximus to bring her to the temple.

Once attired, they progressed to the inner sanctuary. The slaves and attendees at the shrine that day had to wait outside the archway as the Vestals knelt before the small, six-pillared shrine that contained Vesta's hearth. The flame burning inside a flat-bottomed stone bowl within it was lower than usual, so low that Caecilia worried.

"That is not the way it should be," Doria murmured. Pressures outside Rome must have impinged upon Vesta's protective warmth.

Still on her knees, Caecilia extended her hands to the Vestals on either side of her.

"Then let us build it higher, sisters," she said.

The women clasped hands and devoted their energies to their goddess. Vesta, who warmed all of Rome, who provided light to its citizens, and who, twenty-one years before, had taken Caecilia out of a home where she would have been a pawn married off to provide an advantage for her ambitious father, and never allowed to blossom. She had not wanted to be a wife, living in the shadow of a man who was powerful only because he was rich and had bloodlines that could be traced back to Romulus and Remus. The goddess had been more of a mother to her than her own mater. This temple and its environs were her home. She felt terror that she could be dragged from here and have her own flame snuffed out for the whim of a greedy man. She knew she was the toy of the gods, destined to go where and how they willed, but to have a mere man try to hold the power of the gods over her offended her. She was his equal in rank, and more than that in intelligence and strength of will.

But Vesta deserved her best and fullest concentration. Caecilia closed her eyes, reached deep into her heart, and concentrated on the love she felt for her goddess. Her body filled with the joy of it. Warmth suffused her entire frame, transforming her bones into pillars of fire.

When she felt that she could muster no more, she opened her eyes and breathed out. Flames poured from her mouth, and those of her sister priestesses, into the shrine.

Behind her, she heard the visitors gasp. Caecilia had to smile. It had scared her into wetting herself the first time she had seen the senior Vestals breathe fire. But now, the sacred flame leaped high enough to lick at the canopy of the shrine.

A voice in her mind made Caecilia gasp in turn.

"Peace, my daughter," it said. "My fire is your weapon against all enemies. Let it light your mind."

The feeling of deep contentment that enveloped her settled her jangled nerves. The goddess had been watching over her in the Senate. Aemilius would not rob her of her office! Heat poured out of the covered enclosure and enveloped them. Caecilia reveled in its warmth. With its aid, she sent her mind flying above the city, feeling the gentle protection of Vesta. Romans felt safe because of her, nestled like chicks under the feathers of their mother hen. Instead of brute force, like that of the god Mars, the goddess of the hearth provoked those within her aegis to treat one another more kindly, with greater civility, than usual. Violent outbursts were lessened under her hand, and people relaxed. Caecilia was able to let loose of her resentment and enjoy the sensation.

Then suddenly, there was a collective gasp from the six Vestals as the smoke grew red, and was filled with Roman soldiers trapped and pressed shoulder to shoulder, dying under flashing swords and the points of spears.

A cry from outside made her jolt out of the trance before she could see more. Caecilia let go of her fellow priestesses' hands, and rose to her feet.

"Who disturbs us in our worship?"

The wide-eyed patrons turned to point at a slave in short toga and mud-caked sandals. He scrambled toward the Vestals and threw himself at their feet.

Oh, what now? Caecilia thought, her fear returning. He could only have come from the Senate. Had they decided to put her trial forward?

"Speak, slave!" she commanded, pushing her fear out of sight. "What does the Senate require?"

"My lady," the youth panted. He could have been no more than twelve. His narrow, pimply face was innocent of the traces of mustache or beard. "A messenger has come from Cannae. Hannibal destroyed our armies. They march toward Rome itself! They are only five days from here. The Senate begs you to protect the city."

"Our power is not enough to hold back an invading force," said Julia, the next-youngest priestess. She was fourteen. Voluptuous curves lay concealed under the all-enveloping stola, and the bow of her mouth looked like Venus's kiss. If she had not been promised to Vesta, she would have been sought in marriage by many wealthy patricians. But she had yet to learn tact. Her fierce tongue had earned her the name Blue Spider.

"Surely the Senate is taking other measures," Caecilia said, fixing a stern eye on both her student and the messenger.

The youth nodded.

"They have ordered more legions to be assembled," he said, with a gulp. "Four more! And cavalry, many horsemen. Senator Aemilius is raising an army on his estates to the northwest of the city. But they beg the god's assistance. The enemy must not be allowed to cross the Tiber. The city is roiling in panic. People are fleeing to the ports."

"Of course we will do our duty," Doria said, looking to Caecilia for reassurance.

"From whom did the request come?" Caecilia asked the slave. "From Senator Junius?"

"No, holy one. From Senator Aemilius."

"And did he say 'beg'?" Caecilia asked, raising a skeptical eyebrow. She already knew the answer.

The boy's tanned cheeks burned red.

"No, holy one."

"What exactly were his words? I know you were trained to repeat them precisely. Do not fear Vesta's wrath, my child. You are but the vessel."

Another gulp. "He commands you to shore up the walls of Rome with Vesta's magic flames, my lady."

"Does he?" Caecilia said, her voice level, even though those flames felt as if they coursed through her body in fury.

"How dare he?" Doria exclaimed. "We do not answer to him!"

He already thinks he rules me, Caecilia thought. She smiled at the trembling slave.

"Tell him—no, tell Marcus Junius Pera—that the Vestals will do their sacred duty."

"Yes, my lady." The boy sprang to his feet and hurtled out of the temple, leaving behind dirty footprints. The temple slaves sprang to sweep up the soil.

"Serenity, now, sisters," Caecilia said, forcing herself to do just that. "Let us conclude the ritual and be about our duties of the day."

"How can you be so calm?" Ilonia asked, her eyes wide. "Rome is going to be invaded!"

"Silence!" the chief Vestal demanded. "You watched the battle, as did I, in the sacred smoke. We were all astounded and saddened at how many died. Brave soldiers all. But the Carthaginian will not succeed as long as we keep our heads."

She sounded far more confident than she felt. While she had known Vesta to perform small miracles, this felt beyond all possibility to achieve. Yet they must try, or Rome would burn.

CAECILIA LET ILONIA stir the vast pan that contained emmer for the *mola salsa*, the sacred flour needed to propitiate the divine lares and penates in every household, as well as in every other official temple and shrine, until it began to toast fragrantly. The fire over which it cooked had been kindled from the sacred flame. This was the third day in a row that they had had to make such quantities. It was being sprinkled all the way around the border of the city, with particular emphasis on the approaches from the southeast.

"Makes me think of my mother's house," said Julia. At Doria's nod, the girl added salt to the ground wheat. Ilonia stirred it furiously. Caecilia and the others poured their love for Vesta into the mola, chanting the prayer that imbued it with the goddess's strength. At the moment when the mixture turned honey brown, just before it would have begun to burn, she exercised her will on the fire beneath. It subsided to a flicker.

She gestured to the servants, thirty in all. They had their usual stops, at the temples of Jupiter, Mars, Apollo, Athena, the Parthenon, Venus, and so on, plus the shrines at each sentry point around the perimeter of the city. Ordinarily, a peck-measure of it would be destined for the sacred games in the Forum, but the entertainments were suspended until the coming crisis was dealt with. They all helped to scoop the still-hot mola salsa into vessels. As each slave filled his jar, he covered it with a clean woolen cloth. With a bow, the young men shot out onto the road and vanished into the crowd.

The homey aroma kept the Vestals from thinking of war and the horror of having their borders invaded. What news came from the south grew worse with the arrival of every successive messenger. Fewer than fourteen thousand soldiers of eighty thousand survived the bloodbath at Cannae. The remainder limped toward home under the generalship of the disgraced Consul Varro. Besides raising new armies to bolster what was left of their fighting force, the Senate sent ships and wagons to appeal to their allies in the other city states and the provinces. After treating his injured men and replenishing his supplies, Hannibal had indeed turned his force southward. His next target was Rome itself. Men sent their families away and prepared to defend the city. Slaves fled in whatever direction they thought would take them away. The Vestals had their hands full, bespelling the fugitives to bring them back again. Caecilia understood their fear; she was as much a prisoner as they, but none of them could run away from the duties they had to fulfill. Rome must not fall.

With the threat of attack imminent, Junius sent word down to the Collegium that Caecilia's trial would be put off indefinitely. It irritated her not to have the charge dismissed outright. Having the possibility of removal and death hanging over her head added stress that she did not need. Desperate people flung themselves at her feet day after day, praying for reassurance that Vesta's protection would not desert them.

That the trial would eventually take place gave Aemilius liberty to order the Vestals around as though they were his own servants. The same breathless youth who had come on the first day returned morning and afternoon to demand this or that, in his master's name. First, Aemilius wanted prayers chanted to protect his home and his family, as well as his villa outside the city and his farms in the east. That was no trouble. Their chronicler, the priestess Lucilia, kept a long scroll of those who sought to importune Vesta for their well-being. Aemilius's family was merely added to the roster.

Next, he ordered that the Vestals give him the whole day's output of mola salsa for the protection of his property. Caecilia sent a politely worded but outright refusal. The temple of Mars already required an increase, to bless the legions about to march.

"We are stretched so thin," she explained, apologetically. The slave already bore bruises and stripes from a cane or whip upon his arms and legs for bearing bad news. Her heart ached for him. She almost wished the boy would run away. No matter how Aemilius raved, she would refuse to send the spell that arrested his flight. He had gulped and nodded and gone back uphill toward the Senate, though not with the eager trot of two days before.

But here came the poor child again. Caecilia heard his footsteps on the paving stones even before he burst into the temple.

"My lady, the senator demands your presence on the Senate floor," the slave said, not lifting his eyes to meet hers.

"For what purpose?" she asked. One of her own servants came to her with a basin of rosewater and a linen towel, to wipe away the traces of mola making from her hands.

It took a long time before the child could bring forth the words he had been ordered to say. His cheeks turned so red they rivaled Vesta's fire burning in the shrine behind them.

"He says that he has heard rumors that the priestesses of Vesta are not doing all they can to turn back the enemy. Rome will fall, and it is the fault of the Virgins. Since you are supported by the public purse, you're shirking your duty and… cheating all of Rome. If that is true, he says, your order has no reason to exist. He… calls upon you to denounce this claim before the full body of the Senate, my lady." The youth fell to his knees and dropped his head to the floor, trembling. Obviously, he feared that Caecilia would smite him dead with Vesta's fire. Her heart filled with pity.

She went to him and touched him on the shoulder.

"Poor boy," she said. "I wish you had a better master. Aemilius must be terrified that his legions won't be strong enough to withstand Hannibal's. Go back and tell him that we are preparing our reply."

"Yes, my lady." The slave scrambled to his feet and fled.

"That is the direst of insults!" Doria exclaimed, clutching one hand to her ample breast. "We have done nothing but our duty. I feel the protections on every road that leads to Rome. No one could be safer than within our environs!"

"If he disbands us, then Vesta's fire will go out," Lucilia said, her eyes wide. "Then the city and the republic *will* fall, Hannibal or no Hannibal."

"I don't want to die!" Ilonia wailed. Her nose turned red as she burst into tears. "Goddess protect us!"

"Peace, sisters," Caecilia said. Her mind was working furiously.

She pleaded with Vesta for protection. *As I hold the boundaries of your city protected, please help me. Give me inspiration to save my life. I will die for you, but not this venal, greedy man.* Did the goddess expect her to go meekly up the hill to face four score of men who did not respect her power?

The soft voice in the fire came back to her then. No, indeed, she did not. But they should respect it. Perhaps the loss of it would remind them of why they owed reverence to Vesta.

"What shall we do?" Doria asked.

"Only our sworn task," Caecilia said. "We do not answer to the Senate. A higher power commands us." *Oh, Goddess, lead me wisely!* she thought. She looked around at the desperate faces of her sisters, and steeled herself, though her heart pounded in fear. She was taking a risk, one that endangered all of them. She might have company in that dark, underground chamber, but she prayed that extremis would not come to pass. "Vesta's flame is our priority. The Senate can indeed cut off our stipend, but even in rags and living on scraps, we can maintain our sacred calling. Senator Aemilius is right in one thing: we help to guard the gates of Rome. We must go on doing that, to the exclusion of all else."

"WHAT DO YOU mean, you cannot accept my sacrifice?" Patrician Lucius Paulus Germanicus demanded. The old man gestured to the trio of goats that his servants held by the horns on the steps of the temple. "My son leads a century of men out against the enemy. He must be protected by the goddess!"

"I am sorry," Caecilia said, with a sad smile echoed by the Vestals ranged behind her. "Our order has been called into disrepute by the Senate. The goddess knows we have done no wrong, so we continue to fulfill our rites to her and her alone."

"What fool would say such a thing?" Paulus snorted.

"I am afraid that to repeat gossip only adds power to it," the chief Vestal said, satisfied at the outrage on Paulus's face. She eyed the plump young goats with regret. The goddess would accept their spirits, and the savory meat would remain to be consumed by the priestesses and the servants of the temple. "I ask you to return with your offering another time, dear sir. I pray for the safety of your son. He is a true hero of Rome."

She turned, and swept back into the inner sanctuary, ignoring the protests behind her.

"Bank down the fire to its smallest ember," she ordered the other priestesses. "Vesta's flame will always burn, but she will not shed her light on those who treat us, her devotees, ill."

The Vestals followed her order, even though they were uncertain about refusing an order from the Senate. They had the public's sympathy, by and large, except for a few who snarled abuse at them. Caecilia made private note of those, though at the same time, she asked Vesta's forgiveness for thinking ill of them. The moral high ground was at the top of a slippery slope—as indeed was the Senate itself.

Paulus was only one in a host of many whose sacrifices and donations Caecilia refused that day, and the next. According to Timinius, Rome was in an uproar. By all accounts, Hannibal continued his march southward. He was less than a week's march away from the city's gates. That Vesta seemed to have turned her back upon her children was adding to the tension rising in the city. To anyone who came to the temple to demand to make a donation or sacrifice, Caecilia offered a sad smile.

"I am sorry, but we are prisoners here. We cannot accept your offerings."

Timinius kept them well supplied with gossip. Reports came from afar that Hannibal's army had penetrated farther than any enemy ever had in decades. Cities that had been Rome's allies for generations considered betrayal rather than face Hannibal. He had priests of his own clearing the way with foul wizardry. Caecilia, on her mental flights over the city, could feel the magic growing against them. She knew they sensed the dampening of Vesta's protective aura. So could the priests of the other gods in Rome.

"Why are we doing this?" Lucilia asked, as the eyes of the citizens on the street grew unhappy, even hostile, over the course of the next day. Yet another unhappy would-be donor departed, taking his calf and geese with him. "Rome could be invaded while we let the wards die away!"

"Because if we do not defend ourselves, then our office, all our sacrifices and vows, become meaningless," Caecilia said. "Unworthy vessels of Vesta's power will take our place, if anyone does at all. The goddess will withdraw her blessing from Rome. Hannibal is a human enemy. In the long run, he is meaningless. We are under siege, sisters. Our lives and the future of this temple are at stake."

"Must Rome fall, then?" Doria asked.

Caecilia shook her head. She drew them into the small sanctuary, barring even the most trusted servants from entering with them. She glanced at the arched doorway. Timinius looked stricken, but he kept the others back, out of earshot.

"Rome will not," Caecilia said, in a low voice. The small coal in the shrine crackled as if in agreement. "It never will. But Hannibal drew Rome's armies into a trap. We can do the same, with both our enemies and Rome's. It will take courage."

"We have never lacked courage," said Lucilia, her spine as straight as a column. The others nodded.

"We are true Daughters of Rome," Caecilia said, proud of them all. They gave her the heart to continue. "Hear me, then. We will allow the borders to shrink slowly, ever so slowly, and let Hannibal come within range. Then, we will kindle the embers into the largest and most roaring blaze ever. We cannot consume him, but we can break his confidence, and make him easy fodder for the legions."

"In the meanwhile, we will look as if we are neglecting our office," Julia said, with a fierce look worthy of her Blue Spider nickname.

"The Senate already believes that we are," Caecilia said, waving a dismissive hand. "We are prisoners, until the magistrate decides upon our virtue. What of that? We serve Vesta, pure and simple. Go back to your dormitories, and remain there until all this has passed."

Overnight, the aegis of Vesta dimmed and diminished all around the city. For those as sensitive as the Vestals were, great unease filled their hearts.

In the distance, the mass migration of soldiers under the command of the one-eyed general from Carthage felt the vulnerability of their prize. Caecilia sensed his eagerness in the coming conquest, and hardened her resolve against him.

Not on my watch, she thought. *Never while I live.*

THE FOURTH DAY dawned. Timinius fluttered into the dormitory, disturbing Caecilia from her morning ablutions.

"The Senators are here, my lady!" he called into the bathing chamber. Caecilia allowed her female servants to help her dry off and don her vestments. She shook with nerves, but refused to let them show on the surface. That warm feeling within her told her she was right.

Hannibal is walking into my trap, and so is Aemilius.

Even before she entered the anteroom, she could hear Aemilius ranting in the empty temple.

"There she is!" he snarled, pointing at her. Marcus Junius Pera stood behind him, looking unhappy. "The Vestals have failed in their duty! See the perfidy! She is in league with the Carthaginian! The enemy is almost upon our threshold!"

"Vesta does not fail us, honored senator," Caecilia said. "I swear it, and no one has ever doubted the word of a Vestal Virgin. Until you."

"Lock her up," Aemilius ranted. "Hannibal is advancing. If there is anything left of Rome after he has invaded, I will take her outside of the city walls and dispose of her myself!"

The other senators looked shocked. Caecilia eyed him evenly. Either she succeeded now, or she deserved to die a humiliating death. She lifted her chin proudly.

"We have been watching Hannibal. He does advance, but he is about to walk into our trap."

"Trap?" Junius asked, his dark brows rising. "What trap?"

"He is full of confidence, but he has never faced the wrath of Vesta, protector of Rome," Caecilia explained. "We have *allowed* the sacred fire to abate, honored dictator, leading him to believe that we are helpless. He has marched within three days of Rome. But if you have lost all faith in us, there is no point in continuing our ruse." She made her face look sorrowful and resigned. "We will have to put all of our faith in our brave legions, and hope that Mars spares the city when he smites the Carthaginians."

"Who said we lost faith in you?" Junius asked, puzzled. Caecilia realized that all the demands that had come from the Senate were sent by Aemilius only. She lifted a slim, small hand.

"We can do nothing, Senators. You have condemned us all *with your doubt*. We cannot do the tasks set us by the goddess Vesta. If we do not have your confidence, then we fall. If we fall," she lowered a baleful eye on them, "so does Rome. We are prisoners of that doubt."

"Who doubts you?" Junius demanded. "Not us."

"Not all of you. He who cast aspersions on my virtue, and that of the other Vestal Virgins," Caecilia said, trembling as the fury she had suppressed for days resounded in her voice. "He who has taken action at law, saying that I did not worship my goddess properly!"

Everyone turned to look at Aemilius.

"Withdraw your suit," she said.

"It all turns on this?" Junius demanded. Caecilia swallowed. If this did not work, both she and Rome could be lost.

"Yes, dictator. He called my integrity into question. And with my integrity, that of my sisters and our vow to protect Rome. Our fire still burns, but look at the poor thing." Caecilia gestured toward the door of the inner sanctuary, at the last remaining ember. "It *gutters*. It could go out at any moment. And Hannibal is so close."

"Don't be a fool, Aemilius!" Junius said, impatiently. "The Vestals are our shield and guardian!"

Aemilius knew exactly what she was doing, as she had known what he was doing.

"All right," he growled. His fierce gaze stabbed at her, but she held up the shield of a bland smile.

"Do you withdraw your accusation against me?" Caecilia asked.

The word gritted out. "Yes!"

"And against all the Vestals? You recognize our purity and our dedication?"

"Yes!"

Caecilia nearly collapsed with relief, but held herself upright. She had won!

Her smile of satisfaction made the greedy senator snarl. Aemilius withdrew in high dudgeon, stalking out with only a barked command at his beleaguered slave.

Caecilia knew it was unlikely he would give up trying to buy her property from her, but she would live to fight that battle.

"Well, dictator?" she asked.

Marcus Junius Pera turned to the guards and raised both hands.

"Release the Virgins!" he cried. "Let them safeguard Rome!"

"Sisters!" Caecilia called. "Come serve your goddess!"

The other five Vestals came pouring out of their dormitories, followed by the acolytes and worshippers, carrying all the jugs of oil, tinder, kindling, and sacred wood that they had saved in the store-house.

Caecilia stepped into the sanctuary, to the small coal that was all that remained of the fire. Such a small thing, she thought, tenderly. She could have stepped on it with her caliga and snuffed it out, and just like that, they would be overrun by the largest army ever to challenge Rome. But the goddess winked at her through the ember. She dipped tinder in oil and added it to the flame. It caught fire, spreading out. The other sisters stepped in, adding kindling and sacred cedar and sandalwood. Fragrant smoke rose up as the fire grew and grew, until it was a wall of dancing yellow and orange, roaring its hunger. In its midst, the figure of a woman appeared, her arms outstretched.

"A miracle!" Junius exclaimed, falling to his knees. The rest of the senators gasped. "Vesta!"

The goddess smiled gently upon then, then rose up through the ceiling of the temple, and vanished.

Caecilia clasped hands with the rest of the Vestals, and the waking trance enveloped them. She felt the protection of the goddess like a hand of iron spread out from the fire in the shrine, pushing outward, covering the miles in less than a minute.

In her mind's eye, Caecilia saw all of Rome's enemies stop. Surrounded by uncounted horses and men, Hannibal himself, a rough brute with an empty eye socket, stopped short in the middle of a conference with a dark-skinned man in a gold fillet.

"The walls of Rome are too strong," he announced, to the evident astonishment of his companion. "The new legions ready and we too few. We do not have enough siege equipment." His confidence had deserted him. His hand shook as he gestured orders at his troops.

As one, the invaders turned their backs, no longer facing toward Rome. Caecilia knew Carthage was withdrawing. At least for now, Rome was safe. She had done her duty.

If only all her enemies were so easily vanquished, she thought. But for now, she welcomed the worshipers pouring into the temple with their offerings.

Salvage
Shariann Lewitt

"GOT A LOT of metal there, even if the tech's dead. And maybe it's good."

Captain Ana Martinez rolled her eyes. "Did you check the registration this time? I do not want to go through what happened when we hauled in that government wreck…"

"Uh, okay, Captain. Forgot about that one," Void replied. "I'll get on it now."

The Captain could not fathom how anyone could forget about three weeks interrogation in government confinement, but Void had gotten his nickname not from where he flew but from what was between his ears.

"And get Zip for backup," she ordered before he left the bridge. Well, what passed for a bridge on the *Gather*.

Martinez did not have a good feeling about this, mostly based on experience. Nothing Void found ever turned out well. She would have ditched him at their first port if his continued presence on the vessel hadn't been the prime condition of ownership.

But the sensors did show plenty of recoverable graphite-fiber polymer/carbon nanotubes, and an exceptional amount of very saleable silicon-carbide-particulate-aluminum, that clearly indicated ship composition of about two to four hundred years old with possible cryogenics. Over one hundred fifty years and without a government registry meant fair salvage, and they needed to make some jing soon—like before the starboard jump exchange blew. Which it could tomorrow. And then they would be totally screwed.

Even Zip, the best mechanic in known space, couldn't fix an exchange without any parts or a garage. He'd managed to keep the thrusters in shape, and even coax the shaky trawler into doing its job, but that jump exchange needed some serious work and a place to do it, and the *Gather* couldn't put it off any longer.

"We've got maybe one jump in us, two max," he'd said last night, over yet another dinner of Tomu's Bulk Freez-Dri Ramen. "Why do we have to keep eating this stuff, Cap?" he'd asked, poking at the mess in the bowl as if he doubted its organic origins.

Ana agreed with him, but, "They had a special on it at the warehouse. Half the price of the mac'n'cheez. If we've got enough left after the exchange repair…"

"I'd rather spend it on the tow overhaul and a couple of fully charged spare fuel cells."

Zip had his priorities straight. Which was why she needed him to babysit Void. The others were great at their jobs, but most of them had their own notions about what came first. Wong, for instance, was more interested in doctoring and diseases and the possible (oh so very exciting; Martinez was sick of hearing about it) presence of alien pathogens. Or Hakim, who had never met a computer system he didn't love more than any organic being in known space. Prying him away from any wrecked system they found was like trying to convince a spacer to stay portside. Not happening.

And then there was Gordon. No one knew if that was his first or last name, though they were all agreed it wasn't his real name at all. If Gordon hadn't been the best navigator Ana Martinez had ever met in her entire spacefaring life, she'd have spaced him. Not because he was unpleasant (he wasn't) or difficult to be around (he wasn't) or complained (he didn't) but because they all knew he was a spy. Or maybe an assassin. Void had money riding on it. Not that Gordon gave any indication, but they all agreed there was something off about him. Way off. Personally, Martinez thought he was an android, and Zip agreed when she ran it by him in private.

But the rest of the crew wasn't ready to space him so long as he wasn't spying on them and only using the *Gather* as a cover. They were legal, and everyone had their papers. They registered their salvage. Besides, Gordon was the finest navigator any of them had ever seen. And he worked cheap. So he stayed.

Now she only had to wait to see what Zip said about whatever it was that Void had found. An old ship, obviously, but what kind and how old and could they claim rights to it? More importantly, would it be worth anything if they towed it to Vacci II or Constolo, the two nearest ports that had garage slips adequate to the *Gather*'s needs. The kind that didn't ask too many questions and didn't cost a fortune, either.

She sat by the comm, knowing full well that everyone else was on the system, too. Because they needed a break and they needed it now. And this dead and abandoned ship might be their ticket, or it might be a load of junk.

Twenty minutes. Half an hour. Martinez fiddled with the instruments, and wondered whether something had gone wonky in the comm. Wouldn't be the first time.

"Yo, Cap'n, you want to come see this. It's, um, something." Zip's voice, not Void's. "And bring the doc, maybe? Because we may need her."

"Shouldn't we just tractor dock her, and take it from there?"

"Don't know if that's a good idea yet, Cap'n," Zip answered. "This may be valuable, but I'm not sure it isn't contaminated. Maybe the doc should check it out before we dock. And Hakim might want to take a look, too."

Oh no, Martinez thought. "Well, lock it tight, and I'll get over there with Wong. You two get back here and make sure we're good to go. And give Gordon the mass and drift coordinates, so we stay on course."

Not that they had much of a course. They needed something to sell to rent a garage dock, and who knew where something valuable enough for that would show up? Downplanet people thought scavengers had it easy. Find ancient treasures, live in luxury, loot lost civilizations on planets where the populations had gone long ago and had been forgotten for even longer.

Don't we wish. Martinez had never thought that, not for one minute. But she'd never been quite so desperate as she was at this moment. *Gather* had been close to scrap when Zip had put her back together with duct tape and super glue, but years of hard labor had made her too close to salvage herself for anyone aboard to be happy. Least of all her captain, who knew a little too intimately how deep the damage went, and that the rust they sighed over was the only thing holding her together.

Martinez met Hakim, already suited up and ready to go, at the starboard forward port. "You think they got some alien AI, Cap'n? Or something esoteric?" Hakim's words tumbled over themselves, his fingers twitching in his gloves as if examining an unfamiliar keyboard. "Where's Clementina?"

Hakim bounced up and down on his toes.

Martinez got on the comm. "Wong, what's taking so long? Haul your ass over to starboard forward. We're waiting."

Clementina Wong almost never needed a second summons, except to dinner. Admittedly, dinner didn't deserve prompt attention, but a find like this should excite everyone.

Oh. Of course. Hakim. The two of them wouldn't want to wait in the lock together a nanosecond longer than necessary.

"Coming," the doctor replied, with all the enthusiasm of a teenager summoned to log in to PE.

Martinez clocked seven more minutes until an unrepentant Wong showed and pulled her skinsuit on. Good thing that Hakim truly did prefer computer systems, because Clementina Wong looked more like an entertainment star than a spacer doc on a tiny salvage. Martinez wondered why she had signed on, but she wondered that about all her crew. Every private spacer had a story, and it remained private. That was the first of the Three Prime Rules of spacer life.

Second prime was the Family Rule, which meant they were all family. No romance, no sex among the crew. Get your needs met portside, but not in the family. Long ago, spacers had learned the fastest way to break up a crew was love. Or sex. Or any combination of the two.

Looking at the *Gather*'s crew roster, Hakim and Wong looked like a natural pairing, or so Martinez had thought when the doctor had signed on. She'd watched the two of them together just in case. The two in question turned out to be not only in no danger of violating the family rule, but of breaking the Third Prime, which was the No Fighting Rule. They appeared to loathe each other. Therefore, Clementina's late appearance and sullen manner.

Martinez would have liked to see a bout between the computer expert and the doctor. Both were skinny and appeared weak, but the captain knew that Hakim had a fourth dan black belt in Tae Kwan Do, and Wong had taken the Golden Gloves featherweight championship six years running. It would have been fun.

Hakim had already set up a feed on the *Gather* to cache information directly from the derelict. Zip and Void had registered on board twelve minutes before Martinez and her party were ready to leave to check out the new find.

And yeah, Martinez thought, it was worth something. A lot. A freaking fortune.

Except they couldn't claim it for salvage. The damn thing was a stasis ship, and there were humans aboard. Real live(?) humans in stasis.

Even if the registry had been lost or voided, the ship would belong to the people on it if they woke.

Damn her luck. *Damn!*

"Wong, check out whether these people can be revived. Hakim?"

"Working on it," Hakim cut her off.

"I'm going to have to transfer the readings for each of the units," the doctor said. "From a quick survey, it looks like some of the units are working, some have deteriorated, and some have failed. Impossible to know more without detailed information from each unit."

"Got it," Hakim said. "*Gather*'s system is already working on the analysis. Should be finished by the time we get back and peel off these suits."

"How did you find all the passwords?" Martinez demanded.

"I didn't. I've only got about half of them. Still working on the others," Hakim admitted. "Most are pretty straightforward, based on prime numbers. I don't think any of these are idiosyncratic."

"Well, that's a piece of luck," Martinez said. She didn't add that it was the only luck they'd had so far, and they needed about a whole lot more if *Gather* was going to remain spaceworthy. The others (except Void) could probably find jobs, so long as their employers cared more about competence than consistent adherence to law. Law, being different from one place to another, and rather undefined in deep space, meant a number of private space captains, herself included, had a rather fluid attitude toward the concept.

They returned to starboard forward, returned the suits to their lockers, and Hakim and Wong went to analyze the new data. Martinez went to her own quarters to pull up whatever information she could glean and think.

Fortunately Hakim, being either efficient or hyperactive, had uploaded a cursory prelim. She sent the nav data to Gordon tagged URGENT in flashing red, with the instruction to ascertain where the ship had come from or where it had been headed. At least they might be able to track down a registry.

A note popped up in queue from Wong. The stasis equipment dated from three hundred years ago, manufacture Leoto Cluster. That narrowed things down. Then the ship would belong to the people aboard, assuming any of them survived. Leoto Cluster consisted of six inhabited worlds—

but how many of those had been inhabited three hundred years ago? Comp said six. Great. Mining colonies back in the day, now diversified in manufacture, industry, inhabited by some rigid religious sect, whatever.

An idea slowly blossomed in Martinez' mind. More notes rolled across her screen, which she skimmed. This could work. It had better work, or they were well and truly screwed.

"All hands: meeting in the galley at twenty-two hundred hours," she announced, hoping that the comm didn't conk out for once. After dinner, at least, meant that if it did, everyone would be there anyway.

AS PREDICTED, EVERYONE was there. Ramen again, because they had nothing else. Void tried throwing noodles at the narrow air vent above them, but no one else wanted to play. "It's only going to make the place stink," Hakim complained. "If you don't eat now, you're going to be hungry, and we don't have anything else," Wong told him. At which point Void picked up his bowl and chugged half the thing in one go. Thankfully, it chimed 22 hours, and the captain stood up and convened the meeting.

"Okay, so this new salvage has a lot of anomalies. First off, everyone report on your analysis, and then we'll figure out what we're going to do. You all know interplanetary law on stasis ships with no registry and living or revivable inhabitants; the ship belongs to them."

"We could kill them," Gordon suggested.

Everyone looked at him.

"Just saying," Gordon said. "While they're in stasis. I mean, they're three hundred years old."

"No. Just no," Zip said. "We're salvagers, not murderers."

"Damn right," Martinez said. "Now if we can get on with the reports. Gordon?"

The navigator spoke as if he hadn't just suggested mass murder as if it were perfectly reasonable. But then, Gordon possibly was a mass murderer. Maybe Martinez should rethink keeping him aboard.

"Nav system has been dead for decades, can't tell how long. From what I can figure, the ship was hit by something—a meteorite, junk, whatever—that took out part of the engine and nav. It went off course until the remaining engine ran out, and has drifted for an undetermined period time. Undetermined due to half the archives being bashed in by some meteorite strike. Or something."

"Whoever is still alive in those stasis units, they're set up to start a mining colony," Hakim began his report by jumping into the middle without any kind of introduction. "Not economically viable. Which means they'll have to be retrained, assimilated, and integrated into either one of the present day Leoto worlds or somewhere else close to the center. In any case, there isn't going to be anything left from the worth of their ship to pay us a thanks gift."

"Wait, slow down. How do you know they're from the Leoto cluster? How do you know the worth of the remaining ship? And how are you dividing the spoils anyway? I mean, how many survivors are you expecting?" Zip, again sorting things out and being sensible.

"Obvious they're from a Leoto world. Language and computer architecture," Hakim answered. "And as for how many I would expect to survive, there are eighty in stasis. If even fifty percent revive, the expense of repatriating forty humans who are three hundred years out of date is an easy calculation. The ship's worth is entirely materials, not tech. Again, easy to calculate. And there it is."

"Doc, how many are revivable?" Martinez finally cut in.

Wong had the good grace to look sad. "Nothing near fifty percent. Those stasis units were never built for three hundred years, and the fact the ship was hit and half the guidance and computer system was taken out finished the job. I've looked over the data, and so far as I can tell, every single stasis unit shows irregularities. At least fifty of the people in stasis are clearly dead, and I would guess likely more. The rest are uncertain. And of those who may survive, and let me emphasize *may*, I expect not one of them will be the people who left their original world."

"You mean they'll need specialized training and support? Even medical intervention?" Gordon asked.

"Very likely," Wong replied.

"Brain damage?" Gordon continued.

"I don't have enough data to tell," the doctor said, after considering for a leaden minute. "I've never seen readings like the ones I've got here. The changes appear to be strongly hormonal, but I've never even heard of anything like this."

"So what could it mean?" Zip asked.

Wong shook her head and lifted her hands, palms up. "Anyone's guess."

"But very likely brain damage." Gordon stated the obvious.

The entire crew fell silent, and Martinez thought she knew what they were thinking. What she was thinking. One thing to kill living, functioning humans. Quite another to euthanize the remains of people who had been irreparably damaged or who could never become whole. Planetside such people could have a life, but to spacers, the very thought was their worst nightmare.

"Absolutely uncertain," Wong said. "I can't condone euthanasia, not when we have no clue what has happened to those few who may be viable."

"Given the small number, they should have excess to offer a thanks gift," Hakim pointed out. "And I can't guarantee that I can open the stasis units anyway. They've only got half the computer, and I've only got half the passwords."

"Well, why don't you get on it, Hakim? Zip, help him," Martinez started to give assignments.

"How is Zip going to help me? He doesn't know anything about ancient computational architectures."

"He knows a bit about Leoto cultures. Maybe if you can figure something about the programmers or makers? He might be able to give you some insights so you both can figure out the password."

Neither of the men looked happy, but Martinez knew that they both had something to offer, and she wanted this resolved. If and how many survivors, and how badly said survivors were damaged, would make all the difference to *Gather*'s future. If *Gather* had a future.

"Doc, see if you can get some information about what the hormone anomalies might mean for the survivors, if there are any survivors. If anyone does wake up, we'll all do better if we have some idea of what to expect."

"It'll be guesswork," the doctor told her. "Even at best."

"Anything is better than nothing at this stage," Martinez said, and then returned to the bridge. Not because she had any specific job to do at the moment; the course was locked, and last time she'd been flush, she'd invested in the second-best debris deflection system Greleck had available. The thing worked better than advertised, too.

No, she went to the bridge because she needed to wait, and she did not wait very well. Nor did her crew like her to hover over them while they worked. Here, at least, she downloaded a Leoto language learning pod. Well, actually there were seventeen distinct Leoto languages of that time period, but she could get the base and then the variations, which the catalog said would be faster. It gave her something that passed as productive to do.

With the immersion language pod, she also absorbed some of ancient Leoto culture, values, and priorities, which were embedded in the language. Zip knew a lot more about the politics and economics; he also knew the procedures of setting up the mining colonies, but she had absorbed far more of the base assumptions.

The Leoto group had started as a closed religious group with strict regulations and little tolerance for infractions. Mandatory prayer twice a day, a long list of food restrictions (Martinez did check that Ramen was permitted, though she would have lied had it not been, since they would have no choice), and utterly inhumane limits on sex. No one was supposed to engage in sexual relations except to reproduce, and then only after a series of approvals and rituals. Men and women lived separately most of their lives, and everyone was continually supervised and monitored.

Horrified, Martinez ran a quick check on current Leotian culture to see how much they'd changed in the intervening centuries. Not nearly as much as she'd hoped, it turned out. Which might work to *Gather*'s advantage. Survivors would have far less adjustment into modern Leotian society.

If these colonists ran true to form, they would be barely out of adolescence, with only a secondary education and skill training. Which meant they would be easier to retrain than if they'd had professional credentials that would be long out of date. Arrange passage back to Leoto for them, and reasonable expenses could easily be cut by a third.

Hakim and Wong both showed up together, and neither of them was bleeding. Martinez took that as a very good sign.

"We're pretty close now, Captain," Hakim said. "I've got pretty much everything expect the final password to pop the tops, as it were."

"He means open the stasis units," Wong said. "Like I said, it's all guesswork at this point, but I've done as much analysis as I can, given the information available. Which isn't a lot." She glared at Hakim.

He glared back. "To call what is left of that control system a mess would be a compliment. I don't know, if we even find the password and the rest of the code, if the thing will work. And the units could be welded or rusted shut at this point, even if all the circuits connect."

"Zip's working on it."

"This needs a miracle," Hakim replied.

"They were some kind of religious cult. Maybe they'll get one," the captain said.

"Let's just go over and do it."

So they did. They suited up, leaving only Void and Gordon on board. Martinez felt a cold knot in her stomach at the realization, but knew that she couldn't be present in both places. And she had to see whether they were going to make it or not.

In the dark, cold, half pressurized stasis hold, Zip had already begun channeling life support systems from the *Gather*. "Just in case anyone does wake up," he muttered. People were meant to emerge from stasis into warm, fully pressurized, Earth atmosphere environments. This wasn't going to be quite that comfortable. Hakim took the control panel and started programming faster than Martinez could speak. Wong checked unit by unit, locking those that showed no live readings. No reason to release corpses along with the living.

"Ready," Wong said.

"Ready," Hakim said.

Zip floated over to control board as Hakim typed. "Given Leotian mining colonies, I would expect that the release code would start with 'Release the' and then something that would refer to this particular batch. Only we don't know what this batch is. I've looked at their equipment, what's left of it, and their instructions, what Hakim could pull out the remains of that system, and I've been able to eliminate about seventeen classes of operations. But that leaves only about a hundred more."

"Did they only use classifications?" Wong asked.

Hakim gave her the evil eye.

"No," Zip said. "Sometimes they used the destination. Or the name of the ship. Neither of which we know."

"Did they have a sense of humor about these things?" the doctor asked.

"The Leotian culture was not in the least fanciful, especially in that period," Martinez said. "They were a strict religious community. Still are."

"Yes," Zip agreed. Then he began a series in Leotian using a series of religious ranks that Martinez recognized from both her language immersion and from her reading on contemporary culture.

"'Release the promised,' 'release the beloved,' 'release the godly.'" Zip stopped and scratched his head. "'Release the shriven.' I don't remember any other ranks that would reasonably apply. They're too old for baptized or the children, and way too young for the elders or the sacred or the priestly or the vowed."

Martinez closed her eyes. "Release the virgins."

Eight stasis units opened. Eight young, naked, ancient, people floated up, coughed, turned, screamed, and had to be hauled into thinsuits.

"It's okay, it's going to be okay," Wong and Martinez and Zip told them as they roped them together. "We'll get you over to our ship and get you cleaned up, and then we'll figure this all out."

"GET THEM OFF of me! I can't do anything," Hakim said, breathing hard. They'd had their refugees for two days and nothing, absolutely nothing on the *Gather* worked any more. Especially the crew. They were under assault.

This secret meeting had been set up surreptitiously, and getting out of the way of their assailants had not been easy. At least Void had not been needed, and he played decoy, keeping at least two of them amused, but that wouldn't last very long. Privacy had become a memory, but at least the former colonists had never been to the engine room and had no interest in going there. So here they were, crowded in between coil casings and fuel lines. The space configuration meant that no one could see anyone else, but at least they didn't have to worry about being interrupted.

"What are we going to do? And what are we going to do with them?" Wong asked. "I mean, it was fun for a while. But."

"Yeah," Zip agreed. "It was fun. For a while. Until it turned into rape. Or near enough."

The hormone imbalance. Wong had tried to explain it, Martinez thought, but even she hadn't realized at the time that those few who had survived over a century in an overly hormone-soaked stasis unit became something like sex addicts. And since their "guests" were all young and fit and reasonably attractive, it had been fun at first. But the Leotians wouldn't stop. Not to let them work, not to sleep, not to eat, not to figure out where to land them and get on with their business. The situation had become impossible.

Virgins, indeed, Martinez thought. *Don't we wish.*

Beyond having become sex addicts, though, they had been deprived of several vital supports during their long sleep, and their intellectual function had degraded as well. So they didn't understand why the crew needed to do anything other than constantly "play" with their new "friends."

"They're going to need a sheltered environment when they get to ground, and that's going to cost way more than general orientation," Zip observed. "And they're not bright enough to know that they ought to pay us a thanks gift for saving them."

"I think one is missing," Wong said. "One of the boys."

"Yes?"

"Really?"

"Which one?"

"Don't worry."

Everyone twisted to try to see Gordon. "Don't worry, I took care of him."

"What do you mean?" Martinez had never before heard such concern in Hakim's voice for a something not a computer.

"I mean he was a problem. He was quite—unpleasant—to me. A problem. I solved the problem. That's all."

If Martinez had ever had any doubt, it was gone now. She wanted Gordon off the ship. She wanted him nowhere near any of her reasonably decent crew, not even near their damaged Leotian survivors. She wanted very badly to space him but he was, first, their navigator, and second, a member of the crew.

"You did what?" she heard Zip say, and could hear him move.

No. Much as she agreed with him, she had to intervene. No killing aboard the *Gather*, no matter that Gordon fully deserved it. They needed him to get to a garage, damnit.

Which meant she had to think fast. Fortunately, Martinez excelled at thinking fast. That was why she was the captain. Well, that and other things.

"I have an idea," she interrupted the incipient fight. "Hear me out. We agree these people need a sheltered workshop where they can earn a living but be cared for, given room and board, medical care, clothing, everything they need to survive without having to take responsibility for that, right?"

All heads except for Gordon's nodded.

"Isn't there a Desir office on Constolo?"

Hakim smiled. Zip whistled. Wong protested. "You mean to sell these people as slaves to a brothel?"

"Absolutely not," Martinez said. "Desir is a legitimate business, and slavery is a capital crime. No, I mean to offer them the opportunity of a work contract doing the one thing they want to do. All the time. At the end of the contract, they will receive a fairly generous payment, and I will even negotiate that for them. Of course, we will be paid for their passage out of the total. That's only fair. And this hulk becomes our legal salvage as well."

The crew of the *Gather* looked at each other with wide eyes. "Brilliant, Captain. I couldn't have done better myself," Gordon said.

"Except you, Mr. Gordon. You will receive your portion of the profit minus one eighth, since you have deprived us of one eighth of the total sum. And you will depart *Gather* on Constolo. I will give you a recommendation as the best navigator I've ever worked with, and that you are leaving due to personal differences, but I won't have a murderer on my crew. Is that understood?"

"They're all problems. I should have spaced them all." The spy stood and left.

"We should space him," Zip muttered, but Martinez shook her head. "One murder is more than enough for me."

"Let's put it to the Leotians and see what they say. You think they'll go for it?" Hakim asked.

"You think they wouldn't?" Zip asked.

"How many days out is Constolo, Engineer?" the captain asked.

"I think I can nurse *Gather* through one last jump. With that, we can make Constolo in sixty-three standard hours. And then no more virgins, Captain," Zip said.

"Amen," Martinez replied.

"But one thing, Captain. How did you know?"

"Know what?"

"Know the password. The sacred rank. If even I'd forgotten it…"

Ana Martinez smiled. "It's archaic, dropped about two hundred years ago. That's why you aren't familiar with it, Zip. A specific caste for those venturing outward: virgins in body, but also in their new land and endeavor."

Zip gave her a very suspicious look. "You didn't just learn that from some immersion tapes last night."

She smiled. "We all have our right to privacy, Zip. Even our virgins."

The Midwinter of Our Discontent
Keith R.A. DeCandido

"WHAT ARE ALL these people doing in my crime scene?"

Lieutenant Danthres Tresyllione was already in a foul mood. She'd trudged through snow that ranged from ankle-deep to hip-deep all the way from the castle where the Cliff's End Castle Guard was headquartered.

Now she stood in one of the largest rooms in the Amswari Arms, an inn located just off the River Walk—the border between Goblin Precinct, the city-state's slum, and Mermaid Precinct, the docklands—which was completely full: four women dressed in white robes and three men in black robes, the latter trio kneeling next to a bed on which lay the body of a fourth man in black robes.

Danthres was there because of that dead body, as her job as a lieutenant in the Castle Guard was to investigate crimes committed in the demesne.

One of the guards assigned to Goblin Precinct—Danthres didn't care enough to remember his name—was standing by the threshold. "I'm sorry, Lieutenant, but the acolytes won't leave."

Frowning, Danthres asked, "Acolytes?"

"Yeah, apparently the dead guy's a high priest of something, and these are his chief acolytes. They've been kneeling around the bed the whole time."

"Fine, what about them?" She indicated the four women with her head.

"We can't get them outta the room." The guard pointed at one of the women's hands. "See those bracelets? They're like the ones on the prison barge."

Peering more closely, Danthres noticed that all four women were wearing metal bracelets inscribed with runes. Prisoners who served their sentence in Manticore Precinct—the prison barge that sailed out in the Garamin Sea—wore similar bracelets. If the wearer left the confines of the barge, the bracelets became extremely heavy.

"These," the guard said, "are magicked so that they can't leave this room. The only one who can change it is Father Gribnel."

"Who would be the body?" Danthres asked.

The guard nodded.

A flash of light, and then a short, squat figure appeared, wearing a black linen shirt that was too small on him and brown pants that were too big.

"I'm impressed, Boneen," Danthres said, as she blinked away the spots from her eyes that were the effects of the Teleport Spell. "You usually just teleport *away* from a scene."

"I usually don't have to wade through snow. I will be very pleased when this wretched season passes."

"Could be worse," the guard said, "we could live in Barlin—winter there lasts several months, not just a couple weeks."

Boneen pointedly ignored the guard, an action Danthres silently approved of, and instead asked, "Where is your partner?"

Danthres sighed. The plight of the partner in question, Lieutenant Torin ban Wyvald, was part of why she was so cranky. "Stuck in his house, as a snow drift has blocked the door and windows to the entire building."

"Typical." Boneen shook his head, and reached into the pouch on his belt to remove the herbs he'd need to cast an Inanimate Residue Spell. As the magickal examiner assigned to the Castle Guard, one of his primary functions was to cast that "peel-back" spell, which showed what happened in a space in the past, to determine how a crime was committed. It was one of the most useful investigatory tools the Castle Guard had. "I'll need all these people to leave."

"We'll need your help with that," Danthres said. "These women are all wearing bracelets that keep them in the room."

One of the women, a short blonde who looked like she had only just hit puberty, spoke up. "We been stuck in here for a *week*!"

"Yeah, we want out," said one of the two redheads.

Boneen waddled over to one of the redheads and asked, "May I inspect the bracelets, please?"

She held out her arm, and Boneen studied it. Then he let out a very long sigh, which did not encourage Danthres in the least.

"These bracelets are magicked in such a manner as to only be controlled by one person."

Danthres pointed at the corpse. "Who is lying dead over there."

"I assumed as much." Another sigh. "I will need to break the connection."

"And then you can cast the peel-back?" Danthres asked.

"I can attempt it, but if these women were here when the crime happened?" Boneen glanced at the four women.

The blonde shrugged. "We was asleep. We woke up, and Father Gribnel was all, y'know, *dead.*"

"Then I'm afraid the peel-back won't work. The bracelets will interfere with it."

"Wonderful," Danthres muttered. "I hate magick."

"I don't like it, neither," the blonde said.

An acolyte stood up. "The virgins would be silent!"

One of the redheads and the fourth, a woman with close-cropped black hair, both flinched and shrunk toward the wall. The other redhead just swallowed, while the blonde rolled her eyes.

Danthres stared at the acolyte. "Virgins?"

"Yes, of course." The acolyte seemed confused by Danthres's surprise. "Why else would they be dressed in white?"

The minutiae of fashion was something Danthres had never cared much about. She ignored the question and asked one of her own. "Why are you carting around four virgins and keeping them imprisoned?"

"They're not imprisoned—"

"Are too!" the blonde said.

"Be silent!" another acolyte snapped.

"Everyone be silent!" Danthres shouted.

The brunette raised a braceleted hand. "Excuse me, but I need to pee."

Danthres glanced over at the open doorway on the far side of the room, which led to the privy. The door had been removed from its hinges, she noted. "So go ahead, don't let me stop you."

"I can't go when there are other people watching."

Frowning, Danthres said, "You've been stuck in this room for a week, you said. What have you been doing?"

"Going when everyone's asleep."

"Then you should be used to holding it during the day." Danthres then turned to the guard and pointed at the acolytes. "Take those three outside."

"We can't leave Father Gribnel's side!" one of the acolytes said.

Danthres walked right up to the acolyte in question, who was rather short. For her part, while Danthres didn't have every aspect of her father's heritage, she did have the great height that was common to elves.

She loomed directly over him, and put her gloved hand on the hilt of her sword for good measure. "Can't you?"

Another acolyte grabbed the short one by the arm. "We will comply, of course, Lieutenant, and my apologies for Brother Karond."

As the guard escorted the three acolytes into the hallway, Boneen mixed some herbs in a pestle, made a grand gesture with one hand, and a spray of sparks burst forth. Two seconds later, the bracelets all fell off the women's arms and hit the floor with four resounding clunks.

"Finally!" the blonde said.

The brunette blinked. "Wait, we can leave the room? We're free?"

Danthres shook her head. "You can leave the room, but I'm afraid you're not free to go anywhere just yet." She turned to the magickal examiner. "Boneen, you're sure the peel-back won't work?"

"Completely. If it was just one bracelet, I might be able to reconstruct a clear picture, but four bracelets in the room for a week?" He shook his head.

"Fine, then can you use whatever magickal stuff you're saving by not casting that spell and expand your Teleport Spell to get the acolytes and the—the virgins to the castle?"

"I suppose." Boneen sounded incredibly reluctant, but then he glanced at the women and their very thin white robes. "They'd probably catch ill if they had to go on foot through the snow."

"Have one of the guards put them in the Interrogation Rooms. I'll be by later to talk to them."

"Very well."

As Boneen escorted the women into the hallway, Danthres went to the bed, grateful to finally have cleared the room. She caught the flash of Boneen's Teleport Spell in her peripheral vision.

Father Gribnel slept in his full robes, apparently. Now that all the people were gone, Danthres got a better look at the room in general, and saw that there were five pallets on the floor. From the looks of it, the three acolytes got their own pallets, while the women had to double up.

As for Gribnel himself, the blue tinge on his lips indicated poison. Danthres glanced around the room and found a small bottle on the

nightstand. Grabbing it and sniffing it, she smelled only lavender, but that could easily have been used to mask the poison.

Placing the bottle in a pouch on her belt, she checked the rest of the room, but found only a bunch of scrolls written in a language Danthres didn't recognize, and a large coin that she recognized as a voucher for passengers on a ship. According to the etching on the coin, it was for eight people on the *Ellartnev*.

The guard came back into the room and asked, "Anything else you need, Lieutenant?"

"Send for a detail of guards to bring the body to the castle—and these scrolls and coin also. Once we figure out what language it's in—"

"It's Aytrok."

"Excuse me?" Danthres shot the guard a look.

Shrinking visibly, the guard stammered. "Um, it's what they used to speak in Barlin back in the old days. Haven't seen anything written in it in ages."

Impressed that there was someone at the rank of guard who was literate, Danthres asked, "Can you read the scrolls?"

The guard restored Danthres's lack of faith by shaking his head. "Afraid not. It's been ages. The top of one scroll says 'Raebar,' but that's all I can tell you."

"What's a raebar?"

"No idea, but I remember seeing it etched into the façade of one of the buildings back home in Barlin. But I haven't been back there since I was a kid."

"All right." Danthres sighed. "Take care of this, will you? I'm gonna head back to the castle."

"Lieutenant? Why didn't you teleport with the M.E.?"

Danthres shuddered. "Teleporting makes me throw up. Better to walk through the snow."

WHILE THE SLOG back to the castle in the snow made Danthres's mood even worse, it was leavened by the sight of her partner in the squadroom.

Lieutenant Torin ban Wyvald rose from his chair upon Danthres's entry into the large room in the east wing of the castle and said, "There you are."

"There *I* am? I had despaired of seeing you before the thaw."

A smile peeking through his thick red beard, Torin said, "Several guards from Dragon Precinct dug my house out, thus enabling me to finally come to work. This is the latest I've ever reported for a shift."

Wandering through the squadroom, his green cloak billowing behind him as he shuffled scrolls about, Sergeant Jonas said snidely, "And given how late you usually are, that's saying something."

"*Thank* you, Jonas. In any event, I assume that the seven people Boneen delivered an hour ago are our new case?"

Danthres nodded. "Father Gribnel of some religion or other, possibly related to something called Raebar, died in his room in the Amswari Arms, a room he shared with *all* of our current guests." Danthres filled in her partner on the rest of what she knew, which wasn't nearly enough, though it did remind her that she had a bottle in her pouch. Pulling it out, she handed it to Jonas. "See that Boneen gets this, please, Jonas? I need to know if there's poison in it. And find out if anyone in the castle knows how to read Aytrok. We've got some scrolls in that language, and I want to know what they say."

"Of course," the sergeant said, and he departed, green cloak continuing to billow behind him.

"So, assuming he was poisoned," Torin said, "any of the seven of them could have done it."

Danthres nodded. "My money's on one of the women, since they were imprisoned. Let's talk to them, and see which one lies the most."

"Best we split the interviews, otherwise we really will be here until the thaw."

"Agreed," Danthres said. "I'll take two of the women and two of the acolytes, you take the others?"

Torin nodded.

"MY NAME IS Wynna, and I'm from Wehrvin. It's a small town outside Barlin."

Torin leaned forward, as the redhead was speaking in a low whisper. "What brought you together with Father Gribnel and his acolytes?" he asked in a gentle voice.

"My parents told me that Father Gribnel had chosen me for a holy mission. You see, he's our pastor. My family has worshipped Raebar since forever, really. I suppose I do, too—I never really thought about it much."

"And what was the mission they asked you to go on?"

"Oh, they didn't *ask*. They ordered me. And, well, they're my parents; it would be disrespectful to disobey."

"Very well, then," Torin said patiently, "what was the mission they ordered you to go on?"

"To help in the revitalization of Raebar."

"And you went willingly?"

Wynna nodded.

"Then why did they put the bracelet on you to keep you in the room?"

"I honestly don't know. Whatever they wanted me to do, I was going to do it. My parents said so."

"WE'RE JUST WAITING for the thaw, so that ships can sail again."

Danthres sighed as she sat across from Brother Karond, the short acolyte who had snapped at the women. "Yes, I gathered that. The port's been effectively shut down for a fortnight. You're sailing on the *Ellartnev*?"

Karond nodded.

"And where are you going?"

"On a holy mission!"

Danthres closed her eyes and sighed. "I meant geographically, not philosophically."

"Oh. Yes, of course. Erm, to Vikeez Isle to restart the volcano."

After a moment, Danthres recalled that Vikeez was a tiny island on the Garamin that included a dormant volcano and very little else. "Why would you restart the volcano? For that matter, *how* would you restart the volcano?"

Karond's mouth hung open. "Erm, which question should I answer first?"

"Pick one," Danthres said through gritted teeth.

"Ah. Well, the why is simple: to appease the great god Raebar, and show everyone in Flingaria that he is a god to be reckoned with!"

It was Danthres's considered opinion that everyone in Flingaria would need to know who Raebar *was* first, but she let that go, instead asking, "And how?"

"Sacrificing the virgins, of course!"

* * *

"FATHER GRIBNEL WAS the only one who still kept the faith, you know."

Torin nodded at Brother Kew Fortier. "This would be faith in the god Raebar?"

"You've heard of us!" Fortier leaned forward eagerly. "That's good, that's very good! We've been trying so hard to drum up interest. That's why we're going on this mission, you see. We were hoping to get to Vikeez right at midwinter, but the Garamin had to go and freeze." Fortier chuckled. "Father Gribnel actually considered the possibility of walking to Vikeez on the ice, but I was able to talk him down from that. The virgins would have frozen to death in those light robes of theirs."

"You could perhaps have given them something warmer?" Torin tried to make his suggestion sound kind rather than snotty, but he wasn't entirely sure that he succeeded.

However, Fortier seemed to take it in the kind spirit. "Oh, I wanted to, believe me, but Father Gribnel wouldn't hear of it. The four of them had to remain in the pure white robes in order for the ritual to be performed properly. The scrolls were *very* specific on the subject. Once all four are sacrificed in the proper manner, the volcano will restart, and Raebar will make his presence known in Flingaria once more."

Torin refrained from pointing out that he'd just confessed to intent to commit murder four times over.

"I AIN'T *ACTUALLY* a virgin, y'know."

Danthres stared at the blonde. "Excuse me?"

"I ain't a virgin! Everyone *thinks* that, 'cause I look so young, but I'm in my thirties. I slept with plenty'a men *and* women. Y'see, part of the act is I pretend like I'm a virgin."

"Act?" Danthres asked, silently impressed with whatever glamour the blonde was using to make her look young and innocent.

The blonde sighed. "My name's Kaytee. I work for Layla's in Wehrvin. It's the biggest sex emporium this side of the river. Clients are always askin' for me when they want, y'know, the virgin experience."

"So these idiots kidnapped you thinking you were a virgin?"

"Brother Karond's one of my regulars. I been *trying* to explain that it's an act, but he don't believe that I'd lie, 'cause that'd be 'an affront to Raebar,' if you can believe *that*."

"Having spoken to Karond, I can believe it."

"So, uh, can I go back home, now? I got clients back home who're prob'ly wantin' me back."

"Not *just* yet," Danthres said.

AFTER TALKING TO all their suspects, Danthres and Torin had them held in custody for further questioning. When they objected, Danthres tartly pointed out that they'd been stuck in the same room for a week, both by the bracelets and by the weather. They could last a few hours in a different room.

"It has to be one of the women," Danthres said. "They were on their way to their doom. That's definitely motive."

"I don't think they knew," Torin said. "I only spoke to two of them, but they seemed completely ignorant of their actual fate. They just thought they were participating in a ritual."

"One that required them to be magickally imprisoned. And Kaytee, the blonde? She's older and smarter than she seems. Oh, and she also isn't a virgin, so whatever absurd ritual Gribnel had in mind wouldn't have worked."

A voice came from the entrance to the squadroom. "It wouldn't have anyhow."

Danthres turned to see Xaar, one of Lord Doval's secretaries. "I'm sorry?"

Xaar was holding the scrolls in her arms. "I learned Aytrok as a girl. These scrolls have nothing to do with any rituals."

"But they are about Raebar?" Torin asked.

Nodding, Xaar said, "Yes, but they're financial paperwork about how the High Church of Raebar owed more than a thousand gold in back taxes, as well as various transcripts of court documents. Nothing about a ritual."

"If one of the acolytes discovered that the scrolls didn't outline the ritual as Father Gribnel claimed," Torin said, "then they might also have motive to murder the priest."

Jonas came in, then. "You'll both be happy to know that the bottle you brought back from the crime scene did indeed have poison in it. Unfortunately, thanks to the bracelets, Boneen cannot magickally determine who last touched the bottle. He tried a minor peel-back on the bottle itself, but the only people he could tell for sure had touched it were you, Danthres, and me."

Danthres sighed. "Wonderful. So everyone had opportunity and everyone had motive."

"We could just arrest all seven of them," Torin said with a grin.

"Don't tempt me."

Another voice came from the entryway, this one of the guards assigned to the castle. "Um, Lieutenants?"

Danthres turned to see the guard holding Kaytee's arm in one hand and Karond's in his other. Karond had a cut on his lip.

"What happened?" she asked.

"Th' acolyte tried to, whaddayacall, kidnap the virgin, an' the virgin, whaddayacall, smacked 'im inna face."

"Don't you understand?" Karond said to Kaytee. "We can be together, finally!"

"Together?" Danthres and Kaytee both asked at the same time.

Kaytee added, "You get that I'm a prostitute, right?"

"Oh, I know you worked in that place to pay the bills, but that won't be necessary now. I've saved up some silver for a rainy day, and now that Father Gribnel's out of the way—"

"Out of the way?" Torin asked.

Karond whirled on Torin. "I mean, that is—now that Father Gribnel has been tragically called to Raebar, he—"

"You killed him, didn't you?" Danthres asked.

"No! Never! I would never pour poison down his throat like that!" He closed his eyes. "Damn."

Danthres looked at the guard. "We have these two. Go fetch the other three women and the other two acolytes."

Nodding, the guard took his leave to perform that task.

Karond held up his arms. "Look, I just wanted to be with Kaytee so we could live in connubial bliss! If he sacrificed her to Raebar, we'd never be together! I tried to convince him that the ritual wouldn't work, because Kaytee wasn't a virgin!"

"You knew?" Danthres asked.

"Of course, I'm not an idiot!"

Somehow, Danthres refrained from responding to that.

Karond went on. "Even if she was a virgin when we met, she obviously wasn't after we had sex several dozen times. I kept saying that we could find another virgin, but Father Gribnel *would* insist!"

"So you killed him," Torin said.

"No! I mean, yes, obviously. I mean—" Karond's shoulders slumped. "Damn."

As the guard brought the other five in, Kaytee said, "You shitbrain, you really think I was gonna run away with you?"

Karond blinked and stared at her, tears welling up in his eyes. "You—you mean, you *weren't*?"

Torin stepped forward. "Brother Karond, you are under arrest for the murder of Father Gribnel, and for the intent to commit the murder of Kaytee, Wynna, Thamoa, and Voull."

"I had no intention of killing Kaytee! Don't you understand, I wanted to—"

"You still murdered Father Gribnel," Torin added.

Brother Fortier looked mortified, as did the other acolyte. "Karond, how *could* you? He was going to finally bring Raebar back to Flingaria in glory!"

"How exactly was killing four innocent women going to accomplish that?" Danthres asked.

"It was all spelled out in the—"

"Financial documents?" Torin said with a grin. "That's what those scrolls were, according to our expert." He indicated Xaar with his head.

Fortier blinked. "Father Gribnel said they were sacred texts."

"Only to an accountant." Danthres couldn't resist a smirk.

"The rest of us are free to go, then?" Fortier asked.

Shaking her head, Danthres said, "I'm afraid not. You're all under arrest for intent to commit murder."

"All?" Kaytee said. "What the hell? We was the ones gonna be murdered!"

"She's right," Torin said. "Brother Karond confessed to Father Gribnel's murder, and it was these two—" He indicated Fortier and the other acolyte with a gesture. "—that intended to throw them into the volcano."

"True." Danthres sighed. "Fine, release the virgins. We'll just arrest these two shitbrains."

"I toldja, I ain't no virgin!" Kaytee cried.

Coming Attractions
Daniel M. Kimmel

DURING WORLD WAR II, there was a joke in Hollywood that went like this: In the event of an air raid, seek shelter at RKO—they haven't had a hit in years.

RKO was long gone, but the same joke could have been made about Colossal Pictures, if such a thing as air raids still occurred.

It had been several years since Brogard had made first contact with Earth and we had begun our cultural and scientific exchanges. Tiny Graham Studios had been the first to cast someone from another planet in a major release, and the phenomenal success of *The Brogardi* had been a game changer for both worlds. For Earth, it made it clear that audiences would accept our new friends from another planet in their entertainment. For Brogard, it was somewhat more traumatic, as they had no tradition of fictional books, plays, or movies, treating such "lies" as little more than pornography. Yet slowly attitudes changed—although Brogardi who wanted to succeed in the entertainment industry had to come to Earth. They might accept human fiction, but not such material starring their own.

For "Milt" Goniff, Hollywood represented a golden opportunity he never could have had on his home world. He had no interest in being a movie star, as Abi "Abe" Gezunt had become with *The Brogardi*. Instead, he saw the chance to become a power behind the scenes. He arrived on Earth just as every studio was looking for their own Brogardi production. As another old Hollywood joke had it, it was a town where everyone was first in line to be second. Graham Studios had achieved a monster hit by being the first one out of the gate, but the studio that came in second could still cash in.

Goniff arrived in Hollywood holding himself out as an expert on Brogardi culture, although, practically speaking, his employment history to date had been as an accountant. In short order, he was hired on to adapt a remake of *West Side Story*, turning it into the first musical set on two worlds. The bulk of the work had already been done, but then veteran screenwriter Peter Siskind had an unfortunate encounter with a Mack truck. He was checking his email on his portable telenet, and the driver of the truck was ignoring a red light. Goniff did the honorable thing: he took out a full-page ad in the trades memorializing his writing partner, and then he claimed sole credit on the final screenplay.

The mix of the classic score with several original Brogardi compositions turned out to hit the sweet spot for moviegoers who could fancy themselves sophisticated for enduring the alien music and then regain their equilibrium with the more familiar songs. Goniff's contributions were meager, but when the movie cleaned up during the holiday season, his fortune was made.

For his next project, he convinced the studio to allow him to serve as producer. It was there that he met Melissa Calvert, who had become America's sweetheart as well as a major star. *Follow That Blonde* was a bit of fluff, a rom/com liberally borrowing from classic movies that today's young moviegoers wouldn't know.

During the shoot, Goniff turned on the charm. He could be flirtatious with Calvert without crossing the line that might have led to headlines and lawsuits. Although recognizably humanoid, he was, like his fellow Brogardi, blue, hairless, and possessing vestigial gills. The not-so-subtle message he conveyed was that he was interested, but only if she was as well. He had done his homework. He knew how the game was played.

At the wrap party, she gave him a clear signal. "I've enjoyed our time together," she told him. "I'll miss seeing you every day."

"There'll be other movies," he replied coyly.

"Not for us. I'm booked on other projects for the next year and a half."

Goniff turned to the bartender and put up two fingers, ordering another round. Then he stepped in closer. "We could meet outside of work. I'm willing to make the sacrifice."

She looked at him for a moment, and then laughed. As the bartender placed their refills in front of them, she said, "Well, I do need someone to help me run my lines."

Putting his arm lightly on her waist, he said, "And I could always use a second opinion on the scripts I'm looking at."

Her lips lightly brushed his cheek. "Sounds like we'd be good for each other."

There was scarcely any space between them.

"You know what they say," he murmured, "Once you go blue, you'll always stay true."

THEY WERE THE Hollywood power couple for quite a while. Goniff produced a string of hits in which she starred, culminating in her Oscar-winning turn in *Across Two Worlds*, the first movie that was shot on Brogard. It was a significant accomplishment, given the Brogardi attitude toward fiction, but the two planets had come to tolerate each other's ways. There would be no Brogardi film industry in the near future, but they accepted that Earthans had a different take on fiction, while the film tried to stick to the facts about Abe Gezunt—the first Brogardi movie star—as closely as possible. Hollywood biopics were not documentaries, but this one rarely veered away from the historical record, a clear nod to Brogardi sensibilities. Calvert played Linda Reid, the actress whose romance with her co-star had helped make their film a sensation on two worlds.

When the actress returned to Earth ahead of schedule, she hoped to surprise Goniff, but was surprised herself when she found her lover in bed with a young actress he was grooming for his next production. The websites that focused on Hollywood gossip had a field day. The power couple went their separate ways but, as often happened in such situations, Goniff's reputation was enhanced.

Indeed, he found women more eager than ever to accept his overtures. On Oscar night, he was in the audience with yet another young "protégé" when Calvert's name was announced as Best Actress. Whatever her feelings toward her former lover, she knew what was expected of her if she wanted to continue working in Hollywood. She made a point of thanking Goniff for believing in her. He sent her a congratulatory bouquet the next day, not caring if it ended up in a vase or the garbage.

While his career was soaring, the fortunes of Colossal Pictures were not. The trade papers would note that if it weren't for Goniff, the studio would be a candidate for Chapter 11 bankruptcy. He bided his time, watching the various suits come and go, as the corporate overlords made attempt after attempt to salvage the studio. Each had their own approach, and each failed. As time went on, the word around town was that if it wasn't a Goniff production, it might as well have gone straight to video on demand. Goniff didn't mind. In fact, he was paying his publicist top dollar to spread that very word.

So it was no surprise when the call came for Goniff to come to the executive board room. A special committee of the board of directors had been delegated to see if the producer of the studio's only recent hits would be willing to take the reins of the whole operation. As far as the financial people were concerned, Goniff's films had succeeded at the box office and, therefore, he must know the secret of what audiences wanted to see. If he could apply this supposed knowledge to the studio's entire slate, he could turn its fortunes around.

The announcement was big news on two worlds. On Brogard, there was pride that another one of their own had succeeded on Earth, but there was also the queasy feeling that—once again—it had been as a purveyor of fiction. Meanwhile on Earth, there was much comment on how he was the first off-worlder to be handed control of a major studio. On the one hand, it was seen as a gamble that an alien could understand an industry whose primary customers were Earthans. On the other hand, given Colossal's recent track record, it was deemed a "Hail Mary" pass. At this point, what did they have to lose?

Goniff had studied the ways of Hollywood well. He knew he had to trash the slate of films that had been greenlit by his predecessor. If any of them turned out to be a hit, the credit would go to him rather than to Goniff. There were eight films in post-production when he took the reins at the studio. Goniff cannily chose the weakest one to open on two thousand screens in the U.S. and Canada, so that he could say he had made the effort. It was a sappy love story about two teens who had decided to abstain from sex until they could marry. What could the studio execs who approved it have been thinking?

Goniff called in his young assistant, a bright young woman named Sammi Gluck. "I'm looking over the films we inherited. We're going to dump most of them. Release *The Virgins*, and send the rest to pay per view."

"I'm right on it, Mr. Goniff. You can count on me."

She asked if there was anything else and then hurried out of the room to carry out his bidding. Gluck was attractive and ambitious. He'd have to keep a watchful eye on her.

GONIFF HAD ACHIEVED a certain amount of fame and fortune as a Brogardi film producer—the first and, so far, only one from his planet to have achieved success in that field. Meanwhile on Brogard, the most prominent human was Sheila Fenton, a historian who had written a multi-volume history of the planet. The Brogardi were a fact-based culture, and such academics were highly revered for hewing closely to the record. However, her books came at Brogardi history from the outside, and made observations and drew conclusions that were highly controversial, to say the least. Yet, as a historian, she had provided the factual basis for her conclusions, which led to extended and lively debates as to a.) whether an Earthan could truly understand life on Brogard and b.) whether her insights would require Brogardi historians and philosophers to reconsider their own received truths.

It might seem very dry to the average Earthan, but when Goniff learned about it—he made an effort to keep up with happenings on the home world—he saw a potential movie in it. He asked Sammi to look into whether the film rights to the history books were available without drawing any undue attention to his interest, not wanting to tip his hand to the competition.

"They're available, boss, and we should be able to get them cheap. Academics aren't used to selling the film rights to treatises," she reported a few days later.

"Excellent. I want you to set up a shell production company to buy the rights. If she realizes it's a major studio, particularly one headed by a Brogardi, she might guess something's afoot."

Six months later, Colossal began casting *The Outsider*. The screenplay focused not on the history of Brogard, but on the conflict between the human author and her native colleagues, particularly a professor with whom she was having an affair. The names were all changed, so while Prof. Fenton might be appalled, she'd have the money she'd been paid to console her. Should she ever learn what she could have made off the project, she'd no doubt be even more appalled.

Goniff wanted the film to be the studio's big movie for Oscar season. While he'd enjoyed some financial success, he craved the respect of his peers that awards would bring. Lots of schlock had had big box office returns. An Oscar on the mantle was something else.

There was only one actress he considered for the lead: Melissa Calvert. The fact that she had won her own Oscar made her highly marketable. The fact that she was Goniff's ex made her a challenge. It was a challenge he was ready to face. He had Sammi find out Calvert's schedule, and saw she was going to be at a tribute to Sylvester Graham, Jr., the studio head who had brought Abe Gezunt out to Hollywood and transformed him into the first Brogardi movie star. Using some of the profits from *The Brogardi*, Graham had set up a foundation to bring Brogardi culture to Earth, as well as to allow their citizens to come and study here.

During the cocktail party, Earthans and Brogardi mixed freely—many of the off-worlders had become quite enamored of our more exotic cocktails—and Goniff chitchatted with colleagues and would-be colleagues. He was listening to an elevator pitch from a director who was going on a bit long, unless it was an exceptionally tall building, when he spotted Melissa. He turned to the filmmaker and, still amazed at how easily he had acquired the Earthan habit of faking sincerity, he shook his hand and said, "Get in touch with my office, and we can discuss this further. There's someone I need to see right now."

The director didn't know if he had been brushed off or made a connection and, truth be told, neither did Goniff. He was hurrying across the ballroom to his ex-lover, hoping he could reach her before she spotted him and began evasive maneuvers. He was a few steps away when she saw him. She turned to go, but found her path blocked by a waiter with a tray of mixed Earthan and Brogardi hors d'oeuvres which had been carefully vetted in order not to give offense to either group. Turning back, she pasted a smile on her face. It wasn't hard. She was an Oscar-winning actress, after all.

"Milt, how nice to see you."

"And I'm so glad to see you, Melissa. I have a project that I think you would be ideal for, and I'm hoping I can convince you to sign on."

Melissa thought it was a bit crass to come right out with a business proposition without going through the motions of small talk, but she also knew her ex-lover. "Send the script to my office. You, of all people, know how this works."

Goniff stepped in closer; he was not smiling. Fortunately, Melissa was able to read this as well. A toothy grin on someone from Brogard was a sign they were very angry. "Melissa, dear, I know we have our history, but you're the only one who could do this part justice. It's a film that could outperform both *The Brogardi* and *Across Two Worlds* at the box office."

When Goniff got like this, she knew, there was no stopping him. "Okay, Milt, I'll still need to read the script, but tell me what it is."

He told her, and she gasped. In spite of the Hollywood schmaltz that would inevitably be ladled on, he was not exaggerating. This could be the most important cinematic exploration of relations between the two worlds to date. And he was offering her the lead. "How soon can you get me the script?"

He took his telenet from his pocket and quickly texted Sammi. He looked up at Melissa with the tight-lipped expression that showed he was pleased. "It'll be at your house when you get home. Shall we meet for dinner tomorrow and make the deal? Then your agent and my lawyers can work out the details."

He was rushing ahead, as always, assuming he could steamroller any objections and get his way, and it usually worked. This time would be no exception. The next evening, they met at a little bistro he found in Highland Park that was too new to be "hot," although he knew that would change shortly, especially after he leaked to several gossipy websites that that's where he had personally signed Melissa Calvert. It was too juicy a story to ignore, and would be great publicity for the film. What he wouldn't tell them was that after drinks, dinner, and a bottle of wine, they had repaired to his house in Bel Air, where they had relived old times. She still enjoyed his mushroom omelet in the morning.

All during the production of *The Outsider*, they would find time to sneak away for long weekends. When it was nearing the end of the production, Goniff wondered where things might go beyond that.

"We wrap next week," she said during cocktails. She had a gin and tonic, while he tried an Old Fashioned, which he found ironic since it was new to him.

"Yes, I know. I've been looking to see if we could develop some new project for you."

"That's sweet, Milt, but I'm committed to a three-month shoot in Brazil, and leave right after we're done."

Milt looked surprised. "Why didn't you tell me? I'm hurt."

"Now Milt, I signed on for this mini-series a year ago, and was waiting for all the pieces to fall into place." She patted his hand. "Don't you worry. I'll be back in plenty of time to do promotion for the film's release, and," she added, lowering her voice, "whatever Oscar campaign you have worked up."

True to her word, she returned and plowed right into the publicity effort, talking to anyone with a publication, a website, a podcast, or any other form of media that existed on either world. Some Brogardi might still be squeamish about viewing fiction movies publicly, but they had come to accept that factual reporting—or what passed for such—about fictional media had a legitimate purpose.

Inevitably, one of the questions was about the fact that this was the second time she had played an Earthan woman who had been romantically involved with a Brogardi man. While her rekindled relationship with Goniff had not gone public, Hollywood remained a company town with few secrets.

Goniff watched one interview where the reporter was clearly hinting that she was probing for details about what sex with a Brogardi was like. The actress was having none of it. "I'm not comfortable getting into that," she said to the clearly disappointed reporter, before adding, "but there's a reason for the expression, 'Once you go blue, you'll always stay true.'"

The studio boss started wheezing. Sammi no longer asked if he was all right, having learned that that was the way the Brogardi laughed. He had taught Melissa well, including how to give interviews where you provided the necessary soundbites without actually saying anything.

"Can I get you anything, boss?"

"Just a refill on the bourbon," he replied, indicating the bottle of a 27-year-old small batch bourbon at the wet bar. The sale price for the bottle was in four figures, but what was the point of being fabulously wealthy if you couldn't enjoy yourself? He'd certainly come a long way from counting other people's money back on Brogard.

Oscar night was a triumph. Melissa picked up her second Oscar, and the film also won for director, screenplay, editing, and art direction. Sweetest of all was the moment they opened the envelope for best picture and called out his name, since he had personally produced the film. He was not the first Brogardi to win an Oscar. Abe Gezunt had won for his history-making debut. However, he was the first one to win for a prominent role off-camera.

He strode to the stage, his hairless blue head looking striking in his custom designed tuxedo and simple off-white shirt. He accepted the statuette, and then turned to acknowledge the enthusiastic response of the audience of his peers. He was at the top of the heap now. When the applause died down, he looked down at them and began.

"I'm just a modest Brogardi, grateful for the opportunities I have been given by my many Earthan friends," he said, following a text he had had Sammi provide several media outlets as soon as his name was announced. "There are too many people to thank, and I know you all want to get to your parties, so let me just note the wonderful team at Colossal, especially my right arm, Sammi Gluck." He thought mentioning an underling would show how democratic he was. He probably could also avoid giving her a raise this year.

"And then there are the two women without whom this film could not have been made. First, Sheila Fenton, thank you for letting us tell your story." The studio's lawyers were trying to quietly settle with her after she threatened to sue over how she had been ripped off by Goniff. With what the film was expected to make, they could afford it.

"And of course, my dearest friend, Melissa Calvert. She was the only one I considered for the role, and tonight you showed I was right." Cameras picked her out of the crowd to see how she reacted to this expression of gratitude while taking credit for her performance. She had a smile pasted on her face.

After the Oscar show ended, he tried to catch up with her, but with all the parties going on and all the people who wanted to congratulate him— many with the hope that he'd remember them down the road for future projects—he just couldn't find her. By 2 A.M. they still hadn't connected. He checked his telenet for messages, and saw that she had rented a bungalow on the grounds of the Beverly Hills Hotel instead of going home tonight. He summoned his driver to take him there, and then dismissed him.

When he reached the cabin, he tried the door. It was unlocked. Good. She might already be asleep, and when he surprised her, he didn't want it to be from loud rapping. He slipped in. The front room was dark, but there a soft light from an open door that was presumably the bedroom. He tiptoed in, and then stopped dead. She was already in bed. She was not alone. She was lying next to a man with a thick head of hair and skin that was decidedly not blue.

The man noticed Goniff standing there, clutching his Oscar at his side, and turned to the woman nuzzling his throat, "Look, he has one, too."

Melissa stopped what she was doing and looked up. "Milt, what are you doing here?"

"What am *I* doing here? What is *he* doing here?"

"I'm sorry, I suppose I should make introductions," she said, as if this was all perfectly ordinary. "Milt Goniff, this is Matheus Silva. He was the leading man in that miniseries I did. He's a big star down in Brazil. Matheus, this is Milt Goniff, head of production at Colossal Pictures. He produced my movie."

Matheus beamed a toothy smile. "You'll have to pardon me for not getting up."

Goniff tried to ignore him. "Baby," he said to the actress, "what happened to us?"

She laughed. It hurt. "Us? There is no us. There used to be, but that was long ago."

"But I thought we had reconnected."

"You taught me well, Milt. Do whatever it takes. You wanted me for your film. I saw it would be a great career move. It was fun while it lasted, but we both got what we wanted. Now if you'll excuse us…"

He was clearly being dismissed, something he had not experienced for years. He headed back out to the street, looking for his driver, and then realized he had let him go. He summoned a car service on his telenet, and asked to be taken to the studio. The last place he wanted to be right now was his empty bedroom.

It was after 3 A.M. when he got to his office. He exchanged the Oscar for the bottle of bourbon, and went to lie down on the couch. He didn't bother with a glass.

He must have dozed off, because the sun was coming in through the window when he woke. What had made him stir was his door opening and several people coming in. As his eyes cleared, he recognized Sammi. With her was the president of the parent company that owned Colossal, and several other people from corporate.

"I see what you mean, Sammi," said the president. "Perhaps we should have this conversation elsewhere."

Goniff started to speak, but they were already out the door. The last thing he heard was one of the suits saying, "We've had our eye on you for some time. You shouldn't have to put up with this."

He staggered to his feet, knocking the bottle of bourbon over. What was left spilled out. He didn't care. This was horribly wrong. He was Milt Goniff. He had clawed his way to the top. He had turned the studio around, produced the most honored movie of the year, all the while bedding its star. He was the Brogardi who had shown he could succeed in Hollywood without getting in front of the camera. This couldn't be happening.

By the time he reached the hallway, he saw they were already scraping his name off the office door.

Cracking the Vault
Matt Bechtel

KATIE SPILLANE TOOK the elevator down to the front security desk at 2:00 A.M. with a cup of coffee in each hand and her ulterior motive in the front pocket of her hoodie.

"Hi John," she opened, offering one mug to the tired guard. "I brought you a cup of coffee, just how you like it."

John Dunbar raised one eyebrow at the senior, a trick he'd mastered decades ago as a youth to mimic Mr. Spock. "What do you want, Katie?"

Katie sighed, placed the coffee in front of him on his desk, and fished her flash drive from her pocket. "I've got a paper due at my eight-thirty, and I just ran out of ink. Can I please print it here?" She gestured toward the locked front door, and added, "I'd run out to Kinko's, but…"

The movement of her arm toward the sealed glass caught the attention of one of the protestors camped outside the dorm that night, who leapt to his feet and began chanting as soon as he saw her. The rest of the meager crowd followed suit, and the refrain that had become so familiar over the past few months echoed across the quad—

"Release the virgins! Release the virgins!"

The old man sighed, and rose from his seat behind the desk. "Cream and two sugars?" he asked as he took the mug.

"Splenda," Katie said. "You know you have to watch your A1C. And thank you!"

John shuffled his body across the lobby, stared out the front windows, and waved at the chanting protestors. In a flash, Katie took his seat and slid her drive into a USB port. "I promise I'll be out of your hair in a minute."

"Take your time," he said. "I appreciate the company. What class is your paper for?"

"Art history."

"Really? Not coding or computer science or some other topic that would be Greek to me?"

She laughed. "Those classes don't require papers."

"Why are you taking art history?"

"Are you kidding?" she chuckled as she hit control-P on the old Acer's keyboard. "Color, structure, form—I've got to study the masters, even if my work doesn't require paint and brushes."

"I never thought of it that way," John admitted as he sipped his coffee. Then he added, "And by the way, you're an R.A.; you of all people ought to know that you're not allowed to have a coffee maker in your room."

Katie smiled. "Who says it isn't instant?"

John smiled back. "Don't insult my intelligence. This is too good to be instant."

"Truthfully, not many kids in my major take art history," Katie continued as the old inkjet at the security desk belched forth her work. She ejected her flash drive, and with a wide smirk added, "That's why I'm the best at what I do!"

John turned his body away from the front door to face her. "I'm sorry you can't just go to Kinko's tonight," he said.

"Meh. This is cheaper and easier anyhow."

He looked sadly at the young woman, half the age of his oldest daughter. "No Katie. I'm sorry."

She looked up from gathering her paper with honest eyes. "It's okay, John. It's not your fault. You're just doing your job."

"An excuse that didn't work at Nuremberg."

THERE HAD BEEN an unusual rise in the diagnoses of human papillomavirus in the area the previous spring, particularly amongst females aged nineteen to twenty-four. In response, the state health department arranged for free seminars to be held on every college campus, where a doctor would explain how a young woman could protect herself from infection.

When Bethlehem College's president, Father Joseph Webber, was contacted about scheduling a visit to their campus, his response was, "That's okay. There's no need for you to come here. Our girls don't have sex."

The web site launched on the first day of classes the following semester.

"SMALL CROWD TONIGHT," John observed, as he glanced back out the front windows.

"It's Tuesday," Katie explained. "Everyone's got class tomorrow, so no one goes out. Only the real die-hards will camp out on a Tuesday night. Trust me, the crowd'll be back this weekend."

The young man who had restarted the chanting ran toward the building and spat on the front glass. That drew cheers from his compatriots, who began chanting and clapping even louder.

"Wouldn't 'Free the Virgins' fit the cadence of the chant better?" John asked. "Especially if they're gonna do the clap-clap-clapclapclap thing in the middle?"

Her paper printed, Katie slid from behind the security desk as she deftly snagged the handle of her coffee mug. "Probably, but they had already started selling the 'Release the Virgins' T-shirts with the Kraken artwork before the lockdown was imposed."

A cheer rose as soon as she rejoined John and the protestors could see her again. Katie gave them another slight wave, and moved to one of the old couches across the lobby.

"Why did you come here, Katie?" John finally asked, without removing his gaze from the righteous students camped outside.

She laughed. "To print my paper?"

"You know that's not what I meant."

"Because not all of us are Meghan Fitzgerald? Bethlehem was the only college that offered me a full ride."

"Wait a sec, who's Meghan Fitzgerald?"

Katie was legitimately stunned. "Sophomore? Red hair? Lives on the third floor?"

"No, I meant, who is she to not have to worry about tuition?"

Katie laughed. "Her dad's the state attorney general."

John laughed back. "I'll be damned, I swear I never knew that! And fair enough about the financial aid. But why still live in Mackenzie? You're a senior; you could've gotten an off-campus apartment and not had to put up with any of this."

"And I would've had to pay rent and utilities and pay for food," she said. "And I'd have to have roommates. For all its faults, an R.A. gig here does come with a single. Gives me the privacy to stay up late working for my clients and squirrel away money at the same time…"

Katie's voice trailed off, so John said nothing.

"I didn't know all of this was going to happen, though," she finally added.

* * *

A SANDSTONE MONOLITH, Mackenzie Hall was the tallest building on Bethlehem's campus, and the college's parietal rules were enforced there more strictly than at any other dorm, since it housed underclass females. Those factors led to it being dubbed "The Virgin Vault," and the nickname had stuck for generations.

Hence the URL of the web site that launched the first day of classes that fall—www.crackingthevault.com. It was nothing more than a basic online message board, built using a free template with its color scheme matched to the school's. As its header explained, the site was for one simple purpose—sharing stories of times Bethlehem students had "cracked the vault" and had sex in Mackenzie Hall.

It started out slowly, with a few current students using anonymous log-ins to post about skirting security's rounds, staying extra quiet, or sneaking in a nooner between classes. But soon enough, undergraduates were logging in using their real names and "@bethlehemcollege.edu" email addresses, openly bragging of recent trysts. When the link reached an alumni social media group, the board was flooded with four decades worth of true-life amateur erotica.

By Halloween, a search for the college brought up crackingthevault.com before bethlehemcollege.edu. The most-watched local news broadcast even devoted a full half-hour to the site the week before Thanksgiving.

"YOU EVER POST on 'Cracking the Vault'?"

Katie almost spat her coffee back into her mug. "You've known me four years, John. Do you really think I'm the type to share the details of my personal life on a message board?"

"No, but I know you well enough to know that all of this has to piss you the hell off something fierce."

"Of course it does," she said. "That's why I refused when they asked me to help them figure out who put up the site."

The old man was taken aback. "They actually asked you for help? A woman they've been locking up in here?"

"They asked last fall, back before the lockdowns started, but yeah. Hell, I've got a G.P.A. over four-point-oh and a better real-world working knowledge of current internet standards and protocols than any professor here. Of course they asked me."

John raised his mug. "I'm glad you said no," he told her.

She clinked her coffee to his, and they both drank. "Wanna hear what I told them?" He nodded, so she launched in. "The administrative contact for the site is hornycoeds@youmail.com, and anyone can set up a YouMail account with no I.D. or verification because they're a free email provider. The site's hosted by GoHostMe.com—the world's largest and cheapest hosting company, geared toward amateurs who don't really know what they're doing. That's why it's such a cookie-cutter site; whoever posted it just chose GoHostMe's ready-made message board platform, changed the color scheme, and went live. Most importantly, GoHostMe also offers an add-on privacy package. That's why the only contact for the site is the free email address; everything else is blocked, and the school would need a warrant to get that info…"

"Which no judge would ever grant because no crimes have been committed," John finished. "Could the administration pull an end-around and figure out who bought the hosting through GoHostMe's billing records?"

"They could try, but ten to one says the hosting was purchased with a prepaid gift card. And if that gift card was bought with cash, it would be a whole lot of work to come up with nothing. Whichever frat boy started the site did his homework."

John studied Katie before asking, "How do you know all of this?"

She chuckled. "It all comes up on a WhoIs.com search. And trust me, I'm not the only undergrad who got curious and did a little snooping."

John rose from the couch with a groan, bending at the waist to stretch his hamstrings and lower back. "I almost forgot, I've gotta send my wife a quick email. Give me a few minutes?"

"What the hell is your wife doing up?" Katie asked.

"She's not," he said, slowly making his way back over to the desk. "She'll find it first thing in the morning before I get home."

"I thought you weren't supposed to use that computer for personal stuff…" she teased.

John smiled. "I'm not. Not supposed to let night owls print their art history papers, either. But hell, the weekend guy sits here playing poker all night; as long as I clear the browser history, I think I'll be safe."

"Doesn't the IT department keep backup images of the entire server? It would be so easy to bust you!"

"You mean the same people who asked a young woman living in Mackenzie Hall to help them take down the site about life in Mackenzie Hall?" John replied. "Are you actually surprised that a department headed by priests isn't quite up with the times?"

TWO WEEKS BEFORE the semester break, President Webber held a press conference in front of the giant Christmas tree outside of the administration building. Every local media outlet covered the event.

"I will be reading a brief statement, and then my staff will be distributing a memo regarding a change to our on-campus residence life policy," he began. "What you'll receive today has been sent, both via electronic mail and in hard copy, to the families of every resident of Mackenzie Hall. Recent developments in our community, both on campus and online, have endangered the core Catholic values of Bethlehem College. In response, the administration has enacted new security measures, set to take effect the first day of classes next semester, to safeguard the physical well being, the emotional well being, and the spiritual well being of the students living in Mackenzie Hall. We are confident these new policies will rectify the current unrest, and are consistent with the college's Catholic mission. Thank you all, God bless, and Merry Christmas."

Then he left before anyone had a chance to read the memorandum and question him about it. Father Webber's new security measures reversed the college's standard parietal rules at Mackenzie Hall—starting the next semester, rather than keeping male students out after 11:00 P.M., the female residents would be locked in until 7:00 A.M. the following morning.

Protestors began camping out in the courtyard in front of the dorm every night, sleeping on the concrete in solidarity and chanting every time they saw a coed in the lobby. The Kraken-designed "Release the Virgins" T-shirt became the most popular apparel on campus, and even some of the lay professors were photographed wearing them. On top of everything else, traffic on crackingthevault.com took another huge spike when a new category of post was introduced—"Lockdown Sex."

"SO, WHAT DID you put in my coffee?" John asked, swirling the grounds in the bottom of his mug as he hit "send" on his email.

"Pardon?"

"What did you put in my coffee?" he repeated. "I figure you probably roofied me, which I guess kinda makes poetic sense in a way. The old man falls asleep, and a wiz like you would only need five minutes on this computer to steal the lock codes for the entire building. Once you had those, you could open the doors anytime your heart desired."

Katie stood and took two steps toward the desk. "I'm honestly a little bit hurt, John. We've been friends for four years. I'd never drug you."

John just stared at her.

Eventually, Katie sighed. "There was spyware on my flash drive," she finally admitted. "It installed on your computer the second I mounted the drive to print my paper."

"When's your paper actually due?"

"Tomorrow at eight-thirty, like I said. But I'm not really out of ink upstairs."

"How does the spyware work?"

Katie produced her cell phone and read from her screen. "Good morning, beautiful," she recited. "I hope you've slept well by the time you get this. Please call in refills of my prescriptions when the pharmacy opens at seven, so I can pick them up on my way home? Thanks, I love you, and I'll see you in a few hours, John."

"Holy crap!" John breathed.

"I can see everything that happens on that computer now," Katie told him. "Every single keystroke. So even if they change the lock codes daily, I'll know exactly how to bust this place open like a piñata."

John laughed. "They don't change the codes daily. Hell, they barely change them monthly."

"You're kidding me!"

He shrugged. "Trust me, you're overestimating your adversaries." After a moment, he asked, "So, when're you gonna do it?"

"Saturday night, at the stroke of midnight. We've already started a whisper campaign so there'll be a huge crowd, and we're gonna start leaking it to the press on Saturday afternoon to make sure they're here, too. It'll be a massive flood of virgins breaking themselves out of the vault, a giant 'fuck you' to the college that they will never be able to make people un-see." She paused, then added, "Plus, you don't work Saturday nights."

John nodded. "You didn't have to do that. But thanks."

"You're my friend, and I know you and your wife need the extra income. I don't want there to be any chance this comes back on you."

"What do you want, Katie?" His question caught her off guard, so he continued. "What exactly is your end game here? I'm guessing you started the site to embarrass the administration…"

"I never said I…" she started to interject, but then stopped and smirked when John raised one eyebrow at her again. "Wanna hear what's gonna happen on Monday?"

"I'm all ears."

"Remember Meghan Fitzgerald?" John threw his head back and started chuckling before Katie connected the dots. "Yeah, her dad—the state freaking attorney general, working pro bono—is going to file a class action suit at exactly 9:00 A.M. on behalf of all the residents of Mackenzie Hall against Bethlehem College. They never locked in any male students, just females. There's a whole boat-load of laws he can argue that they broke, even up to the Fourteenth Amendment. Right as they're gonna be dealing with the P.R. mess of our Saturday night jailbreak, we're gonna hit 'em again where it really hurts."

"How strong does Meghan's dad feel your case is?"

"Doesn't matter. I mean, the money would be nice, but he'll never, *ever* survive the shit storm."

"He?"

Katie closed the two steps between them and sat on the far edge of John's desk. "You asked me what's the end game?" she began, her voice sharp with anger. "What I want? It's the same thing I've wanted for a year —Webber's fucking scalp. At first, I would've been happy enough just to see the old man resign out of embarrassment, but now? There's no way this ends without his termination, with cause."

John exhaled and rolled his eyes. "That's a hell of a scalp to have gone hunting after, Katie. But don't get me wrong, I get it."

"No, you don't," she insisted. "*Our girls don't have sex.* On top of how stupid and dangerous it is to have such an utterly clueless old fool in charge of a college… he never should've called us girls."

"I have three daughters," John replied. "None of them went here. That wasn't by accident."

Katie suddenly straightened up. "Hey, speaking of which, I don't have to ask you if you're gonna…"

John waved her off. "Please! I went to State back in the '70s. I've got stories that would dwarf anything on your web site."

"So you *have* read the board!"

He shrugged with a half-smile. "Call me curious."

"Do you remember Desiree Miller? Graduated last spring, but lived here her first two years? Sandy blonde hair, legs that went on forever? Did you see her post?"

"I remember her, and those legs," John confessed. "Was she the one who posted about her first lesbian experience, getting tipsy on cheap boxed wine while doing laundry with a freshman who lived down the hall, and getting naked on top of the counter where everyone folds their clothes?"

"That's the one."

"What about her?"

"I was the freshman," Katie said, proudly. "I doubt I would've posted it anyway, but there was no need to repeat her story."

"You're a brilliant, beautiful young woman who's lived here four years," John replied. "Please tell me that's not the only time you 'cracked the vault,' or else you really did spend too much of your college years working."

Katie grinned ear to ear as she slid off the desk. "It's just the only one that's been posted so far," she said. Then she wandered back toward the front doors and waved goodnight to the crowd outside. As soon as they saw her, they resumed their familiar chant—

"Release the virgins! Release the virgins!"

John joined Katie behind the glass and returned her his empty coffee mug. "Soon enough," he said.

The Coffee Corps
Alex Shvartsman

I QUESTIONED MY life choices when the address I arrived at for my job interview turned out to be a Dunkin' Donuts.

For a moment, the impulse was to just keep driving. Don't get me wrong—there are plenty of good companies eccentric enough to conduct a job interview in a coffee shop, but if I wanted to work for one of those startups, I'd be enjoying the warm weather in Silicon Valley, instead of navigating through the stop-and-go traffic of Braintree, Massachusetts. Still, this was the first interview I'd managed to land in two weeks. I sighed, pulled the car into one of the building's three parking spots, and went in.

"Kyle!" A man and a woman sat next to each other at a little plastic table. The woman waved me over, pointing at the empty seat across from them. She wore wide-brimmed glasses and what looked like a Christmas sweater. The guy was tall, bald, and leather-clad, his left eye covered by a patch. He looked like a Caucasian version of Samuel Jackson's Nick Fury. Both of them were overdressed for early summer.

I walked over feeling a tad overdressed myself, in my suit and tie.

"Kyle Palermo." the woman smiled as I slid into the seat across from them. "I'm Abby and this is Pierre."

"Hello," I said.

"For you." Pierre slid a white foam cup toward me.

"Thanks," I said, "but I'm trying to cut down."

Pierre looked like I'd just kicked his favorite puppy. "It's company tradition," he said. "We drink, then we talk." I couldn't place his accent.

Abby half-shrugged, as if apologizing for her companion's manners, and nodded toward the cup.

I took a sip. The coffee was black, bitter, and piping hot. Pierre smiled, revealing a missing tooth. I sighed inwardly. Three months ago, I could have had any job I wanted. Now I was being interviewed by Velma from Scooby Doo and a pirate.

"We've looked into you, Mr. Palermo. Your resume is impressive," said Abby. "Other than, of course, the matter of your termination from your previous job."

Up until recently, I'd worked for one of the largest banks in New England. No prospective employer was going to ignore why I no longer did.

"They say you hacked into the payroll records and posted everyone's salaries on the company intranet," said Abby. "Caused quite a stir."

"That's true," I said. "They were screwing over a lot of the IT people. Inept bootlickers constantly rose to the top. Some were getting paid double what more-qualified employees earned. It wasn't right."

"You were paid well, weren't you Mr. Palermo?"

I nodded.

"Do you regret what you did?"

I took another sip of bitter coffee. After they'd canned me, they'd also blackballed me, so no other firm in the financial industry would touch me with a ten-foot pole. "I only regret that they found someone good enough to trace the hack back to me," I said. "They had to have outsourced that."

"Our organization values privacy," said Abby. "Are you willing to sign a non-disclosure agreement—and stick to it, this time—provided we convince you we're not a kakistocracy?"

I nodded, impressed with her vocabulary. "Sure, assuming I take the job."

She scribbled something onto a brown napkin. "We'd like to bring you in as a consultant for a month. Then, if everything is to our mutual satisfaction, we can discuss full-time employment. This is our offer." She pushed the napkin across the table.

I turned it over and looked at the number. It had a lot of zeroes. "This is for a month of work?"

Pierre grinned, showing off that gap in his teeth again. "Includes overtime, bonus, and hazard pay," he said.

"Hazard pay?"

Pierre plunked a thick stack of pages onto the table. "The non-disclosure agreement," he said. "Sign, and we tell you more."

I picked up the pages and began skimming. I've signed my share of NDAs over the course of my career. Most are two pages long, cookie cutter, and boring. This document was special. It mixed the most confusing of legalese with dire threats. I was pretty sure whoever signed this wouldn't be allowed to tell people their name or shoe size, let alone any details on whatever this job entailed.

I pushed the stack of papers away lest I catch bureaucracy cooties. "No, thanks."

The two of them exchanged a look.

"You don't know what you'd be missing," said Abby.

A pair of teenage girls jostled me as they carried their fancy whipped-cream-topped concoctions to an empty table.

I pushed my chair back and got up. "I'm sure I don't. If I may make a suggestion, perhaps consider using your office for your next interview. Might go over better."

Abby rose. "Wait. Come and let us show you what we do. No NDA. Then you can decide if you want the job."

Pierre looked none too happy about this turn of events. He was about to say something, but Abby held up her hand, and he kept his mouth shut. I made a mental note of the power dynamic in their relationship.

Abby walked over to a door sporting a plastic Employees Only sign. "As it happens, we *are* interviewing you at our office. You just earned yourself a grand tour."

I EXPECTED A kitchen, a closet, maybe a cramped little office. Instead, there was a short corridor that terminated in an elevator door. Mind you, this was a one-story building. Pierre hit the button, and the door opened, revealing a cabin large enough to transport a dozen people. We piled in, and the elevator began to descend. What sort of an outfit would hide their offices underneath a Dunkin' Donuts in Braintree, MA?

"What are you, some kind of spies?"

Abby grinned. Even Pierre's lips rearranged themselves into an approximation of a smile as the elevator dinged and the door slid open. My jaw dropped.

The open space was several times larger than the coffee shop above it. Desks were lined up in neat rows, and a series of doors hinted at more rooms along the far wall. A dozen people stared at their monitors. And in the center of it all—

"Welcome to your local neighborhood branch of the Coffee Corps," said Abby.

I didn't respond. I stared at the pentagram encased in a circle drawn in what looked like neon-green spray paint on the concrete floor of the basement. It was large enough that an average sedan could fit inside the pentagon that made up the star's center. Strange runes were drawn along the circle's circumference.

Abby turned to Pierre. "Get the sample, please." He nodded and walked off. "Have you read any H.P. Lovecraft?" she asked me.

"Yeah," I said, not liking where this was going one bit. Was this some sort of a weird Satanic cult? "Some."

"Oh, good," she said. "Makes it easier to explain. The Coffee Corps is an independent agency of the U.S. government, charged with defending the homeland against the Old Ones."

I blinked several times, and searched the space for hidden cameras. Someone was bound to tell me I was being punked any minute now.

"There are regions that are especially vulnerable to their encroachment," said Abby. "Certain islands in the Pacific, the Bermuda Triangle, and New England among them."

"Um… okay."

"An optimal defense is to pepper the area with installations that utilize druidic protective runes, Sumerian chants, and other such techniques. Each installation is capable of shielding approximately ten square miles."

I thought of the ubiquitous Dunkin' Donuts locations throughout New England. "So you masquerade as a coffee chain because a few thousand pentagrams drawn in public parks might be a tad weird?"

"Weird, and prohibitively expensive. Imagine explaining why you need a few billion dollars for supernatural defense to the House Committee on Appropriations. Or, worse yet, raising taxes to pay for it. We're set up to be self-funded, like the post office."

This sounded almost crazy enough to make sense. I pointed at the pentagram. "Couldn't they build these under the post office branches, then?"

Abby shook her head. "Different mandate. The post office has got their hands full exterminating the venomous gorkas."

"What's a gorka?"

"Thanks to the USPS, you won't ever have to find out."

I banished from my mind the image of my sexagenarian mail carrier battling some mythical beast. "Wait a second. If I remember those stories right, aren't the Old Ones way too powerful for humans to fight?"

"Old Howard was a terrible pessimist," said Abby. "If we weren't willing to fight against odds, we would have never defeated Hitler's sorcerers in World War II, or thwarted the body snatcher invasion in '74."

My head swam. Sorcerers? Body snatchers? "Don't take this the wrong way, but how do I know you all aren't escapees from an insane asylum?"

"We'll show you lots of evidence in due course, but you know how photographs and video can be faked. We keep a live specimen around for new recruits. Ah, here we go." She pointed to Pierre, who was returning with a large glass container in his hands. He plunked what looked like an aquarium with a sealed top onto the nearest desk. Inside it was a monster.

The thing behind the glass looked a little like a tarantula—it was black and hairy and the size of a man's fist, but instead of spider legs it had tentacles. It scurried back and forth at the bottom of the container and tried climbing the walls, but the tiny suckers slid off the glass, leaving trails of goo. The thing had at least a dozen eyes, little white bulbs spread across the top of its body that pulsed like a frog's vocal sac.

"Baby shoggoth," said Pierre.

I stared. The thing seemed quite real, and more than a little terrifying.

"I thought shoggoths were as big as houses?"

"This breed only grows as large as a Golden Retriever," said Abby. "You still wouldn't want to run into one without a gun or a large cup of coffee."

"A... wait, what?"

"Watch," said Pierre. He lifted the lid, and I instinctively pulled back. He picked up a coffee mug from the desk, and poured a bit of liquid over the shoggoth.

The creature hissed and scuttled away from where the liquid landed, but a single drop hit one of its tentacles. The coffee ate through the shoggoth's flesh as though it were sulfuric acid. In moments, only a film-like white strip remained where java had connected.

"Coffee is poison to the Old Ones," said Abby. "It also keeps the minds of everyday people fortified against being driven to madness by the eldritch forces."

I made myself look away from the alien creature in the tank. "So you sell coffee, which also helps fight the bad guys. What about donuts? Do they have a secret superpower, too?"

Pierre stared down his nose at me with his one eye like I was a simpleton. "Donuts are delicious," he said.

"If you join us, you'll get to work on computers that are powered by both magic and science," said Abby. "I guarantee, it's like nothing you've ever experienced before. Plus, we can really use your skill set. But first..." She offered me the NDA again.

Without an argument, I signed on the dotted line. And initialed pages. And signed a dozen more times. "There." I pushed the stack of legalese away. "What do you need me to do?"

Abby and Pierre exchanged glances again.

"We're being hacked," she said.

WHOEVER WAS ATTEMPTING to hack the Coffee Corps was good, but I was better. Once I figured out the basics, I was able to beef up network security to levels that would make even a dragon turn green with envy. Assuming it wasn't green to begin with.

It took me a few weeks to get up to speed. The Coffee Corps computer network melded science and magic in ways I couldn't have imagined. Supernaturally enhanced code compiled smoothly and sometimes fixed its own bugs. Subroutines coded with bits of magic were sneaky and powerful; I could have probably hacked into the Pentagon and was tempted to, until my co-workers warned me that its cyber-security daemons were actual demons. The magic programming language was based on—what else?—Java. An enhanced version called Java Espresso, spliced with elements of APL for incorporating special symbols like runes, sigils, and hieroglyphics. I took to coding in Java Espresso like a fish to water.

Automation was a beautiful thing, too. Instead of keeping a dozen naked monks covered in blood on the payroll, we just played YouTube recordings of their chants on a loop. Prayer wheels, beads, Hail Marys: so many holy supplications relied heavily on mindless repetition, and nothing was better at mindless repetition than a computer.

The job quickly became routine—as much as preventing eldritch horrors from taking over the world could ever be routine. It felt like any other office, except with better coffee.

I called out to the office manager without taking my eyes off the screen as I typed. "Hey Dana, the printer is on the fritz. Also, Azathoth seems to have reshaped the Orion constellation again."

"The Outer Ones aren't our department," Dana replied. "E-mail Victor Stringer over at Starbucks about that. I'll get someone to look at the printer. Meanwhile, don't forget, the biweekly status report is due by—"

The ground lurched, upending chairs and toppling computer monitors. The air filled with the smell of rotten eggs and brine. The din sounded like granite slabs being turned to gravel by a giant rock crusher. Cracks appeared in the floor, and chunks of concrete rose upward in one spot as people scrambled away. Something very large was clawing its way out of the ground.

I lost precious seconds, immobilized by panic. Then I recovered enough to glance at my screen. Our security system was down—all of it. The digital chanting ceased and the screens went blank. The hackers I thought I had routed must've been toying with me, misleading me into a false sense of security even as they burrowed in deep, preparing to gain total control at a crucial moment.

They were fiendishly clever, but there's only so much a hacker can do remotely. One of the contingency plans I'd created since joining the Corps was a redundant set of servers that had never been connected to the internet, its operating system clean, complete with all of our cyber-security measures, and ready to activate and take over for the compromised computers in just under a minute.

With our digital defenses disrupted, the pentagram alone was not enough to ward us from a physical incursion by the eldritch forces. A jumble of tentacles, each thick as a man's torso, burst through the ground. They flailed above the break like snakes seeking prey to zero in on. While most of the staff scrambled away from the monster, Pierre rushed toward it with what looked like a modified fire extinguisher.

He was buying time, but couldn't hope to defeat the alien monster on his own. I needed to get us back online. There was no time for subtlety—I yanked fiber cables from our compromised server like so many weeds, and began frantically reconnecting them to the backup.

Pierre pointed the extinguisher at the writhing tentacles, and pressed the discharge lever. Dark liquid sprayed from the hose. It was a mix of cold brew coffee concentrate diluted with a minute amount of holy water and other substances with names in Latin and Sanskrit. The stuff was basically an equivalent of napalm to the Old Ones. The monster roared with pain and rage. The tentacles didn't burn away the way they had with the miniature shoggoth, but they changed hue from jet-black to gray, and beat frantically against fractured concrete to shake off the chemical mix.

For a moment it looked as though Pierre had the situation in hand, but the extinguisher ran out of charge after about twenty seconds of continuous use. The tentacles sprouted farther from the hole, smashing desks and equipment. Pierre retreated several steps toward the pentagram.

I had all the cables in place and was booting up the backup system. I needed a little more time before it was online.

The tentacles slithered toward the pentagram like hungry pythons. A single tiny disruption to the incantations written on the circumference of the circle would mess up the wards and render impotent our non-digital defenses. "I need another thirty seconds!" I shouted.

My compatriots must've been as scared as I was, but they knew the score. If the monster reached the pentagram, we would likely all be dead or wishing we were dead shortly thereafter. They converged on the tentacles as one, hitting them with rocks and chairs and anything else they had on hand. People I was just getting to know as friends, mild-mannered office workers with whom I shared funny cat pictures on the office intranet or discussed the latest episodes of *The Walking Dead* around the water cooler, were engaged in combat against an evil alien creature.

Up until then, the mission of the Coffee Corps had seemed hypothetical somehow. It was clinical, like playing a complicated video game. I had wondered more than once if drone pilots felt that way; felt removed from combat and the reality of warfare they were engaged in when flying remote-controlled missions half a world away. The scene unfolding in front of me brutally stripped the veneer of distance, the illusion of civility. We were fighting a war against a terrible enemy over the highest possible stakes.

Dana the office manager flung the contents of her coffee mug at the nearest tentacle, then hit it several times with her paperweight until the tentacle flexed and sent her sprawling toward the wall. Bob from Accounting swung at the tentacles with his commemorative 2016 Cubs baseball bat signed by the whole team. He loved that thing, but didn't hesitate to liberate it from its display case. He got a few good whacks in before it splintered against alien flesh.

Dana got up and held her iPhone like a crucifix with its screen facing toward the tentacles. She loaded one of the chants we used on YouTube and played it at maximum volume. Of course, without it being amplified by the pentagram and the plethora of sorcerous sub-routines run by our computers, it was no more threatening to the monstrous invader than a mosquito bite.

Abby emerged from her office holding what looked like a shrunken human head in one hand and a short obsidian wand in another. She stepped between the tentacles and the pentagram and held up the artifacts, reciting an incantation in a guttural ancient language. The tentacles halted for a moment, then parted, snaking around her like a river split by a tall peak.

I watched the events unfold, feeling guilty that I couldn't join in. But I needed to ping the auras and ensorcell the scripts that generated the firewall in order to activate the defenses once the computer was ready. So I watched my friends and co-workers try and fail to hold the tentacles back. Their efforts bought a few precious seconds, but not nearly enough. I silently vowed that if we survived this calamity, I'd keep the backup server running 24/7 to make the transition way faster.

The tentacles were an arm's length from the runes encircling the pentagram when Pierre began to chant.

The one-eyed bruiser recited the complex incantation with staggering precision. The warding prayer in an ancient language I didn't recognize—some version of Hebrew, perhaps?—flowed from his lips and filled the room, drowning out the terrible noises that came from beneath the earth. When he spoke, the tentacles flattened against the ground as though crushed under the weight of enormous boulders. They twitched, and I could see powerful muscles straining against the arcane forces holding them down, but they seemed incapable of overpowering the magic so long as Pierre continued to chant.

Dark circles appeared under Pierre's eyes, and several days' worth of beard growth covered his previously clean-shaven cheeks. Each second drained hours of Pierre's life force but his feet remained firmly planted and his voice never wavered.

He kept the monster at bay for nearly twenty seconds, until finally the computer was ready. I entered a command, and the security system came back to life. The sounds of mantras and incantations from a dozen different cultures erupted from the speakers. Tibetan prayer wheels turned, powered by electricity. Sacred warding pictograms appeared on LCD monitors that hung along the office walls.

The Old Ones' creature howled in pain and retreated, concrete and earth settling lower where it had first broken through. It left several of its tentacles behind, severed clean by the re-established wards. Black ichor leaked from the cuts.

Pierre ceased chanting. He took several deep breaths as he surveyed the demolished office space around him.

"That was incredible," Bob told him. He still clutched the stump of his bat, white-knuckled. "Your Aramaic is flawless."

Pierre shrugged. "I learned to fight the Old Ones back when calculations were performed on an abacus and men spoke their own conjurations."

Then he spat upon the limp dead tentacle at his feet.

THE SKYPE CALL came minutes after we'd fought back the tentacle monster. We were administering first aid to the wounded when a meaty face filled the large screens hanging along the walls and all the monitors.

"Status report," said the white-haired man without preamble. He looked to be in his late sixties. He seemed familiar, but I couldn't place him.

"We have things under control now, sir," said Abby. "We were—"

He cut her off. "I know. It was an orchestrated attack. They hit dozens of Corps branches across New England. Most managed to fight off the physical assaults, but several branches are down, and the hackers are in control of the networks of at least a dozen others. They didn't have backup servers set up the way you did. Nice job on that, by the way."

"Thank you, sir," said Abby. She gave me a tiny nod. "To be fair, it's not something any of us were prepared for. The Old Ones have never shown any aptitude for human technology before."

"They employed human coders," said the man. "Highly competent ones, by the looks of things."

No kidding. I could think of only a few hacker groups with that sort of talent, and I highly doubted any of them were aware of magic. That left government-sponsored groups.

Abby must have been thinking along the same lines. "Who was it, sir?" she asked. "Russia? China?"

"That's why I'm calling," said the man. "We traced them to your backyard. Cambridge, to be precise. The hackers are from MIT." The man pursed his lips. "As a Harvard man, I always knew those underachievers from the wrong end of the street were up to no good. A SWAT team is on the way. I want your squad to join them. Assist in recovering control of our networks, and assess any future threats this new brand of techno-cultists might pose."

"Yes, sir." Abby saluted.

"How?" I knew I shouldn't speak up, but I couldn't help myself. All eyes in the room turned to me. "How did you manage to trace them? I've been trying to do that, too, but I'm having no luck at all."

The man looked at me, then glanced elsewhere, as though he was reading something else on his screen. "I have my ways, Mr. Palermo," he said. He must've looked me up on the fly. Then he smiled. "When we created the internet, we built in certain admin privileges."

The man re-focused on Abby, telling her when and where to link up with the SWAT team, but I was barely listening because I thought I finally recognized him. When he ended the call, I grabbed the sleeve of Bob's shirt as he was passing by my desk.

"Was that…?"

"Yeah," said Bob. "That's Al Gore. He's the government liaison to the Corps, though he spends most of his time spearheading the effort to prevent Venusians from heating up Earth in order to terraform it."

I was dumbfounded enough that my response was mostly reflex. "Wouldn't that be, you know, venusforming?"

"I suppose." Bob shrugged, and headed toward his cubicle, remnants of the Cubs bat still in his hands.

Since the bad guys held the networks of many of our branches hostage, bringing a computer expert on this mission seemed like a no-brainer to everyone involved. Except I hadn't signed on to be an action hero. But I also didn't have it in me to say no. I'd manned the computer while my co-workers battled an otherworldly monster with nothing but office furniture, and while that was strategically the right thing to do, it made me feel guilty. When Abby asked me to come along, I was too embarrassed to say no in front of everyone. By the time Abby, Pierre, and I climbed into the SWAT team bus, I was already regretting that decision.

I expected the SWAT team to look like they do on TV: a bunch of fit, somber young men in bulletproof vests armed with machine guns and smoke grenades. The four characters we met on the bus were anything but. A rotund middle-aged man in a Rush T-shirt that was at least two sizes too small and cargo shorts took up both seats in the front row. Sweat stains spread around his armpits. He wore an actual fanny pack. Behind him, a gray-haired lady in her sixties clutched a broom. A tall pointed black hat lay in her lap. Next to her sat a leather-clad black woman in her early twenties who had a sword slung over her shoulders, its intricate pommel sticking out from behind her back. A Samoan man with the physique of a sumo wrestler towered over them in the last seat. His goatee, mustache, and fancy red cloak could probably pass as Dr. Strange cosplay.

Overall, they couldn't look more like a gaggle of Comic Con attendees if they tried.

"Hello," I said as we squeezed past them and toward the empty seats in the back.

They nodded. The swordswoman smiled at us. No one said a word.

"Battle sorcerers," whispered Abby when we took our seats and the bus peeled off toward Boston with blatant disregard for speed limits and traffic laws. "They tend to be somewhat peculiar."

I nodded. The dress code at the Coffee Corps was casual, so as to blend in among the coffee shop customers on our way in and out of our secret bunker. The SWAT magicians clearly didn't have this problem. I figured their secret headquarters was probably in some comic book store.

The bus pulled up in front of 32 Vassar Street. The Stata Center, an avant-garde tower of strangely curved walls and teetering columns that housed the MIT computer science and AI lab, among other departments, towered over us. The building looked like it was designed using non-Euclidian geometry, and seemed like exactly the sort of place bound to become infested with a bunch of cultists.

We piled out of the bus and into the lobby. Our colorful group got a few curious glances, but mostly people ignored us. They'd seen stranger things in Cambridge. The SWAT sorcerers eschewed the elevator in favor of stairs. We climbed eight flights to the top floor. I was annoyed to have become more winded than the heavyset guy wearing the Rush T-shirt.

The leather-clad woman took point and unsheathed her sword. It looked like a katana to me, though that guess was based purely on the repeated viewings of *Kill Bill*. I mentally dubbed her Ninja Girl. She kicked the door open and entered the eighth floor. The rest of us followed.

Inside, the facility looked rather mundane. We moved past offices and study rooms filled with computer desks. The place appeared deserted, it being a holiday weekend. We'd made it half-way across the floor, opening and checking every room, when I heard a low rumbling. It was as though someone had recorded the sounds of an upset stomach, amplified them, and mixed in the hissing of steam. Then I saw them: a trio of shoggoths, man-sized versions of the sample Pierre had showed me on my first day at the Coffee Corps, slithering toward us across the tiled floor.

The elderly woman waved the back end of her broom like a giant pen. Crimson symbols appeared, shimmering in the air before her.

"Keep going," said the Samoan. He raised a scepter-like short staff. "We'll deal with these."

The two battle sorcerers got between the shoggoths and the rest of the group. We hurried along. I, for one, didn't have to be asked twice. With the sounds of combat behind us, I followed Abby down the corridor where the lights seemed dimmer, the far end lost in the dusk, even though the halogen bulbs in the drop ceiling appeared to be functioning. The remaining sorcerers tensed like bloodhounds who'd caught scent of prey. Even I sensed something unsettling coming from that direction.

The man in the Rush T-shirt held up a fist, and motioned toward one of the doors. The sorcerers burst through, and we followed.

The room we entered would have looked like a normal computer lab if not for the arcane symbols drawn in blood on the chalkboard, or the half-dozen students who sat in front of their computers, unblinking. In front of them perched a nightmarish creature.

It cocked its head like an owl, if owls were five feet tall and covered in thousands of sharp scales instead of feathers. Its saucer-like black eyes zeroed in on our group. It screeched, its open beak revealing jagged teeth, and opened its wings in a threatening manner. More razor blades glistened from its eight-foot wingspan.

The young woman held up her sword and got between me and Big Bird. I felt a ping of discomfort—being protected like that seemed un-chivalrous somehow. But I suppressed the thought: she was doing her job, ensuring that the computer nerd got to the computers and did *his* job. Also, she was far more qualified to deal with this sort of thing.

The last of the battle sorcerers pulled a cell phone out of his fanny pack and fiddled with it. Big Bird attacked, furiously flapping its wings. The movements were almost too fast for me to follow, but Ninja Girl managed to parry and possibly even hurt the thing; a number of severed blade-like scales fell to the ground as they fought. Abby dragged me off toward the far corner while Pierre pulled a pistol and shot at the bird's head, seemingly not worried about the possibility of hitting the battle sorceress with friendly fire.

The fight lasted several seconds—barely long enough for Abby to usher me a handful of steps away. Then the cell phone loaded the incantation, its tinny speakers filling the room with sounds of some ancient language.

Big Bird shrunk away from the sound, but then rallied and flew over Ninja Girl and toward the battle sorcerer holding the phone. Ninja Girl managed a long, deep cut at the creature's belly as it passed overhead, but its wing connected with the man's upper arm and shoulder anyway. Blood seeped from his shredded arm. He stumbled out of the way, and tossed the phone to Ninja Girl. She caught it with her left hand and retreated toward the door, blocking Big Bird's escape. The monster flew back and forth across the small room frantically, like a sparrow that had accidentally flown inside a building and was trying to escape. Then it threw its weight at the window, shattering the glass and tumbling into the balmy mid-afternoon air.

Before any of us managed to catch our breaths, one of the shoggoths pushed its way through the door. Its bulbous eyes undulated across its hairy body like oversized pustules. I didn't know if it was one of the three monsters the battle sorcerers had engaged earlier, or if there were more of these things in the building. Neither option appealed to me.

The wounded sorcerer and Ninja Girl exchanged glances.

"We're on it," she said. Then she addressed me directly. "We'll buy you time. Do your thing." Then, to her wounded compatriot, "The barrier."

He nodded, withdrew a lavender-colored crystal from his cargo shorts with his good hand, and dropped it on the floor. He spoke a few words in what might've been Latin, and crushed the crystal under his heel.

The walls of the computer lab began to glow. The same lavender color intensified as the two battle sorcerers charged at the shoggoth and pushed it out the door. Less than fifteen seconds later, the walls, the door, and the windows could no longer be seen. It was as though we were inside an opaque lavender cube. I probed its sheen covering the floor with the toe of my shoe. It was rock-solid and felt like linoleum.

"A barrier spell," said Abby. "Rare and very expensive, but nothing is getting in or out, not even an Elder God."

"Don't worry," said Pierre. "It will dissipate in a few hours. We won't run out of air before then."

I shuddered, silently thankful that I'd used the restroom before we left Braintree.

Abby glanced at her watch. "Reinforcements will be here by then. But you should get to work."

I walked over to the students who had remained immobile through all the excitement. Their eyes were milky white, with no pupils or irises. I waved my hand in front of the face of the nearest one, eliciting no reaction. "I'm no optician, but this doesn't look right," I said, mostly to break the uncomfortable silence.

"Optometrist," said Abby. "If you're going to crack jokes, get it right."

"Maybe I meant they need fake glasses with googly eyes for lenses," I said defensively.

"Look at that." Pierre pointed at a pentagram variant drawn on the floor of the lab.

"Huh." Ninja Girl frowned as she examined the arcane drawing. "This is designed for virgin sacrifice. Guess the owl-thing had another use for these geeks planned after they were through attacking our computers."

"Virgin hackers at MIT? Guess that's a Venn diagram with a pretty large overlap," muttered the overweight battle sorcerer, as he used magic to tend to his wounds.

"Hey, now. That's a hurtful stereotype," I said.

Ninja Girl pointed to the blank, pasty faces of the computer geeks. "The proof's in the pentagram. Come on, let's fix the damage, and then maybe we can figure out how to release the virgins."

We spread across the room searching for clues, studying the writing on various blackboards and notepads. I pushed the wheeled computer chair away from one of the screens, its occupant still zombified, and began interrogating the machine.

Pierre eyed a bunch of numbers and letters on one of the boards. "What sorcery is this?" he asked. "I don't recognize the language."

Abby studied the board for a moment. "That's trigonometry," she said. "It seems to calculate the Earth's distance from the Sun. Let me see." She got closer. "This is bad," she said. "Very, very bad."

Pierre may not have known the math, but he recognized something, because his eyes narrowed and his brow wrinkled with concern. "Aphelion?" he asked.

Abby nodded.

"What is it?" I called from the computer.

"Aphelion is the point in the orbit where a planet is farthest from the Sun," said Abby. "Earth's aphelion is also when our magic is at its weakest against the eldritch forces. Whatever these people were doing, they were laying the groundwork for an invasion, probing our defenses. The monster we fought and the others were some sort of an opening move. Now we know when the main attack will take place."

"When?" I asked.

"The next aphelion is tomorrow." She consulted her phone, but the barrier cut off WiFi. "I'm fairly sure it's on July 3, at 4:11 P.M. Eastern this year."

Garfield and Will Smith both had it right. Of course the scary aliens would invade around Independence Day, and on a Monday to boot.

"There go my barbecue plans," I said.

I worked as fast as I could. The lavender cube was growing uncomfortably hot. I wiped sweat off my brow with a sleeve. The MIT whiz kids knew their stuff. There are maybe two dozen people around the world who could force their way past their protections. Fortunately, I was one of them.

After about an hour, I pushed the office chair away from the desk and sighed.

Abby and Pierre stared at me like patients waiting for the doctor to tell them whether the tumor was benign.

"Here's the deal," I said. "These overachievers coded the most sophisticated worm I've ever seen. It's propagating across computers, cell phones, even smart fridges: anything with an internet connection and a processor. It's been spreading fast; millions of systems have been infected by now."

Pierre wasn't a tech guy, and must've been struggling to keep up. He looked like a light bulb went on over his head as I explained. "Like a virus?" he asked.

I didn't have time to rant about the difference between worms, viruses, and trojans. "Yes. They're both malware."

Abby was faster on the uptake. "What's it do?" she asked.

"All those devices are going to play a recording of a summoning incantation, at the same time. One guess as to when."

Abby frowned. "4:11 P.M. tomorrow?"

I nodded.

"So." Pierre stared at the computer monitors with disdain, as though they were a bunch of Benedict Arnolds, about to betray humanity. "How do we stop it?"

"We can't," I said. "But we may be able to subvert it. Use their own code to send an updated version of the worm, if you will. Get it to play 'Never Gonna Give You Up' instead of 'Cthulhu fhtagn' or something."

"Great," said Abby. "And how do we do that?"

"This thing was coded in the beefed-up magic variant of Java," I said. "Very similar to Java Espresso, but it seems they cooked it up from scratch. We need two things: a few hundred top-notch programmers who can poke at it, and an insane amount of computing power to crack their encryption in time."

"That's a problem," said Abby. "There are only a few dozen people in the world who know Java Espresso."

"A few *dozen*? That's not going to work. Not on the super-tight deadline. And we need time for the updated worm to disseminate, too."

Abby stared at me helplessly.

"How is it that so few people know?"

"It's top secret, remember? And we never had it used against us before," she said. "It's not like undead octopi are good with computers."

"Well, they've got smarter cultists now," I said.

"We can turn off the internet," said Pierre. "I'll call Gore."

"That won't help. The worm is on each device. It's even smart enough to turn on phones and tablets that happen to be in sleep mode."

"Great." Pierre made a fist. "We've defeated terrible threats for millennia, only to have the world destroyed by a half-dozen zombie-nerds."

"EMPs," said Abby. "We can fry all electronic devices across the globe. It won't be pretty or fun, but it beats everyone getting eaten by the Elder Ones."

I had a better idea, but I was sure Abby and Pierre weren't going to like it. "Whatever we do, we'll have to wait until the barrier releases us. So I'll keep at it and see what I can figure out."

IT WAS ANOTHER hour and a half before the barrier glowed and began to dissipate. It was still solid enough to keep us in, but the internet access came back. I was ready by then. I hit "Send" on the e-mail with a long list of recipients. Then I got up from the chair and stretched my aching back.

Both of my colleagues stared at me.

"It only took me a couple of hours to pick up the basics of Java Espresso because I was already an expert Java coder," I said. "So I sent the tutorial to a few hundred of the best hackers and coders I know, along with what needs to be done. And I asked them to post it around on forums and on the Darknet."

"You did *what*?" Pierre advanced on me, but stopped just short of grabbing me by my shirt.

"That's incredibly reckless," said Abby. "And way above your pay grade."

"It's also our best chance to succeed without knocking the planet back to the pre-microchip age. Gives us enough brainpower and computer power to get this done by tomorrow afternoon."

She thought for a moment. "At the very least, you should've consulted us."

"No," I said. "I just told the world magic is real, and shared around a copy of the owner's manual. That makes what Snowden did child's play by comparison. There's no telling how the Powers That Be will react, but it probably won't be pretty. At least this way, I'm the only one responsible."

Pierre and Abby looked at each other.

"What if it doesn't work?" said Pierre. "What if they simply don't believe you?"

"Can't guarantee that it will. But it doesn't matter if they believe me. I promised ten grand converted to Bitcoin to whoever cracks this egg first. And that's just the icing on the cake: these people will drop everything for an opportunity to try to break this sort of encryption—that I can guarantee. I know them. I *am* them."

The lavender barrier was becoming translucent. We could see reinforcements—our fellow Coffee Corps members—outside.

"Guess I better break the news to our bosses," said Abby. "And get those EMPs in place, in case your stunt fails."

Before I could respond, the barrier went down, and agents rushed toward us.

EVERYONE KNOWS WHAT happened next. By evening, the sensational story about an impending alien invasion was all over the news. Most people didn't take it seriously, but any hacker worth their salt took one look at the code and rolled up their sleeves.

At 4:11 P.M. the next day, over ten million computers, tablets, phones, and all manner of smart appliances capable of emitting sound played a spell designed to ward against the Old Ones. A few hundred thousand devices never received the patch, and played the summoning spell, but even during aphelion, they were vastly outnumbered and overpowered by the a cappella choir of Siris and Cortanas controlled by the good-guys' version of the worm.

I walked off in the chaos of the aftermath, leaving behind the Stata Center overrun by dozens of Coffee Corps agents. I laid low for the next twenty-four hours, working on countering that worm along with everyone else. I sent the Bitcoin prize I'd advertised over to a high school kid in South Korea—I hope the Corps will try to recruit him as they beef up their cyber security division in light of this new type of threat. In a few minutes, I plan to head over to my office under a Dunkin' Donuts in Braintree, and face the music.

I don't know what's going to happen to me. They might give me a medal or ship me off to some overseas CIA prison, never to be heard from again. Whatever the case, I wanted to tell my side of the story. So I'm doing the whistleblower thing yet again, uploading my account of recent events to the internet.

You may choose to believe me, or not. But even if you disregard this as some ill-advised attempt at Dunkin' Donuts Lovecraftian fan fiction, do yourself a favor: have a cup of coffee every once in a while, will you?

The Vestals of Midnight
Sharon Lee

YOU'VE BEEN THERE, right? The moment when you're startled out of a sound sleep because someone is walking on your land who doesn't belong there?

Who *seriously* doesn't belong there?

Curled on my side, eyes closed, snugged into blankets still warm from Borgan's presence, I reached for the Land...

It was early—or late, depending on your inclination and service. Borgan'd left ten minutes ago, to go out for the day's fishing. Those who prospered in the dark were thinking about pulling themselves into their places for a snooze, while those who had no cause to hide from the sun's face were drifting toward wakefulness...

There.

I snatched at the shiver of wrongness; pushed the Land to *show me*; and sat up straight in bed.

There?

Who in God's name would try to sneak up on the Enterprise?

I mean, the Enterprise *is* on my Land—by which I mean, it's in Archers Beach, of which I am, for a bunch of complicated reasons, mostly having to do with sin, and bloodlines, and—I'm sorry—magic, the Guardian. Geography being what it is, the Enterprise is in my—call it *my jurisdiction*. In theory, this means it's also under my authority.

Feel free to tell that to the Enterprise. I'll wait.

Still keeping a tight fix on that sliver of wrongness on the Land, I opened my mundane eyes to my bedroom. Breccia the cat was sitting up tall at the bottom of the bed, ridiculous floof of a tail wrapped primly around her toes; her eyes serious. Outside, I could hear the ocean playing with the shore; the view out the window was grey sea-mist against dawn-grey sky.

The imminent rising of the sun was causing the stranger on my Land some concern, and they weren't making any particular effort to hide that worry—or themselves.

Which in turn worried *me.*

I threw back the covers, pulled on jeans, sweater, socks, sneakers; nodded to Breccia.

"Hold the fort," I told her. "Be right back."

Then I reached to the Land again, and stepped from my bedroom…

…into the dooryard of the Enterprise, which was shrouded in something much denser and more malevolent than mere fog; heavy with a despair that reminded me forcibly of a Black Dog.

There was magic building. Specific, sophisticated magic, and the Enterprise was its intended target. I drew on my own power, and looked closer, seeing the sticky ball of compulsion and command revolving in the thick air; saw, more importantly, the dark figure at the heart of the darkness, cloak billowing in a breeze I didn't feel; the spell very nearly complete, spinning between the palms of their hands, spitting sticky black sparks of malice.

I took a deep breath, drew a tad more power, and spoke.

"That," I said, conversationally, "would be a bad mistake."

The Land boomed; the air crackled. The dark figure jumped, the bomb they'd created snapping out of existence with a pettish little *fsst,* like a wet firecracker.

A breeze I *could* feel rushed through the clearing, chilly and tasting of salt. The unnatural fog shredded, and I was facing a stocky woman wearing a long black gown under the black cloak, bodice laced with blood-red ribbons, sleeves dripping with crimson lace. Her face was pale and round, and she was wearing sunglasses.

"How dare you interfere with me?" she snapped.

"In the job description," I said. "I'm the Guardian of Archers Beach, and you were about to do something really stupid, which, just as a side effect, could've killed us all."

I paused, then added, in case it wasn't clear, "*You* would have been included in *us all.*"

She took a breath that strained the bright ribbons.

"That… entity," she said, moving a hand glittering with dark gemstones toward the Enterprise, "has stolen from me."

A word here about the Enterprise. In these parts—these parts being the state of Maine, on the East Coast of the United States—an "enterprise" is a kind of a cross between a junkyard and a flea market. You can find all kinds of *stuff* at an enterprise, from silver teapots to Nixon/Agnew campaign buttons; from slate chalkboards to yellowed lace doilies, to bags of mismatched Legos®.

The Enterprise in Archers Beach also deals in *stuff*: magical stuff, hexed stuff, stuff nobody heard of, stuff nobody wants, and stuff somebody might want way too much.

The assertion that the Enterprise had *stolen* from this nice lady didn't particularly shock me. I'd long wondered where the Enterprise's *stuff* came from. Artie, the *trenvay* whose duty the Enterprise was, could only tell me that "things come in," from time to time, on their own schedule, and with their own ideas. He didn't know where they came from, or necessarily how they arrived. They appeared, was all. Artie's part of the business was to make certain that those things which came in with a purpose or a name attached were delivered to their proper recipients, and the rest were kept... quiet.

But that's getting ahead of things, just a little. There were courtesies to be observed between visitor and Guardian. She should have offered first, being a stranger on my Land, but I could afford to be gracious.

On my Land.

So, I bowed, and said easily, "I'm Kate Archer, Guardian of the Land; heir to Aeronymous, late of the Land of the Flowers."

I got the impression that I'd startled her; that maybe she'd blinked behind those dark glasses. If so, she recovered fast, and produced a very nice bow, indeed.

"I am Annora of Shadowood, in service to the Queen of Daknowyth."

Daknowyth. The Land of Midnight, that would be. Not quite my favorite of the Six Worlds, but it did explain the sunglasses and the concern about the coming dawn.

"So, what exactly did the Enterprise steal from you, and how would blowing it up get whatever it is back?"

Annora bristled.

"I am on the business of my Queen!" she snapped.

"You're on the business of your Queen *on my Land*," I countered. "Since the business of your Queen seems to include *blowing things up* on my Land, I'd—"

"If you had bothered to understand what I was doing," she interrupted sharply; "you would have seen that my intention was to smother everything magic-touched in this area. My... items, which are not so touched, would then have been easy to remove."

"That might have been your intention," I said. Admittedly, I'm not very good at spell-craft; for all I knew, her sticky bomb really *had been* only a fire-blanket. But smothering the Enterprise wasn't any better, in the long run, than blowing it sky-high. Worse, really. The Enterprise is used to getting its way.

"Still not a great idea to interfere with the Enterprise."

"Am I to reason with it?" Annora inquired, with a certain amount of justifiable sarcasm.

"No," I said, giving her the point; "that never works. We'll have to reason with the *trenvay*—the spirit of the place—involved." Which *some*times worked.

"Now, how about—"

"Kate?"

The door to the Enterprise opened, spilling yellow light into the dooryard. Annora hissed and moved a hand; the light dimmed perceptively as the shadow that was Artie came forward.

"Kate," he said again, ignoring Annora entirely. "We got a problem."

"I should say *so!*" Annora snapped, and took a deep breath, like she'd remembered where she was, and continued more moderately. "You can cease to have a problem. Merely release them to me."

Artie turned his head, and considered her for a length of time just shy of insulting before turning back to me.

"Who's this?"

"This," I told him, "is Annora of Shadowood, on the business of the Queen of Daknowyth."

"Daknowyth," Artie repeated, like you might say *jelly fish*. He turned back to me.

"What's the trouble?" I asked, to forestall a long detour about Daknowyth, its Queen, and its history, or lack of same, with our very own Changing Land.

"Well," he said, rubbing the back of his neck in a fair semblance of bewilderment. "We got something come in, all right—couple of somethings, if it come to that—but it ain't—*they ain't*—in the usual way."

He paused, and looked me straight in the eye, which was when I knew—*really knew*—just how worried he was.

"An' if we don't get 'em outta there soon, there's no telling what'll happen."

THE ENTERPRISE IS one smallish three-room shed, and the yard behind it. Every square inch is covered in stuff, and sometimes there's stuff inside the stuff.

Mundane folk—by which I mean people who are magic-blind— mundane folk are the Enterprise's fair game. All summer long, ordinary people walk into the Enterprise, meaning only to stay a couple minutes, ducking in out of the sun, maybe, or just mildly curious. Certainly, they never mean to *buy* anything.

And yet, all summer long, those folks go home with this or that little souvenir that, when questioned, they have only the haziest recollection of having purchased; an ugly little thing, but for some reason, they just can't seem to bring themselves to get rid of it. No one would suggest that there was anything… magical… in that. Magic wasn't real, after all, and for most of the people in the world, it's just not there. They don't *feel* the energy sparking all around them; they don't *hear* the strange music intended to pull them into a dance they can't hope to survive; they don't *see* the beautiful woman beckoning to them from the wood, and they *certainly* don't follow her off the path.

Magic folk—like me, like Annora of Shadowood, like Artie—magic folk have their own defenses and strategies to answer the lure of the Enterprise. That's not to say that we're not occasionally caught unaware, but the mischief made with us tends to be minor.

No, its half-magic folk—those who *can* see the weird, but who have no magic of their own—who're in the most danger from the Enterprise— and the risk to them is utterly non-trivial. In most cases, it's life-changing. And not in a good way.

In the old days, they were locked up in attic rooms, or insane asylums. In these enlightened times, we've got drugs for that. The weakest can't prevent magic seeping into them, filling them up until they're no longer, really, themselves.

The strongest make it a policy never to walk down dark alleys, speak to strangers, or to look too nearly into the shadows cast by the street-lights. I don't imagine that they ever sleep sound, but I believe most of them survive.

"The light is increasing," Annora said, voice calm, though the Land brought me the sharp stab of her concern.

I sighed.

"Right. Let's get this thing done."

THERE WERE NO mundane customers in the Enterprise this early in the day. That might've been the reason for the extra fizz in the air. Magical being that I am, and Guardian of the Land, too, I could still feel the aisles crowding me, and something a lot like something big, hungry, and with lots of teeth breathing down the back of my neck. The air was alive with whisperings; no words that the ear could actually catch, mind, but you were left with the idea that the Enterprise found you, just faintly, ridiculous.

"What is this place?" Annora asked from behind me. "Why has it not been tamed?"

Behind us, to the left, something… growled.

"A little tact might be in order," I said, when the growl had subsided into whispers again.

"Enterprise is old," said Artie, who was bringing up the rear. "Older'n me, and I'm plenty too old. Back when Kate's grandma was a saplin', we got to talking about it one day with the Ol' Forest. Best we could figure, then, was the Enterprise is more gate than anything else, an' most of it's Out Beyond, blowing in the Wind Between the Worlds. Figured that was how stuff come in like it does. I never figured any better. Ain't like it talks to me, really."

"Surely, it will amend itself out of respect for the Guardian," Annora said.

I didn't laugh, but the Enterprise did, lights flickering, and wooden floorboards groaning.

"So, Artie," I said over my shoulder. "Where are these things that just came—"

I stopped, because here they were, of course, and their danger was horrifyingly real.

They were in the second—middle—room of three, as surrounded by the Enterprise as it was possible to be. The room was slightly lower than the first room—three steps down from the floor I stood on, to the floor they stood on, pressed in on all sides by rustic bureaus, spinning wheels, three-legged stools, rocking chairs, and an unstrung harp.

Six youngsters, ranging in age from maybe-eight to maybe-twelve, stood in two rows, facing the far wall, the three tallest in front. They were wearing dress native to each of the Six Worlds. Black gown and cloak for the dark Daknowyth miss with the white-as-opal eyes; sky-blue tunic for the pale winged one from Varoth; crimson and black for the fiery redhead from Kashnerot; waterskins, high boots, and a demi-cloak for the haughty dark-haired youth from Cheobaug; bright silks and a crown of sweet flowers on the head of the child from Sempeki; jeans so old they were white, tennis shoes, and a black T-shirt with a band logo faded 'til I couldn't read it, from our own, the Changing Land.

"*Kids?*" I snapped, and turned to Annora, flinging out a hand in an *explain this* gesture.

"Vestals," she corrected. "Each has accepted the Word of the Queen of Daknowyth, and bound themselves to her honor."

"Do their parents know?" I asked.

"In every case, they are kinless," Annora told me with dignity. "The Queen of Daknowyth is not a thief."

"Kate…" Artie said from behind me, and I could hear the strain in his voice. "They can't stay here much longer, and I mean *much*. They're all of 'em empty!"

Turning back, I saw what he meant.

The room was dim; expectable, given the hour and the fact that the Enterprise was poorly lit by design.

The kids, though—the kids were standing in a spotlight of pearly light, each casting a shadow of lambent silver. I realized then that I was looking at innocence; at purity, if you'll allow it. None of them possessed the least shred of magic. All of them could see the weird; taste it; hear it. Their one defense was their virtue—and that wasn't going to be enough.

Magic, in case I forgot to say earlier, abhors a vacuum. It will strive to fill any empty vessel with itself. The Enterprise, being old in guile and in magic, desired nothing more than to fill each of those kids up with itself, and possess them, utterly.

The Land trembled with the Enterprise's lust, and I started to feel a little sick. No time for that now. *Now*, I looked deeper, and—yes; there were dark flares and flashes just beyond that nimbus of purity, chewing away at the edges, but not, I noticed, too quickly. The Enterprise was enjoying this game, and had a mind to stretch it out.

"That will do!" Annora stepped forward, and I dropped back a step to let her have a full view of the situation.

"These are not yours to take!" she cried, power thrumming in her voice. "These are the Vestals of Midnight. They are under the shield of the Queen of Daknowyth, which I, her appointed representative, now extend!"

That quick, something black, supple, and complex flowed out and over the room, drifting like a sweet cloud over the heads of the six kids. It was, I saw, intended to envelope them, like armor, whereupon they could be led out of the center of the Enterprise's ravenous web.

Except, it never settled.

The... things that had been gnawing at the edge of the circle of light abruptly merged into a blare of oily lightning, stabbing straight into the heart of the cloud.

Thunder boomed. Sparks flew. The furniture lunged forward, legs clattering like hooves on the old wooden floor.

The red-haired boy yelled and thrust out a hand, catching a flying sugar bowl in one hand and throwing it at a book that was flapping toward them like a raven.

The kid from the Changing Land kicked out, in perfect form, smacking a charging spinning wheel with the flat of her sneaker, sending it crashing back into a bookcase filled with ugly knick-knacks.

"Hey!" Artie yelled. "You be careful! Them things is worth money!"

In the doorway, Annora gestured. I felt power surge, saw a second iteration of the black shield flow into being—only to be torn to shreds by the Enterprise's outrage.

It was only a matter of seconds before things started breaking, and there was no assurance that the kids would survive the battle of wills.

On the other hand, Annora *was* drawing the Enterprise's fire.

I reached to the Land, and through it spoke directly to the kids.

"Let's go! Run! This way!"

They tried. The girl from the Changing Land and the boy from the Land of Wave and Water each grabbed the hands of the two kids nearest them and dragged them forward. The first three steps were fine—not a run, but brisk enough—the fourth step was like they were walking through mud; the fifth step—well, the Changing Land kid managed a fifth step, but none of the rest of them did.

The Enterprise roared!

Dust blew up in a swirling plume, crockery broke, a stool danced a tango across the floor, slammed into a rocking chair, and knocked it onto its back.

Annora groaned. I could see her struggling to raise yet another wave of energy, but the Enterprise had its dander up, now; the air so thick with malice it was barely possible to breathe.

"She's gonna blow!" Artie yelled, and I heard boots pounding on the floor behind me.

I reached to the Land, drew power into my bones, and Spoke with words of fire.

"That's enough."

The dust devil congealed and fell to the floor with an audible thump.

The furniture froze in place.

The roaring stopped.

In the abrupt silence, one last piece of crockery fell off of a shelf and broke, quietly, on a musty hooked rug.

Beside me, Annora of Shadowood drew in a very, *very* long breath.

I could feel the weight of the Enterprise's attention, focused directly on me; and it wasn't the best feeling I'd had in my life. I felt the whole power of the Land singing in my blood: potent, alive, strong. I *was* Archers Beach, and my Word here was law.

"Release the virgins," I said. "Do it now."

The Enterprise hesitated. It… *growled*.

Oh, yeah?

"Are you," I asked, gently; there was no need, after all, to shout; "going to make me come down there?"

The growl… died. The kid from the Changing Land shouted and rushed forward, still holding onto the hands of the kids from Sempeki and Kashnerot. Behind them came the other three.

I swung back from the doorway, they jumped up the stairs, and I waved them on. "Go! Outside! Annora!"

But Annora was already moving, sweeping them ahead of her, out of the Enterprise, into the dawnlight.

Me, I stood there a second longer, listening to the Enterprise brood.

"I'll come back," I said. "When I do, we'll talk about your role in the Age of Science."

The Enterprise... whimpered.

"It'll be fun," I told it, and turned on my heel and went away.

ANNORA WAS STANDING beneath the big tree at the edge of the Enterprise's dooryard, surrounded by the Midnight Vestals. Artie stood a little apart, hands twisting together.

"Kate." He started forward. I paused.

"How's the weather?" he asked me, jerking his head toward the Enterprise.

"Subdued. I'll be back to do some work. In the meantime, maybe you'd better clean up."

He grimaced.

"Some of that stuff was actual antiques," he said, half-accusing.

"So now the stuff that's left is worth more," I said, and moved on.

The Land showed me Artie standing behind me, indecisive for a moment. Then he squared his shoulders and walked into the Enterprise, closing the door behind him.

Annora had pulled her hood over her face. Right. It was dawn. Time for her to go.

Just one more thing, though.

"The Vestals of Midnight hold the Queen of Daknowyth's honor?" I said.

She bowed. "For thirteen years, they do. At the end of their service, they are returned to their native Lands, provided with all and every comfort."

I turned to look at the kids; met the eyes of the Changing Land girl.

"You good with this?" I asked her.

"I'm good," she answered. And, like she felt maybe that was a little brief, added, "We'll have tutors. Three meals a day. Better'n what I got now. An' nobody'll touch us, on account we belong to the Queen."

"And by the time we are released to our own lives again," the boy from Cheobaug added, grimly, "no one will be *able* to touch us."

Kinless, Annora had said.

I nodded.

"Come see me," I said to them all. "When your service is done."

"I'll do that, ma'am," said the girl from the Changing Land; the others murmuring their promises behind her.

The child from Sempeki stepped forward, bowing and offering the flower crown.

I bent my head gravely, and felt it settled gently on my hair.

The child stepped back, and I raised my head to look at the six of them, shining sweet and pure in the growing light.

"I regret that you were ever in danger on my Land," I said, which was nothing more than the plain truth. "And I salute your valor and your loyalty to each other."

I stepped back, and glanced at Annora.

"There's no Gate here, anymore."

"That is of no concern," she said calmly, "we ride upon the back of the winds."

Unexpectedly, she bowed, much lower than she needed to.

"The Queen will be told of your service to Daknowyth, Kate Archer. You have also my thanks. Use my name as your own."

"Thank you," I said, with no intention of *ever* invoking *that* debt.

"Yes," she said, and opened her arms.

"To me," she said, and the kids moved in close, taking shelter in the expanding shadow of her cloak, until…

I stood alone in the dawn-light, the power of the Land singing in my blood.

Paradisiacal Protocols
Gordon Linzner

INGRID WANG FOLDED her arms and scowled. Despite the tropical heat, the head of Wang International wore her usual navy blue business suit. It helped her think.

Beneath thick cloud cover, gray Caribbean waters churned sluggishly. The gloomy atmosphere perfectly matched her mood here, on the shore of St. Thomas. If you could call where she stood a shoreline. These days, one could barely find a foot of sand at high tide in this area. Decades ago, it had been one of the most beautiful beaches on the island.

Wang turned to her sole companion, her assistant Lin Hamamura. It was too early in the day for anyone else to be out.

"This is insane," she muttered.

Hamamura adjusted the shoulder strap of his briefcase as he riffled through the files therein. "So you have observed. Many times." His apparel was far more casual: sandals, khaki shorts, and a loose-fitting shirt illustrated with palm trees.

"I know, Lin. I'm obsessing. How can I not? Look where we are. This is the last half of the 21st century. The people of St. Thomas and their sister islands continue to suffer from decreasing resources and ever more frequent and violent storms. The natural environment is in chaos. Their capital city, Charlotte Amalie, is this close to being permanently flooded." Wang held her right thumb and forefinger a centimeter apart, then closed them with a snap. "It's hard to believe this island belongs to one of the most powerful countries in the world."

"A country that was one of the most powerful," Hamamura qualified. "They threw that all away over the past quarter century."

Her smile mixed fondness with frustration. "I spoke hyperbolically, Lin."

Her assistant smiled back. "Of course, Ms. Wang. Although many of their citizens still think their country among the greatest, despite contradictory evidence. I was merely keeping the record straight."

"As is your job." Her tone grew more business-like. "Summarize what progress has been made on our negotiations."

Hamamura pulled a folder from the briefcase. He was fully aware of its contents, of course, but the act gave him something to do with his hands. "As we anticipated, the United States refuses to outright sell any of its territories, despite the increasing weakness of their economy."

"Or because of it. But they remain open to a long-term rental deal, similar to the British handling of the Three Territories of Hong Kong last century?"

"They are willing, though still somewhat leery after the Thorpasphere fiasco. Fifteen years is still fairly recent."

Wang snorted. "Alucard Thorpe didn't have a fraction of our company's resources. Or any more sense than his father. He overreached by trying to obtain dominion over every single island in the Caribbean. Of course he would end up declaring bankruptcy within a year."

"It was obvious to everyone but him," Hamamura agreed.

"Yes. Well. I believe… no, I know that over the next few decades, Wang International can turn these islands around. Certainly by century's end. Improving the lives of the inhabitants, restoring their industries, we will not only foster good will, but eventually make a profit as well."

After a silent moment, Wang added, "Enough reflection, Lin. You helped reinforce my determination. Let us return to our rooms."

Hamamura nodded agreement. "I can have the preliminary paperwork for St. Thomas drawn up by this afternoon."

The woman paused, taking in the salt breeze. "Include St. Croix and St. John. We can get a better deal as a package. The interdependency will work in everyone's favor."

"Indeed," Lin replied, making mental notes. "By noon tomorrow, I will have completed your application to re-lease the Virgins—"

"Not all of them," Wang corrected. "Just the U.S. Virgin Islands. We can investigate the British ones at a later date."

"Of course. One recalcitrant government at a time."

"It would be nice to have at least some of my reclamation projects underway before the next Carnival."

"I have no doubt we can do so, Ms. Wang."

She paused to look across the Caribbean Sea one more time. The sun was just starting to break through dispersing clouds.

"It's good to be rich," she observed, "but so much better to use that wealth for good."

Brass Tacks
Cecilia Tan

WHEN I TOOK the job as department secretary, I knew I'd be dealing with things like requisition forms. I knew that whiny students (and professors) would come with the territory. It hadn't occurred to me that my previous work as a stage manager and costume designer would come in handy.

Or that I'd end up a *de facto* STD counselor.

But when yours is the campus department that runs sex magic rituals, it all comes with the territory.

A half-dozen virgins were milling around in the hallway outside my office, waiting for someone to tell them what to do, and I was still trying to finish hemming the sleeves on the white robes they were supposed to wear. Gerald, his long black hair partly caught in his glasses, was looking over my shoulder, as if he could make the machine stitch faster with the power of his mind.

If only magic worked that way.

"You know, there's no proof that the color of the robe makes any difference at all," I said with a huff. I (probably) wouldn't be so cheeky to the other faculty, but Gerald and I go way back. In our undergrad days, I'd even dabbled in some rituals with him, before I figured out that the only reason I was taking those Esoteric Arts classes was because I was attracted to him, not the subject. There's nothing worse than getting graded on a crush.

"Tom, please. I just want every detail to be absolutely perfect." His accent and manner of speaking were sort-of British—by way of Hong Kong. It was one of the things I found sexy when we were eighteen. Now it just annoyed me that it took him twice as long to say anything. His fingertips alighted nervously on my shoulder, and then flitted off again. "I know there are plenty of black ones in the department inventory, but... the re-calibration of the Axiometer is a massive responsibility, you know? The administration entrusting me with it is a huge honor."

A huge pain in the ass, you mean. I didn't say anything aloud, of course. Just gritted my teeth and pulled the sleeve free of the presser foot.

"And you said you would help," he added, just a touch of desperation in his voice.

That was all it took to turn my annoyance to sympathy. He really was in a rough spot, trying hard to impress the higher-ups. If he didn't make tenure this year... best not to think about that. There were not a lot of other career options for academic sex magicians. Universities who offered Esoterics as a discipline were few in number, and it wasn't something that crossed over into mundane job hunting. I, at least, could always work for a non-magical university if things didn't work out at Veritas.

"Almost done. But next time just put a sign on the bulletin board asking for a grad student to help, all right? Or at the theater department. Just say it's for a show." I handed him the last robe.

"I shall! Next time, I promise. I absolutely shall." He snatched up the other finished robes on my desk, hugging the entire bundle in his arms. "Tom, you're a life saver!" He leaned over and startled me with a quick kiss on the cheek before he rushed out the door. "Come along, virgins! Follow me to the changing room, please."

The troop of them headed downstairs, and I sat there for a long moment with the faintly damp spot on my cheek cooling in the air.

I was sure he didn't mean anything by it. The faculty in Esoterics were notoriously handsy-seeming compared to the norm. That happens when you have to shed your inhibitions around sex in order to perform your spells properly. I knew not to take it seriously.

And yet it had stunned me for a second. I laughed at myself. For a moment, I was transported back to being that flustered undergrad whose stomach had plummeted every time my crush had walked into a room. How amusing to know I was not 100% jaded.

Merely 99%.

Now I had to hurry to put the "Closed for Ritual" sign on the door to the downstairs chamber. It wouldn't do to have some clueless freshman stumble down there in the middle of the action. I grabbed the tape dispenser and hurried out the door.

TWO HOURS LATER, I was working on the department expense report—entering the cost for two bolts of white satin among other things—when I realized none of the ritual participants had come back upstairs. The dinner bell at Scipionis House rang, and my Pavlovian stomach growled.

If I really wanted, I could lock up the building and leave. Gerald and the junior faculty doing the ritual with him could let themselves and the virgins out when they were done. But I decided to see how things were going for myself.

The ritual chamber under the building was the size of a large auditorium, two or three stories deep. The observation deck was built just below the vaulted ceiling. I let myself in with my master key, and looked down on the proceedings.

The cavern was circular, and at its center sat a giant stone dais. At the center of that stood Gerald, raising an athame—or maybe it was a phurbu? —over his head, his hair plastered to his neck with sweat. In his black robe, he looked like something from a death metal video, except for the tired and frustrated expression on his face. The white-robed, blindfolded virgins were seated cross-legged on the stone at regular intervals around him, and the junior faculty helping out stood at the edges. They looked equally sweaty, but mostly bored.

"Any sign?" called Maryelizabeth Singh from directly behind him. She was adjunct in both astronomy and astrology, and I knew she was just moonlighting in Esoteric Arts as a favor to Gerald.

"Nothing yet." Gerald lowered the ritual blade, looking at the Axiometer at his feet. From my distance, I could barely see the brass instrument, but with the acoustics of the rounded space, I could hear his sigh perfectly well. "I am starting to suspect that this is not going to happen."

Jim Buford, another adjunct who specialized in ecstatic states, stepped forward. "We're only a few minutes from sundown. Should we try it again after nightfall?"

"There should be zero interaction between the Heliosphere and the Axiometer," Maryelizabeth said, "which measures purely localized, personalized phenomena. Besides, I'm leading a study session up at the telescope tonight, so I need to jet."

Jim was undeterred. "Day/night effects are observed in every cultural magical system we know of! I'm just pointing out that it's a really common thing for some magic to work better at night."

Maryelizabeth folded her arms. "And I'm pointing out that I'm an expert on which things do and which things don't. You are aware that is one of the main pillars of astronomological study?"

Gerald put an end to the argument by ending the ritual. "Enough. Release the virgins. I'll email with suggested dates for another go."

Maryelizabeth sidled close to him. "You know who's great with picking auspicious dates for rituals?"

"Astronomologers, I know. I'll email you first, I promise." Gerald twisted his hair into a ponytail, and bent to unblindfold the nearest virgin.

I headed back upstairs to see if I had any free Ben & Jerry's coupons in my desk to give to the virgins. I had gotten the idea from the cognitive science department, where they often gave them to test subjects in lieu of payment.

I doled the coupons out without making a single joke about Cherry Garcia. Soon enough, the students were all gone, and Maryelizabeth had run off to the observatory. But I lingered, perhaps thinking I might catch Gerald on his way out.

Or not. He came up the stairs from the chamber with Jim. As they came into my office to leave their robes in the laundry hamper, Jim was saying to him, "Hey, what do you think about grabbing a bite to eat?"

"Oh, sure." Gerald looked exhausted and highly distracted. "What did you have in mind?"

"There's a new cocktail lounge in Harvard Square," Jim said, circling around him. "Candlelit velvet vibe with small plates to share. What do you say?"

Gerald was clearly still totally spaced out with ritual energy. Even a failed ritual takes a lot out of you. "Oh, um, sure. To share? How about it, Tom? Want to come along?"

It was obvious to me that a "candlelit velvet vibe" was not conducive to a third wheel tagging along. Jim was glaring daggers (or was it athames?) at me. "No, no. I'm all set. You go on."

"All right." Gerald seemed to focus on me then. "Oh, and thank you again for all your help." He handed me the wooden box that held the Axiometer.

"For all the good it did," I said, taking it from him. My plan was to lock it away for safekeeping once they were gone.

But so much for plans. I ended up going back to working on the department reports, and decided to order dinner to my desk. Pizza or Chinese? I didn't need the dairy clogging up my sinuses, so I opted for Chinese. Just like mom used to make? Well, no, not remotely, but I felt oddly unsettled, and it was still comfort food. I set the box that contained the Axiometer aside, and turned my attention to my computer.

One container of fried rice and two spreadsheets later, I realized the wooden box was vibrating.

Hm.

I glared at it, wondering if there was a prankster in our midst. It was a pretty simple thing to, say, put a snake to sleep by refrigerating it for a while, put it in a box, and then have it wake up later when the practical joker was long gone. The box had a simple metal latch. I picked up the chopsticks I'd been eating dinner with, and carefully flipped the latch with one while holding the lid down with the other.

Then I flipped the lid open, brandishing the sticks one in each hand like some kind of miniature weapons.

No snake. But the Axiometer was whirring. The contraption had a series of concentric brass rings around a central core, with a small gem at the very center. One of the brass rings—not the outermost one, which was fixed in place, but the next one in—was spinning. It definitely should not have been. Gerald must not have properly grounded himself after the ritual, and was still attached to it. If I remembered rightly, that ring represented the attraction between two poles, and the motion was the result of the sexual energy flowing between them.

I tried not to think about what that might mean regarding what he and Jim might be doing. There wasn't anything I could do to stop it, so I just latched the case shut and put it into the safe.

I SLEPT BADLY that night. A fan or air conditioner in the apartment above mine had been making a constant humming sound all night long, and it kept waking me up. I arrived at the office with a migraine threatening. Gerald, on the other hand, seemed disgustingly chipper. Morning class sessions had just started when he slipped into my office, all smiles.

"Let me guess," I said. "You want some advice on retooling your failed ritual."

His face fell. "Tom, please, don't use the word *failed*. It's so… judgmental."

"Fine." The department folder with his ritual proposal was still at the top of my filing stack. I flipped it open and looked at the main diagram. "You sure they were all on the compass points?"

"Quite sure. And with that many virgins, there was plenty of unfulfilled potential fueling the spell. At least, if the Axiometer was any indicator."

"Isn't that what it's for?"

"Isn't that what what's for?"

"The Axiometer." Honestly. He was a brilliant Esotericist, and we supposedly spoke the same language… and yet. "Isn't it for indicating, um, those kinds of feelings?"

"Oh, yes, exactly. Its purpose is to ensure compatibility amongst people going into ritual spellwork together." He rounded his hands like he was holding an invisible grapefruit. "The three rings are for mind, body, and heart, and when all three reach the same wavelength, the central diamond glows. Raw attraction spins one, emotions the second, and thoughts the third. We got all three to spin at different times last night, but they never synched up and the gem never lit." He took the folder from me and riffled through his own instructions without really looking at them. He sighed. "If I change anything, this is going to have to go back through ethics review, isn't it?"

Which could take all semester. The review board was not always quick. "I'm afraid so. Let's be systematic, shall we?" I started tacking the pages of the proposal to the cork board on my wall. The compass point diagram, the participant roster, the equipment list. (Aha, so it *was* an athame, not a phurbu.)

"I never had a ritual go pear-shaped like that before." He stood beside me, and I was suddenly aware of how warm it was in my office. The heat had kicked in this week, and some of the rooms in the building were sweltering. "It's always just… worked."

"Okay, well, I'm no expert in the subject, obviously, but the devil is in the details, no?"

He pushed his hair back out of his face, only to have it flow right back where it had been, like a black satin curtain. "I suppose. I mean, the whole thing is—not to toot my own horn or anything like that—but the thing is a lot of the trappings are simply to put people in the proper frame of mind. 'In the mood,' as it were. So if everyone in the ritual is sufficiently, well, *into it,* it should work, even if the details aren't perfect."

"Into you, you mean." I stood back a step. "Stop trying to be modest. You're saying if everyone wants you, it should work."

"Well, yes." God help me, he actually blushed. Normally, it took a whole beer to get him that flushed, an unfortunate Asian trait that got us into trouble when we were underage more than once.

Thank goodness those days were in the ancient past. "Maybe you ought to try it without the blindfolds next time, then."

He blushed even harder. "Come on, Tom. I'm not that much to look at."

"You are the most gorgeous man to walk these halls and you know it, so stop pretending. If you wanted to *add* blindfolds, you'd have to go through ethics review, but taking them away should be no problem." I took a pencil, and crossed them off the equipment list. "Next. Do they have to be virgins?"

"No. The energy you get from them is purer, but anyone who is giving off, um, attractive energy, could work."

Well, then Jim should have provided plenty, I thought, but of course I didn't say. It wouldn't do for me to be quite so catty, even if it was almost Halloween. "Well, non-virgins are certainly easier to recruit. Did you need all eight? Wouldn't just four at the cardinal points be easier to manage? Or could you even do this calibration with just two people who were sufficiently... simpatico?"

He folded his arms, tucking his chin as he glared at the diagram. "I thought you said you're not an expert on this." He sounded annoyed with me.

So much for trying to help. "I'm just brainstorming. If you don't like my suggestions, ignore them." I unpinned the papers quickly and slid them back into the folder. "I'll book you for the main chamber next Friday." I put the folder back into my desk file drawer and shut it, perhaps a bit harder than necessary. "Good luck."

Gerald blinked, one part of his genius-level brain catching up with the rest, I guess. "Tom. I didn't mean to make you angry."

Tsk. It wasn't his fault I had a headache. And it wasn't exactly his fault, either, that he could get under my skin like that. "I'm not angry, Gerald. I'm just busy," I said, shooing him toward the door of my office. "Paperwork, you know."

"Okay. If you're sure. I mean, I truly am sorry if I cheesed you off. I'm not good with picking up social cues."

A sex magician who couldn't read social cues. Circe save me. "Gerald, it's *fine*. Now go on. Get."

He left, and I sat behind my desk, wondering why my heart was skipping and my hands were sweating. Time to cut down on caffeine? With the chilly weather, I'd started picking up a double-shot macchiato on the way to the office. Maybe I wasn't used to it.

A grinding sound attracted my attention, and it wasn't my teeth. Something in the safe behind the bookcase. I locked my office door and unlocked the safe, only to find the Axiometer had popped out of its box and was trying to drill its way through the wall. I suppose this was why the thing needed recalibration.

It took some wrestling to get it back into the box. Like a gyroscope, it seemed to have its own gravity pulling me this way and that. Two of the rings were spinning now. I latched the box and then tied a couple of the blindfolds around it. That would hopefully keep the lid on it.

I WAS GETTING ready to leave that evening when the phone on my desk rang. "Thomas Chen, may I help you?"

"Tom, it's Gerald. I, um, need to ask you a favor."

"That might depend on what the favor is, but you can always ask." I rubbed my eyebrows. The headache was back.

"Any chance I could borrow the Axiometer overnight tonight?"

"Hot date with Jim?" Oh, Circe, did I say that out loud?

"Excuse me?"

"I said, 'going out on a limb?'"

"I promise I'll have it back first thing in the morning. I have a theory I want to test."

"Ritual equipment is really not supposed to leave Sassamon Hall," I said, but I was just giving him a hard time. The Axiometer had sat on Professor Hilliman's dining room table all summer. "But I suppose I could make an exception for you."

"You're a dream, Tom. Okay, second favor. Could I ask you to bring it by my house?"

"You really want everything, don't you?"

"Please, Tom? Look, I know it's the dinner hour. How about I'll scare up some supper for both of us. To thank you. In thanks. You know. Because I truly to appreciate it."

He sounded worried I wasn't going to do it. Maybe I had been a little too harsh on him. "It's fine, Gerald. I'm about to leave here. Let me just swing by home to feed my cat, and then I'll be right over. If I make her wait too long, she'll pee on something."

"Oh, goodness. Wouldn't want that. Sure. Come on by as soon as you're done." He gave me the address of a house a few blocks from the campus, not far from my apartment.

I noted it in my cell phone, and went to unlock the safe while I still had him on the phone. Before I even got the combination done, though, I could hear the Axiometer rattling around. "I hope the thing works for you, though. It's been going nuts."

"Nuts? What do you mean?"

"It spun itself right out of the box earlier. It's like it's got a mind of its own." I opened the door. The box was in splinters, and the blindfolds had been shaken loose entirely. "I think you left it on when you were done with it the other night."

"Ah!" He sounded a bit happier about it than I expected. "Could be, could be. I think I can do something about that. Um, if you just bring it? If you can?"

"I can handle it. See you soon." I wrestled it into one of the tote bags left over from the Passion & Problem-Solving conference the department hosted last spring, tied the handles together for good measure, and headed out.

AS I MADE my way up the walk at the address he'd given me, I could see candlelight flickering through the bay window in his living room. Was the place set for a ritual or for a romantic dinner? Either one put a stutter in my breath. I slipped my shoes off in his mud room, where a note on the door said to let myself in.

I found myself in the dining room of a Victorian-era house. The table was set for two, with a red brocade table runner and white taper candles, a bottle of red wine breathing next to two long-stemmed glasses. The place settings had both chopsticks and forks. Romantic dinner for two, indeed.

Gerald came out of the kitchen wearing a chef's jacket and apron, carrying a bamboo steamer basket. "Please, sit!" he said with a wide smile.

I was frankly a bit bowled over by the entire scenario. "All this for me?"

"I never get to cook anymore," he said. Then he paled and almost dropped the basket. "Wait, don't tell me you don't like Chinese food."

"No, I—"

"Oh, Circe. I just assumed! I'm so sorry—" He looked about ready to flee the scene.

"Gerald! It's *fine!*" My heart beat double-time. "I *love* Chinese food. But, what is going on with you? With all this?"

He set the basket down on the table with a nervous laugh. "I have a confession to make. But, um. Maybe you should show me the Axiometer first."

I pulled the brass contraption from the bag. All the rings were whirring in perfect balance. I set it on the table, and it stood on end of its own accord.

The gem was glowing in time with my breath.

Gerald stepped close and swallowed. "Here's the confession. I think the ritual didn't work because I, well, I spent the whole time thinking about you."

I put my hand in his, and the glow brightened. "So it's your fault this thing has been spinning non-stop since the other night."

He shook his head. "No. Well, yes, but it's you, too, Tom. You and me." His blush was deepening again. "You said it yourself this morning: it only takes two. I kind of suspected you might be kind of interested, but you know, I'm bad at reading people."

Which is why a tool like the Axiometer exists in the first place, you beautiful genius-fool. "I have a confession to make, too." I had to take a breath to make sure my voice would come out steady. A secret held that long takes a while to pry free, but there it was: "I've had a crush on you for over ten years."

He looked gratifyingly surprised about that. "Why didn't you ever tell me?"

"Because everyone in the world has a crush on you, and I figured another Asian guy would be the last thing you wanted."

The surprised look grew. "Is that some kind of... of... American attitude?"

"Well, now that I say it out loud, it's obviously kind of ridiculous," I admitted. "Maybe it was just my excuse for never telling you. Or maybe I just need a little help to get over my hangups."

"You know who's good at getting past hangups? Esotericists," he said seriously as he leaned close.

I could feel the heat of him on my cheek, our faces were so close. "Good thing I know one of those. Does this mean the Axiometer's working?"

"Yes. You made me realize I was complicating things far too much. And, you know, courting, a romantic dinner… there's a ritualized aspect to i—"

I decided I better not let him slip into lecture mode. The gem was blindingly bright right through my closed eyes as our lips met, or maybe that was just how intense the kiss was. Yes, that's it, a kiss so searingly perfect it was like lightning, like fireworks.

Old Spirits
Brian Trent

THE BROWNS WERE tired of explaining it by now, and the exhaustion showed in their weary expressions and slouched postures. It was past 8 P.M., and the grocery store was closed, the register lines deserted, the warren of aisles gloomy and dark. Beyond the windows, the predicted snow had begun to fall with the same languid, dream-like speed of a flipped snowglobe.

"The disturbance started with the eggs in Aisle 14," explained Edith Brown, co-founder of Brown's Family Grocer. "The stock boys kept discovering crates of smashed, raw eggs on the racks. As if someone with a particularly rotund pair of buttocks just plopped down on them."

Their lanky guest pulled thoughtfully on the ends of his beard. "Did you ever catch any, um, portly hind-quartered people squatting in Aisle 14?"

Edith adjusted her glasses and regarded him. "You just got into town, right? So you don't realize that everyone around here looks like they walked out of a Far Side cartoon. But no, residents of Goshen Falls are not in the habit of sitting down on our eggs."

Her husband, Gil Brown, anxiously cracked his knuckles and added, "Besides, we checked the security cameras, and never caught anyone doing that."

"What *did* the security footage show, Mr. Brown?"

"The eggs just… just… implode! Collapsing under an invisible weight. And that's when we realized…" He looked to his wife.

Edith sighed. "That's when we just had to admit that our store has a ghost. A vandalizing ghost who apparently *hates* eggs, and who has now expanded its reign of terror to Aisle 2."

The bearded visitor scribbled in his notebook. "What's in Aisle 2, Mrs. Brown?"

"That's where we keep the liquor."

"Was someone sitting on the liquor bottles, too?"

Gil said, "Not exactly. In Aisle 2, the invisible presence was levitating liquor bottles off their shelves, and hurling them at the cold storage door. Crates of beer, boxes of wine, magically hopping off the shelves and smashing into the steel door. Even the shelving would be torn from their moorings and thrown into the door." He pointed to the unlit back of the store.

"Go on."

Edith folded her arms across her chest and said, "There's not much more to say. Goshen Falls is a peaceful town, and we don't ordinarily have a poltergeist problem. So once Gil and I realized what we were up against, we saw no recourse but to reach out to psychics, and then to parapsychologists. Of which you are the latest, Doctor...?"

The man flashed a huge grin. "Call me Harold."

Gil Brown's exasperated face fell an inch lower. "The psychics didn't last long. Each one of them ran out of here screaming. It was annoying."

"*Very* annoying," Edith agreed. "The parapsychologists fared better, but ultimately proved just as unhelpful. Except for that scientist from Yale. He concluded that we were dealing with a disturbed haunt who apparently had a bad experience with eggs and beer in life and—"

"He's insane!" Harold roared. "Bad experience with eggs and beer? Madness! Total and unvarnished insanity!"

Edith narrowed her eyes skeptically. "Can we see your credentials again?"

Harold handed over a laminated badge and, as she squinted to read it, he turned to Gil and asked, "Will you show me the security footage, please?"

Gil led the way to the management office, where a viewing station showcased a grid of digital CCT displays—fifteen screens to encompass all the aisles, and an additional screen for the deli section in the back. He began flicking through a menu of dated recordings.

"I don't think I can pronounce this word," Edith said, coming up behind them with the visitor's credentials in hand. "I mean, I must be reading it wrong. It says you're a... um..."

"Paleoparapsychologist," the paleoparapsychologist said. "But really, call me Harold."

"Harold," she repeated uncertainly. "The paleo..."

"Paleoparapsychologist."

"Here we are," Gil said, hitting PLAY on the remote. One of the screens displayed Aisle 14. Eggs, milk, creamers, and various cheeses, all sitting innocently in their refrigerated cabinets and racks. The minutes ticked away in large, white numbers.

At the 19:21:26 mark, several egg crates abruptly collapsed, shooting thick gouts of yolk onto the aisle floor. Seconds later, another crate of eggs followed the same fate. Then another. The glass cabinets trembled from the assault.

"That's Act One of our tragedy," Gil muttered, punching up the feed for Aisle 2. "Now watch this."

Aisle 2 materialized, with its cases of beer, bottles of liquor, swan-necked ice wines, assorted brandies, cognacs, and vodkas. A fluorescent light flickered and stabilized.

At the 19:24:40 mark, an entire case of beer began to shake. It hopped off the shelf, floating in the air as if beset by an unseen Jedi, then hurled itself against the freezer closet. The impact caused the beer cans to erupt, fizzing and spilling messily on the floor. Another case of beer followed. And another. The floor was soon a sudsy lake of liquid and pulverized cans.

Gil gave a despondent sigh.

"This ghost is a vandal!" Gil said decisively. "Must have been a vandal in life!"

Harold shook his head. "No, I think this ghost is quite a bit older than the Vandals."

Edith handed the credentials back to her guest. "Doctor…"

"Harold."

"What exactly does a paleoparapsychologist do?"

"We investigate ghosts, of course."

"But the paleo part?"

Harold smiled. "Old ghosts."

"Older than the Vandals," Gil muttered, sifting his memory for old historical facts, and remembering only that he had failed History because of his enduring and distracting crush on his fourth grade teacher, Miss Maloney.

"*Much* older than the Vandals," Harold agreed.

Edith felt a stirring of doubt. "We had this parapsychologist from Wisconsin who said our ghost is a female, and hails from the Prohibition era, and that's why she's attacking our alcohol. What do you think?"

"I think she's *crazy!*" Harold screamed. "A certifiable loon for even *thinking* of something like that! How does that explain the eggs, eh? *It doesn't!* Madness, I say!" He fled the office and marched to the register lines, the desolate grocery store reverberating with the echo of his voice. "I think she got one thing right, though. This ghost is obviously a female!"

The Browns followed him warily. "Really?" Gil asked. "How can you—"

"But from the Prohibition era? Please! Stark insanity!"

Edith's scowl turned ten degrees sharper. "Why don't you tell us what you think then, Doctor."

"Harold." He lowered his notebook and took a breath. "Okay, I will. You are dealing with a horny female ghost suffering with extreme sexual frustration."

The Browns regarded each other.

"I think you should leave," Edith said.

"I wasn't done," Harold said.

"I think *we're* done."

"Oh, you will be if this situation remains unaddressed. Things are only going to get worse. A lot worse."

She hesitated. "Why?"

"Because your haunting isn't just *any* horny female ghost suffering with extreme sexual frustration."

"What else is it?"

"A dinosaur," he said firmly, nodding his head. "Your grocery store is haunted by the ghost of a dinosaur, and she's *very* troubled."

THE CALL TO the police was rather more adversarial than Edith Brown had expected it to go.

"We have a crazy person here!" she yelled into the office phone. "Please send an officer to remove him from the premises!"

The dispatcher on the other end of the line sighed audibly. "Mrs. Brown, has he threatened you?"

"Well, no… but he obviously belongs on the funny farm—"

"Calling it a funny farm is extremely insensitive nowadays. Both to people who actually work on farms, and to mental health specialists."

"But—"

"Ma'am, in case you haven't been reading the town paper with all of your... um... egg hauntings, we have real work to do. The eighth burglary in as many days has just been reported—this time an actual bank heist— and we're no closer to catching the mysterious bastard responsible. So with all due respect, if your visitor isn't threatening you—"

"He's trespassing!"

"You told me you invited him there."

"We needed help!"

"Yes, well, *I* needed to bake my son's birthday cake on Monday, and didn't much appreciate you telling me that I had to go to Watertown because a ghost smashed all the eggs in the place."

Edith snarled. "Carol—you can forget about your son's Christmas cake this year!"

"Guess I'll have to go to Watertown then—"

She slammed the phone down, and spun angrily around to their visitor.

Harold the paleoparapsychologist stood on the edge of the bread aisle, a most peculiar object in his hand. It looked, for all the world, like a large, glowing ostrich egg, obviously plastic and battery-powered. Harold flashed his unsettling grin, his glasses reflecting the red light like scarlet coins. "Nice, huh? I manufacture these little beauties myself!"

Edith marched straight over to him, puffing herself up to chase him from the premises...

...when to her utter shock, he suddenly flew backward as if struck head-on by an invisible car. His body smashed into a rack of pastries, raining down devil dogs, angel food cake, and various other theologically and non-theologically labeled snack foods. The weird glowing sphere he'd been holding tumbled from his grasp, bounced twice on the linoleum floor, and went skittering along to finally stop at a free-standing rack of corn chips. Then, without much fuss, the egg collapsed into a thin pancake of plastic, the glass light inside popping like the flash bulbs on ancient cameras.

Harold staggered to his feet, cradling his stomach. "Ow."

Gil Brown helped him stand. "Are you okay?"

"Oh sure. I do six thousand abdominal crunches a day, you know. Got rock-hard abs, *specifically* to protect against this threat."

"You do sit-ups to safeguard against dinosaur attacks?"

"*Ghostly* dinosaur attacks, Mr. Brown. They have a habit of hitting you square in the midsection when they get upset."

The old man blinked his bewilderment. "Still… six *thousand?* Isn't that kind of—"

Edith interrupted. "How can you expect us to believe that our problems owe to a ghostly dinosaur?"

Harold raised an eyebrow. "Did you think that only humans turn into ghosts? Kind of bigoted and anthropocentric, don't you think, Mrs. Brown?"

"*Every other* parapsychologist we spoke to said—"

"Every other parapsychologist is a lunatic! Do you *still* not see what's going on here?"

She began to snarl a reply when her cell phone rang, and she snatched it up, fuming now. "Brown's Family Grocer! Store hours are nine to eight, so please call back when…" she trailed off, phone to her ear, and her demeanor rapidly changed. "Oh, hi, Ranger Santiago. Yes, um, sorry about that. A rack of pastries got knocked over. Yes, I know it was very loud. We'll be sure to keep the noise down. Okay, goodnight." She ended the call, and buried the phone in her pocket, looking ashamed. "Gil, that was our friendly neighborhood park ranger. He said we're disturbing the birds of the sanctuary with all this ruckus." And she glowered at Harold.

Harold shrugged. "Dinosaur attacks are loud."

"We don't believe in saurian spirits!"

"Irrelevant. You've got yourselves a saurian spirit who, if my calculations are correct, is about to head straight to the spirit aisle. Like, right now."

By the time they arrived at the end of Aisle 2, it wasn't just cases of beer that had been smashed, but the entire shelving, too; the ghost had uprooted the gondola shelves from their peg hooks and thrown them against the freezer door with enough force to gouge the metal. A few five-gallon water jugs had also been hammered into the barrier until they burst.

Edith's shoulders sagged under the weight of knowledge that insurance companies don't cover vandalism by a reptilian ghost.

Gil stroked her hand soothingly. "It could be considered an Act of God," he suggested. After forty years of marriage, they could read each other's expressions as if pages of text were encoded in the creases of their foreheads and the wrinkles around their worried eyes.

Harold folded his arms, surveying the destruction. "No, an Act of God is what happened to the poor creature troubling your store. That asteroid! Think about it: one day, you're hunting about the Cretaceous grasslands, the sun on your scales, the warm breeze carrying with it the scent of new flowers... flowers date back that far, you know. And then *bang*! An asteroid slams into your planet like a cue ball striking a rack."

"Maybe she wants to get into the freezer?" Gil suggested. "There's plenty of frozen meats in there." He stepped through the puddles of spilled beer, avoiding the shattered shelving, unlatched the freezer door, pulled the door wide, and stood back, waiting.

Nothing happened. Packages of frozen meats were visible inside the freezer. Wintry vapors escaped into the warmer air of the store.

"She's not hungry for meat," Harold laughed. "I mean... not for frozen pork and rack of lamb, anyway, *am I right?*"

"Our ghostly dinosaur wants to get laid, is that what you said?" Edith sneered.

"Sixty-five million years of celibacy can make *anyone* frustrated. This dino-ghost is a virgin... was probably just going into heat when that asteroid dashed all her mating options to smithereens."

"But what does that have to do with our freezer? And the eggs?"

"Do you two have any children?"

"We have three children," Gil said. "Grown up and moved away."

"Then surely you both understand what's going on here! Watch." He reached into his briefcase and took out another plastic egg, flicking its light on with his fingernail. "Notice the shape? You see, your haunting began with eggs being wrecked. And then—"

Something invisible struck him head-on, pitching him like a rag doll across the store and straight into the candy display. As various Skittles and M&Ms scattered and rolled, Harold's glowing plastic egg bounced around like a particularly outlandish sweet. It came to stop in the middle of the soup aisle...

...and then flattened.

A roar of anguish thundered the store, shaking the very walls. The Browns clutched each other in terror. Immense footsteps pounded the floor. A display of cakes was flung aside. An entire freestanding rack of cereal was knocked over to become wedged at a nearby register line.

"Wow," Harold managed, rising once more, clutching his stomach again. He lifted his shirt, showing a nasty red bruise. "Lucky we're not dealing with a triceratops, am I right? No, I'd say we've got ourselves a bipedal customer, probably from the raptor family." He prodded himself. "Still, great abs, huh?"

Edith looked thoughtful. "Are you saying that this dinosaur is desperate to lay her own eggs? That—" Her cell phone rang again. She glanced to the caller ID, pursed her lips, and sent the call to voicemail. "It's Ranger Santiago again... calling to bitch about all the racket. Really, Doctor Harold, if you know this ghost is going to attack you whenever you display an egg, perhaps—"

"It's not *attacking* me. Not intentionally, anyway. It just wants to have eggs... it's own eggs, to nurture and hatch! The instinct runs deep. And my artificial egg-decoy is particularly mesmerizing to it, because electricity has solid mass in the afterlife."

"But it's *ruining* our eggs," she moaned.

"It doesn't *mean* to ruin the eggs." Harold led them back to the egg aisle. "Listen to me, this ghost... let's call her Petronia. She died during the dinosaur era. It was probably a very fast, violent death. That's how ghosts form, you know. You know the expression: 'He got the stuffing knocked out of him.' Well, that's sort of correct. A really fast death just knocks the vapor right out of you."

"That we knew," Gil said. "Professor Pang from Peking explained that normal deaths release a spirit gently, but sudden violence and emotional deaths—"

"Professor Pang from Peking is insane, and he's no paleoparapsy-chologist! And he sure as hell doesn't have abs like me!" Harold approached the store's back window, lifting his shirt to admire his chiseled washboard stomach in the glassy reflection. "Check and mate!"

Edith said, "Let's say we buy what you're telling us. Why now? Petronia would have become a ghost a long time ago. My husband and I have been operating this store for decades, and never ran into this kind of trouble before."

Their visitor shrugged. "Who knows? I had a near-death experience once... did too many sit-ups. I found myself in the afterlife where, strangely enough, I was still doing sit-ups. Anyway, it's gray and fuzzy in there. Like wandering around in a fog. Maybe Petronia got lost in that fog. She's lonely. Wants a mate, a brood, some company. And now that she's back, she figures that she can hatch a new generation from your store's eggs… not realizing that these are hen eggs, and while there *is* a relation, they keep imploding under her weight. And that's making her upset…"

Gil nodded excitedly. "So she's throwing a tantrum!"

Harold grinned and turned from his reflection. "Exactly! So now you have a grieving poltergeist from prehistory messing up your store."

But Edith frowned. "Seems a little too neat. I mean, her tantrum is extremely specific, don't you think. Why Aisle 2? What's the deal with the steel door?"

"How do we get rid of this ghost?" Gil interrupted.

Harold blinked. "How would I know?"

The Browns gaped at him. "What?"

"Why would I have the faintest idea of how to get rid of your ghost?"

"*You're* the paleoparapsychologist!" Edith snapped.

"Sure, I'm great at *identifying* these kinds of spirits. But I've never gotten rid of them." An expression of astonishment filled his face. "Why… would I?"

Edith shouted, "Because… that *should* be a part of your job!"

Harold looked horrified. "Does a naturalist studying elephants get *rid* of elephants? Does an equestrian exterminate horses?"

"But you know how to manipulate them! That glowing egg—"

Their guest retrieved yet another plastic sphere from his briefcase and switched it on. His reflection in the back window mimed this, so that there seemed to be two glowing eggs at the rear of the store. "I see your point. Maybe… just maybe… I could use these artificial eggs to lure your prehistoric poltergeist away from her preferred haunt and—"

Slam!

His body was knocked straight into the window, bursting through glass and into the snowy marshlands outside. This time it was obvious that the impact had been quite a few inches higher than Harold's magnificent abs. His body flopped and rolled in a useless, dead heap.

"*God he was annoying!*" Edith cried, opening the door to view the scene.

A supernatural cry of rage and frustration echoed throughout the store behind her, following by another round of useless, battering attacks against the freezer door.

* * *

THE BROWNS HUDDLED together outside, staring down at the dead paleoparapsychologist. The man's backpack had disgorged its contents onto the snow: his notebook, several dozen workout books, and the last of his plastic dinosaur eggs.

"Maybe we should just stop carrying eggs," Gil suggested.

Edith shook her head miserably. "And then what? We stop carrying liquor, too? There'd be a town-wide riot! No, honey, we have to deal with this problem." She squinted at the dead body on the ground. "And we'll have to call the police about *this*. Carol from dispatch is going to flip her lid. Who will believe this? I'm not sure *I* believe us!"

"Harold's theory *does* seem to fit the evidence."

"It does," she admitted grudgingly. "Kind of arrogant for us to assume that only humans become ghosts. Still… I feel like there's a piece to the puzzle that we've been missing."

Gil kissed her cheek and smiled. "Then let's figure it out."

"This ghostly dinosaur. I get why she's trying to sit on the eggs. She wants her own to hatch."

"Okay…"

"But why attack the freezer?"

"Maybe she wants to get inside?" Gil suggested, but then added with a frown, "Except you saw me open the door. I open that door regularly, so the delivery guys can bring in new meats. So if she wanted to get inside, why wouldn't she just… go inside then? And what's in the freezer anyway that has her so frustrated?"

Edith rubbed her chin. "Remember what Harold said about electricity? He said it has solid mass in the afterlife. Ghosts wouldn't have a problem walking through doors… unless…"

"The freezer is a labyrinth of electricity!" Gil cried. "All that wiring for the cooler units, compressors, breakers…"

"And Petronia can't cross those lines of electricity. To her, the electrical lines would be solid." Edith hesitated. "So maybe she wants something inside the freezer but can't get to it and…" She saw her husband's expression. "What?"

"I think I know what she wants," he said. "I'm sure of it, now. It all makes perfect sense now that—"

A flashlight snapped on, temporarily blinding them both.

"Let me guess," Edith sighed, shielding her eyes at the approach-ing dark silhouette holding the mag-light "Ranger Santiago, I presume?"

"You two goddam weirdos are being *really* noisy again," Ranger Santiago grunted, lowering the flashlight but not turning it off. His beam went from Edith to Gil, and then swept to the frozen ground to illuminate the last of Harold's plastic dinosaur eggs. "What the hell is that?"

"A plastic mockup of an egg designed by a late paleoparapsychologist in the hopes of attracting the ghost of a depressed and very horny dinosaur of the raptor family," Gil explained.

"Of course." Santiago moved the light another few inches, illuminating Harold's backpack and surplus of workout books; he hadn't noticed Harold's body yet, a few meters away in the darkness. "I don't care what weird shit the two of you are into. I *do* care that I've just caught you littering in a protected bird sanctuary! I care about that very much!"

Edith stiffened, realizing that another few inches and the flashlight would reveal Harold's corpse.

To her immense relief, the ranger thumbed off the beam. "And you realize," he growled, "that I've warned you three times today about noise, right? I have no choice now but to file a formal complaint with town hall, citing you for noise *and* littering!"

Gil's heart sank. "It wasn't our fault!"

"This here is a protected bird sanctuary, and the slightest disturbance can have devastating and potentially unpredictable consequences on our feathery neighbors. Do you want to stress the falcons out? Want a baby osprey to choke on that copy of..." He turned the flashlight on again, brightening one of the book covers. "*Superhero Abs in Just Six Thousand Crunches a Day?*"

He thumbed the light off again.

Unfortunately, without any warning, and in the worst case of bad timing imaginable, the moon peeked out from behind the clouds.

It was only for a moment, as if the lunar orb was jumping from one cloudy continent to another. The falling snow lit like dandelion fluff, the ground sparkled as if covered by diamonds, the grocery store glowed as if under an enchanted, silky sheen of magic gossamer...

...and Harold's dead body was revealed at their feet.

Yet there was something *else* that had materialized in the splash of moonlight. Several meters behind Ranger Santiago, the Browns spotted a freshly dug pit, a shovel, and several bulging sacks imprinted with the words FIRST BANK OF GOSHEN FALLS.

"You?" Gil cried. "You're the…"

The ranger glanced at the bags, then back at them with a crooked grin. "I'm the what?"

Edith quickly, desperately, said, "You're the nice ranger who totally *hasn't* been responsible for the series of robberies in Goshen Falls. Really, it's none of our business! Isn't that right, Gil?"

Ranger Santiago shook his head. He reached into his jacket and produced a silver pistol.

"Now wait," Gil began. "You don't need to do that!"

"You know, I had myself a nice little operation here. No one suspects a park ranger of robbery, and no one would *think* to look back here for the loot."

"We won't say anything!" the couple insisted in unison.

Santiago shoved the cold muzzle of the revolver against Gil's forehead. "Sorry, can't trust that. And even if I was the trusting type—which I'm not, not at all—I couldn't believe the word of two people who insist their grocery store is haunted." He cocked the pistol hammer. "Any last words, Mr. Brown?"

"If you fire that gun," Gil said, "you'll give the birds around here a heart attack!"

Ranger Santiago hesitated. He chewed his lower lip thoughtfully, glancing at the forested thicket of the bird sanctuary. "I wouldn't want that…"

Edith Brown saw her moment. With the man distracted, she dove for the snowy ground, like a child on a Slip 'N Slide, her arms coming around the unlit plastic egg. Santiago noticed the blur of movement and jerked the revolver, firing a single round. At such close range, the blast sounded like a cannon, and every bird in the sanctuary erupted in startled caws.

"Edie!" Gil screamed.

But the bullet had not hit Edith Brown.

Ranger Santiago stared at the body of Harold the paleoparapsychologist. "Who the hell is *that?*" He paused, jaw dropping. "Jesus, are those *real* abs? How could anyone… whoa!"

He broke off, as Edith tossed something strange and seemingly magical at him.

Ranger Santiago never did understand what the spherical, glowing object was that came sailing at him through the wintry air. Never understood that Edith's action had been one of the purest desperation, and his own reaction one of purest reflex: he caught the glowing egg as if in a slow-motion replay of a football pass.

Santiago had time to demand, "Okay, what is this thing, really? Why would—"

And then the ghostly dinosaur slammed into him from behind.

THE BROWNS STOOD before the freezer door, afraid to hope. Gil drew the latch and yanked the door open, spilling icy vapors into the store. He was aware of a presence behind him—an anxious, pacing, growling presence that made the hairs on his neck stand up.

"I still don't understand," Edith said.

Gil stepped into the freezer. "Honey, we don't have one ghostly dinosaur in our store. We have two of them."

"What?"

"You were so upset about the egg and liquor situation that I didn't tell you what I've been finding in the walk-in freezer. I figured you'd had all the bad news you could handle."

Edith watched him. "You've been finding vandalism in the freezer, too, haven't you?"

He nodded. "Something in here has been shredding our meats, clawing at the racks. I just assumed it was the same thing that was destroying the eggs and beer. But now it all makes perfect sense. Petronia has been trying to get into the freezer. A second dinosaur ghost has been trying to get out. But really, they both just..."

"...have been trying to get to each other!"

Gil placed his hand on the power switch in the freezer. "The poor things! Harold must have been right: these two virginal lizards had just managed to find each other when the asteroid hit. They got lost in all the chaos and fog and whatever else followed."

Edith said, "And we ended up accidentally trapping one of them inside our freezer's electrical grid. Yes, how perfectly obvious."

"Completely obvious." Gil agreed. "So there's really just one thing left to do, honey."

She took a deep breath and cried out, "Release the virgins!"

Gil snapped off the power, and scrambled out of the freezer.

For a moment, nothing happened. A moment after that, nothing continued to happen.

And then, Brown's Family Grocery shook with a bellowing duet of Cretaceous-era voices, the two ghosts colliding in a frenzy of passion that made both Edith and Gil blush.

"Let's give them their privacy," Gil muttered.

"Wouldn't mind a little privacy of our own," Edith purred, steering him toward the door. Just before stepping outside, though, she said, "I wonder if ghosts can procreate. I mean, wouldn't that be something, if Petronia lays ghost eggs, and they hatch into ghost babies, and then the entire town becomes filled with ghostly dinosaurs?"

They climbed into their car, driving off, laughing as they went.

A year later, the joke wasn't remotely funny.

The Running of the Drones
Patrick Thomas

USUALLY, WHEN SOMEONE wants to hire me, they come to my office to discuss the case, at least the parts they want me to know. Clients don't always tell the truth. More often than not, they lie about something, even if it's just one of omission. It goes to show you that even on an alien world like Liberty, most people aren't all that different than back on Earth.

Even with an elucidator implant, I had no idea what these three guys were trying to tell me, despite being able to make out their words.

And they were definitely guys. Sometimes with externals—that's what we call anyone not native to Liberty—guessing is a crap shoot. There are a lot more genders than just male and female, but these three fellows were most certainly male. It didn't take a detective to figure that out. They were walking around naked without any shame. To tell the truth, if I was as well-endowed as these guys, I might be more inclined to go around in the buff, too.

"Gone... Procreationless... Help!" said the one on my left. They were all roughly humanoid, with brown chitinous body plates with two antennae that made them look a little bit like an Earth beetle.

"Are you sure you guys want an investigator? It sounds like you might be looking for the Empirical House." A very special place that services certain needs for most races and genders. "Helping with procreation isn't one of my specialties." Well, that wasn't exactly true, but I tended to limit myself to female and humanoid, and these guys only qualified on one of those fronts.

The stubby one to my right spoke up. "Return must or forever unmated."

This wasn't helping. "Do you drones want me to find something for you?"

All three jumped up and down like they had won something, then the one in the middle took over the talking.

"Yes. Forgive my fellows. They have not had much contact with outsiders, so they have not learned to adopt their speech. I am Thur. You call us drones, so you know our race?"

I nodded. "Sure. There's probably not anyone in the free city of Tore who doesn't know about the Wornets." They were unusual externals. Each generation turns a building into a hive. Most were genderless, a lot like bees on Earth. Once a year, a new queen leaves the hive to go off and found a new one.

She tends to leave in a hurry, because right on her tail are dozens of drones doing their damnedest to reach her first and ensure the next generation is born. It's a huge pastime for the masses to watch as they race through the streets of Tore. The running of the drones is a city holiday and the biggest gambling event going. Think the Super Bowl, Indy 500, Kentucky Derby, and World Series rolled into one. Folks pick which drone they think is going to get to the new queen first to father the next generation. In fact, the consummation happens wherever in the city he catches up to her.

It draws a huge crowd.

"Isn't the running of the drones tomorrow?"

"Yes, but there is a problem. Our new queen, Vere, is missing."

"That's more than a problem. When and where was she last seen?"

"Last evening, when she went to slumber."

"There's one thing about the running of the drones I've never quite understood. What's to stop any of you from getting to her before the race? Say, in her slumber chambers?"

"I could say tradition, but it would not make it so. For one thing, the king drone from last cycle guards her."

"But he's a guy. What's to stop him from being the winner two years in a row, and beating you all to the punch?"

"But we would not strike a female with a closed fist. What manner of brutes do you think we are?"

The elucidator sometimes makes communication interesting by translating the meaning, but not the intent, of the words. "An expression that means you get there first."

Thur nodded, oddly in a circle going clockwise. "That is the other thing. Old king cannot mate with new queen."

"Why? Tradition?"

The one on my left laughed. I decided to call him Lefty. "Not... have... part."

"Left it behind when he won." Stubby seemed to be snickering.

I struggled not to cross my legs and wince.

"Leaving his dronehood behind in the queen ensures that his seed stays where it needs to be in order to fertilize hundreds of eggs. It is also why few would even try to approach the queen beforehand. Our life consists of two opposing desires: to keep our dronehood intact, and to mate. At the start of the race, the queen will release pheromones which will block out the logical part of our brains. The running will only fuel our desire, so that whoever gets to her first will not think before he mates. He will lose much when she clamps down to claim his dronehood at the end, but *only* he will experience the joy of procreation. But with no queen, none of us will win, and our hive will die out," Thur said.

"So, you want to hire me to find your queen before the race begins tomorrow morning?"

The three drones nodded, again in circles.

"We do," Thur said.

"You do understand how business works outside of the hive, right?" Not that I haven't done cases for free, but if I make a habit of it, my secretary tends to get on my case. It's not that Sylvia's worried about getting paid, it's that she's worried that she'll have to start supporting me again.

"Yes. Payment for services. However, we do not have any Tore francs." How the elucidator translates the local money.

I took a deep breath, trying to debate how I would handle this.

"What we do have is Wornet comb."

The drone reached in the sack he was carrying, and pulled out a piece of Wornet comb about the size of a football. I let out a long, slow whistle. People in Tore are not exactly charitable. The latest generation of Wornets aren't just given a building to set up a hive in because it's a nice thing to do and people like to watch them race. It's a business transaction.

A Wornet hive doesn't produce honey but they do make comb, which is why they are supported, sheltered, and likely taken advantage of. It's the Tore way.

Their comb is one of the most valued substances on the planet. And a unique one, at that. Comb can be eaten to improve health. I'm not talking a snake oil or New Age unprovable kind of thing. It will actually help heal damaged organs and close up wounds ridiculously fast. Often, there is no trace of being hurt in just days. Plus, comb has a natural analgesic to block pain, and grants a mild euphoria.

"Enough for retainer?" Stubby asked.

It's the most I'd ever been offered for a day's work. "Sure."

"We will give you an equal amount of comb once our Vere is found."

That was when the cynical side of my brain kicked in. No one was going to walk in my office and offer me the Hope diamond or the Maltese Falcon so easily. I had heard some things about the hive's living situation.

"Is this yours to give?"

"Wornets made it. We are forced by Baron Nezzel to turn over most of the comb to him. We save some for ourselves and for emergencies. And in my opinion, Nezzel is not entitled to what he takes. He has held the hives since slavery was legal, and indentured us since it was outlawed. We are all born into servitude with no chance at freedom. At least until now."

"What you mean?" Aristos didn't usually willingly let a moneymaker get away from them. "How would you do that?"

"We have a patron who is arranging for the next hive house to be ours, not Nezzel's."

"Our hive be born free," Stubby said, sticking out his chest.

"That certainly would provide motive for this Nezzel to take the queen and try to convince Vere to stay away from that house and go to one of his."

"Our… thoughts… also," Lefty said.

"In our own hive house, we won't have to remove the dead from the last hive," Thur said.

"Why would you have to do that?" I asked.

"Hives live ten seasons. Nezzel has eleven houses. We are told he makes the drones dispose of the dead Wornets," Thur said.

"Lovely."

"No… Is… horrible," Lefty said.

"That was sarcasm, when you say something and mean the opposite," I said.

"Seems foolish," Stubby said.

So was assuming someone was going to give you something for nothing. The drones seemed like nice guys, but naïve. "Are you sure your patron is giving you a good deal? You could be jumping from the frying pan into the fire."

Thur stared at me. "You're very strange, Samuel Troubell. Why would we want to be cooked and then leap into a blaze? We are not suicidal nor cannibal. But we can arrange for you to meet our patron."

"Seems as good a place as any to start."

THE PATRON WAS not at all what I expected. Typically, they're aristos with too much money who want to get more by taking advantage of others. Instead of heading to Innertown, we went to New Terra, the section of Tore where most humans live. We went into an office that was smaller and dingier than mine.

Even more surprising, the patron wasn't an aristo. He was human.

Despite the lack of status conveyed by his office, the man was impeccably dressed, with a perfect haircut. He stood as I walked in.

I extended my hand, and he shook it.

"Mr. Fortier, I'm Samuel Troubell."

"Yes, Thur told me they were going to try to engage your services. I've heard good things about you. And please, call me Q."

"I have to admit I haven't heard anything about you. Could you please explain to me what you're doing for the Wornets?"

"Certainly. For generations, as far back as they've been on this planet, the Wornets have been enslaved or indentured to the family of the current Baron Nezzel. In fact, his family bought the title with the money made off selling the comb from the hive. This is largely because, while they have a valuable product with their comb, they don't have any regular money. They work so hard at gathering what I would call nectar and making the comb that they have never acquired any traditional currency. My plan is to get a building for them to live and work in, and then teach them how to sell their comb and become self-sufficient."

"Where are you getting the money for this?" I asked.

"New Terra has a thriving entertainment industry which has broached over to the rest of the city. Nothing like the Warplex games, but money is made. I have several friends who are going to put up the loan with a reasonable interest rate. The term is ten years…" Not to sound cruel, but no one would make it any longer, since the Wornets die after a decade. "…but by my calculations, the Wornet will be able to pay if off in less than two. Then they'll be able to take the money they make thereafter to buy new buildings, to ensure that their future generations won't be enslaved."

"But even two years leaves one or two new generations vulnerable," I said.

"The loan is enough to cover the cost of three buildings. A little padding if my calculations are off."

"What do you get out of it? Are the people putting up the loan paying you, or are you taking a cut of the Wornets' comb?"

"I'm not making any money off the investors, nor off the Wornets. Although they have agreed to provide me with comb should I ever need it."

"So, you're doing this out of the goodness of your heart?"

Q grinned. "Why is that so hard to believe?"

"It's been my experience that when large amounts of money are involved, very few people are looking out for others when there's themselves to take care of."

"You're a private investigator. Check me out."

"I already did." Or rather, my secretary, Sylvia, checked the records. Unless he was hiding it under the floorboards, Q had barely enough money to pay his rent.

"What happens to this deal if Vere doesn't race?"

"We'd lose the loan. The investors have timed an announcement to coincide with the end of the race so they can get publicity out of it and promote their current shows. Of course, the running of the drones can happen another day, but it will lose the Mardi Gras atmosphere and the publicity. But what I'm really worried about is if the queen doesn't come back. Each generation only has offspring once. If Vere dies, in nine years there will be no more Wornets."

"That's about what I figured. So, if someone kidnapped her, just a delay of the race would be enough to tank the deal?"

Q nodded. "Unfortunately."

"Thank you for your time, Q. I think it's time I go see Baron Nezzel."

I SENT THE drones back to my office to stay with Sylvia. It didn't seem like the best idea to have them go with me to talk with Nezzel, and they'd be safe with Sylvia. Only a fool takes on a Calamari in close quarters. Too many fast-moving tentacles.

Nezzel was more what I expect in a patron. An opulent office in a mansion in Innertown, the wealthiest ring of the city. The aristo kept me waiting over an hour. When he did come in, Nezzel was dressed in garish but expensive robes. There was jewelry everywhere he could stick it without actually making a hole in his body. Nezzel was a G'morran—purple skinned, three-legged, but otherwise humanoid. These days, most of the G'morrans on Tore are part of a strict religious theocracy with, oddly enough, a human mobster at the top. I got the distinct impression that Nezzel had broken away from the theocracy, and worshipped no god but wealth.

The baron turned his nose up like I stank. "A Terran? You can tell Tony that I'm not about to increase my tithes. Good day."

"I don't work for Savage. I'm investigating here on another matter."

"You're a Guardsman?" The guard was Tore's version of a police force.

"Used to be. Private now."

"Then I really don't have to listen to you or answer any of your questions, now do I? Good day."

"Of course not. It's still a free city." Actually, it wasn't all that free, but that's what they called it. "Of course, then I'll have to call my friends on the newsfeeds to let them know that the new Wornet queen is missing, and tomorrow's running of the drones won't be happening. I'll make sure I drop your name as their patron, and the fact that you wouldn't help with the investigation. Good day, yourself."

I turned to walk out, but I didn't take three steps before the good baron spoke up.

"Wait, perhaps I was being too hasty. The new queen is missing, you say? This is the first I'm hearing of it."

"That's odd, because I have three separate sources that say you were contacted when it first happened, and you didn't seem overly concerned. Since your fortune is built on the sale of comb, I find that odd. If the running of the drones doesn't happen, in nine years you'll be out of business. Seems to me that that would be something that would concern you, Baron."

Nezzel laughed. "I doubt anything has happened to the new queen. She's probably nervous and has stage fright. It's happened before. The drones and the queen are all virgins. Tomorrow, she's going to have sex for the first and only time, in front of the whole city, and it will be carried live on the skyvid. Then she's going to give birth to hundreds of children. It's enough to make any woman nervous, especially a one-year-old."

I'd done my research. Wornets mature to adulthood in three months' time, and they have a collective consciousness which teaches them basic skills. By the time they hit a year, the queen and the drones are basically adults.

"When has it happened before?"

"Many times. Sometimes the new queens just need a bit of time by themselves to pull things together. I'm sure she will be back in plenty of time for the running of the drones. Her biological needs will see to that."

I was a fair judge of character. I didn't like the baron, but oddly enough, I didn't think he was lying.

"The drones are convinced she's been kidnapped. Until I learn otherwise, I'm working under the assumption that they're right. Assuming you had nothing to do with her disappearance, do you have any enemies who would want to see you ruined? Have you or the drones gotten any threats?"

"Everybody loves the drones and the hives. Me, on the other hand, I'm not so fortunate. The list of those who've gotten the worst in business dealings with me is too long to mention, but I would still have nine years of resources to tear down anyone who attacked me. It would be a losing proposition for them. However, I regularly get threats from the more extremely religious of my own people."

"Death threats?" I asked.

"On occasion. There may be many among my former people who would be very pleased to see me penniless. What none of them seem to realize is that I have been careful to diversify. I long ago realized that the next generation of the Wornets is never a given, so I have other businesses and investments. True, they're not as profitable, but I would be okay, although I might have to trim some of my expenses."

Either the baron was a good actor, or he really had no idea that the current generation of the Wornet were seeking a new patron and looking to become independent. It seemed in awfully bad taste to tell him if that was indeed the case.

"Have you gotten any threats recently? Or has anyone who has been sending you threats been more persistent than the others?"

"Why, yes. A young G'morran named Yaton has been quite descriptive regarding what he wants to do to me. He started out studying as a cleric, but the G'morra threw him out for being too extreme."

Considering that religion makes women subservient and anything resembling fun a sin, that's saying something.

"The holy council is against unsanctioned violence. Yaton apparently is not. He's attacked me on two different occasions."

"Why is he not in jail? Did you call the Guardsmen?" I figured I knew the answer, but wanted to see if I was right.

"My security team might've been overzealous in how they handled the troubled young man. I didn't see the need to involve the Guardsmen."

Translation: They beat the crap out of Yaton, and didn't want to risk getting charged as well.

"You have an address for this Yaton?"

"As a matter fact, I do."

THE ADDRESS WASN'T in the worst neighborhood, but it wasn't far off. Back in my Guardsman days, I would've never gone in without backup. Then again, wearing a Guardsman uniform was sometimes like having a target painted on your back.

The neighborhood was in one of the inner rings outside of Innertown. Tore was laid out in rings, with two main roads going north to south and east to west. The inner circle is all aristocratic and Muridae, with the tetrarch's palace at the center. The city grew outward around Innertown. The new buildings tended to be nicer, so people with some money moved into the outer rings. Those who couldn't afford to leave stayed in the inner ones. I always found it amusing how short a distance there was between the richest and the poorest. Here they call the middle-class outer ringers.

I debated about calling on Raza for backup, but when I saw where it was, decided against it. You don't bring in a flamethrower when a torch will do.

Weapons are contraband in the city, but that doesn't mean people don't have them. I caried a walking stick that houses a blaster and a blade. Plus, it could be used as a club.

Fortunately for me, I knew the gang that ran Bloomtown. Even better, I knew their leader. I'd done him a solid back when I was still a guard and he was a kid. Flower never forgot it when he grew up.

Yeah, I know Flower doesn't sound like a tough gang name, but he's a Tusko. Flower names are scary to them, because on their home world, the native flowers were deadly. It's the equivalent of being named Venom or Snakebite.

Even though Flower and the Dark Blossoms—yes, that's their gang name—liked me, I couldn't barge into their neighborhood uninvited without going through the protocol.

I walked slowly off the main road. By the time I was a block in, I'd picked up a tail. I walked calmly down the middle of the street until I got to what the Dark Blossoms used as a checkpoint for visitors.

"Hey Troubell, long time no see."

"Hi, Magnolia." The elucidator translates all their gang names as variations of flowers. Magnolia was a female with burnt orange skin who was bonded to Flower. It was a kind of a non-official marriage. She had two tusks protruding up from her lower jaw. They were longer, thinner, and pointier than the males had. "Yes, it has. I'm here to ask for passage."

"Did you bring tribute?"

I held up a heart-shaped box and shook it. "Of course."

"I'll take you to see Flower. Daisy, you take post," Magnolia said.

My tail stepped out of the shadows and nodded at me. I nodded back. Daisy was a guy.

Magnolia took me through the door of a shoddy looking building into an office which, while not as opulent, was every bit as nice as Nezzel's.

Flower had his scary face on, with both his tusks protruding from his lower jaw halfway up his tan face to his eyes. It didn't pay for a gang leader to not be intimidating. When he saw me, the scary face fell away, and was replaced with a smile.

Flower got up from behind his desk, and came out to give me a hug. "My friend Troubell. It's good to view you. How can we assist with your current case?"

I smiled as we sat down in chairs on either side of the desk.

"What makes you think I'm here on business, and not just visiting?"

"Bah." Flower rolled his eyes and moved his hand in front of his face in a downward motion. "When you come for a visit, the tribute you bring is beer. When you come on business, you bring chocolate, the best crop you Terrans brought with you."

He wasn't wrong. Flower held out his hand, and I gave him the heart-shaped box.

"The new Wornet queen is missing. The drones think she's been kidnapped."

"That mean there won't be any drone running tomorrow? Bad for business. We took lots of bets on race. Hate to give back. You have any inside information on which drone is the fastest, to help us with odds?"

"Nope. I've only met three, and I haven't seen them run. I'm following up a lead on a G'morran named Yaton, who lives in your neighborhood."

"You think the G'morran took the queen?"

"I'm looking into that possibility. Have you or the Dark Blossoms seen anything out of the ordinary?"

Flower looked to Magnolia.

"Yaton brought a trunk in yesterday, but we did not stop him. His tribute was paid up for the month. It's not good business to bother regulars who pay on time and in full," Magnolia said.

"This trunk big enough to put a Wornet queen in?"

Magnolia tilted her tusked head and shrugged. "Probably."

"I'm going to check this out. You good with that?

"Yaton is paid up, so no serious injury until you are sure he has the queen."

"I can work with that. Thanks."

"You want help with this, Troubell?" Flower said.

"I didn't bring that much tribute with me."

"Bah. For a non-Tusko, you are alright guy. And if the Wornet queen is in Bloomtown, it will bring unwanted attention from Guardsmen and the Tetrarch. Be worse than attention if queen is dead. Then Guardsmen be looking for a scape-grunt. Not all Guardsmen like you were. Be better for us if we help with rescue. Or recovering the body."

"Thanks, Flower. Let's go take care of business."

Flower snapped his fingers. The guard by the door stepped out. By the time we left the building, about twenty Tuskos filed in around us.

We followed Magnolia to a shoddy looking building. It was the type where folks rented a room and shared facilities.

"You two go to the roof. Magnolia with Troubell and me. The rest of you, surround building. No one in or out until I say so," Flower said.

Yaton had a room in the basement. Flower and Magnolia weren't exactly stealthy, but in their line of work, they didn't exactly need to be.

It wouldn't be that unusual to hear Dark Blossoms in the building. They did regular patrols to make sure nothing bad was going on, and that the people who paid them tribute were safe.

Magnolia pointed to a door on the end.

I smiled. "Should we knock?"

Flower and Magnolia chuckled.

"Bah." Flower kicked in the door on the first try. Tusko were a good ten inches shorter than humans. If an external is shorter than you, it's prudent to assume they come from a higher gravity world and are stronger than you. There are exceptions, but not many.

Yaton was sitting on the mostly bare floor over a pot that was burning incense. He had folded himself into some sort of bizarre yoga pose, with his three legs twisted around each other in a pattern that seemed impossible for him to have gotten into without dislocating something.

Yaton scowled. "I paid my tribute, and you are disturbing my prayers."

"This won't take but a minute. And if I'm mistaken, I'll have the door repaired," I said.

Flower again waved his hand and said, "Bah."

The room was nowhere near as nice as the Dark Blossoms' office was. What passed for paint and stucco was flaking off the walls and ceiling. The floor was the local equivalent of poured concrete. A small bed roll covered one corner. Yaton wore a gray robe, and had a spare on a wall peg. There was a pile of food on a table that didn't need to be refrigerated. The only other thing in the room was a large wheeled trunk with a padlock.

"Open it," I said.

"No. The object inside is of religious significance. It is not permitted for heathens to look upon it."

"It shall be opened. If you won't, we shall." Flower brought a canned ham-sized fist up over his head, and started to smash it down on the trunk.

"Wait!" I said. "If she's in there…" Yaton's eyes open wide, and Flower stopped. "…you might hurt her."

"Good point. Can you open it?"

I nodded, and put the bottom of my walking stick in the metal loop on the top of the lock. Then I leaned, hard. The padlock snapped. We found the unmoving Wornet queen in a fetal position inside.

"This is not covered by your tribute. Come near," Flower ordered. Yaton was already running toward the corner of the room, where he tossed aside the bed roll to reveal a grate, which he lifted up and then dove through the hole, twisting his limbs like a contortionist until he was gone. The opening was too narrow for me or the Tuskos to fit through.

Magnolia ran outside.

"Sorry that Yaton slipped our grip, Troubell. Magnolia will have Dark Blossoms check the sewage system, but I doubt we'll find the G'morran."

"He got away from all of us, Flower. There's enough blame to go around. Help me get Vere out and see if she's still alive."

Chitinous skin makes it difficult to find a pulse, and not everyone breathes out of the same orifices, or even uses them. Most sentients do have some sort of circulation system. I laid my ear on the drone queen's chest, and heard a faint thumping.

"She's alive."

I picked Vere up in my arms, bride style.

"What are you going to do with her?" Flower asked.

"I think it might be safest to keep her at my office until it's time to get her to the race tomorrow."

Flower nodded. "We'll give you an escort, just to make sure nothing happens."

"Appreciated."

We went outside to find Magnolia and some of the other Dark Blossoms waiting. The rest I assumed were searching for Yaton.

The queen shifted in my arms, waking up.

"It's all right, Vere. You're safe."

"That's good," she said rather dreamily, as if she'd been drugged. She wrapped her arms around my neck and laid her head on my shoulder. "Anyone ever tell you you're cute for someone who is not a Wornet?"

"Thanks."

"Looks like Troubell may get lucky before the running," Flower teased.

I explained to him what happened to the winner's dronehood when a queen's neither regions clamped down at the end. Flower crossed his legs, but his girlfriend Magnolia laughed uproariously.

WE MADE IT back to my office without incident, but almost had the running of the drones right there in front of Sylvia's desk. Vere was apparently leaking pheromones, and the three drones moved toward us as soon as they smelt her. By this point, she was walking. When she saw their reaction, she couldn't stop grinning, assumed a sultry pose, and stroked her antennae.

I stepped in front of her, which anyone who has ever seen the running of the drones knew was a dangerous place to be. Luckily, my Calamari secretary slid out from behind her desk, and ushered the three drones out of the office quite firmly using her purple tentacles.

"Troubell, how about you and me go into that room by ourselves?" Vere's voice sounded like buzzing, which I'm guessing would be seductive to a drone.

"Sorry, Vere. I'm just here to watch you," I said.

"Maybe if you watch long enough, you'll want to join in," Vere said.

"Samuel, you seem nervous around an interested humanoid female," Sylvia sang through her undulating tentacles. "That seems very unusual for you. Why is that?"

I relayed how the queens finished off their romantic encounters, and Sylvia's tentacles tittered.

"I knew it had to be something bad for you to be skittish."

"No need to be skittish around me. I will make you feel *good*," Vere buzzed, rubbing my chest with her hands.

I jumped back like she was on fire. "The thing is, I like to repeat that feeling as often as possible. I don't think your way would work out great for me."

"I bet I can change your mind." Vere's hands took a southward plunge.

I grabbed a waiting room chair and held it between us. "I think I'm going to go sit guard in the hall."

"I'll join you," Vere said, but Sylvia reached out a purple tentacle and pulled her back.

"No, my dear. You have a duty to your people. And if you did that to Samuel, I would never hear the end of his whining. You will stay in here with me."

Vere's face squished together, which I took as her version of a pout. I left for the hall while the getting was good.

IT WAS A long night, but we got Vere to the race on time, where she was placed into a barred cage to make sure none of the drones got to her ahead of time. The drones moved restlessly behind the starting rope, knowing that anyone who crossed early would be stunned by the race commission officials, and left unable to participate. I stood on the sidelines and waved to Thur, Lefty, and Stubby.

"Good luck, guys."

"We still don't know what that would be, to win or to lose," Thur said.

I didn't know either.

Barron Nezzel pulled back the latch on the cage and nodded to Vere. The new queen blasted the drones with pheromones that sprayed out of her posterior.

Vere took off running. It was obvious that the drones were struggling not to follow. Nezzel got into the cage and closed the barred door behind him.

Projecting for the crowds, he yelled, "Release the virgins!"

The rope was dropped, and the drones took off like horny naked bats out of hell.

The reason Nezzel got in the cage was a simple one. Once those pheromones hit the drones and they started moving, they weren't stopping for anything until one of them got to Vere. That was the second part of the running of the drones—audience participation.

Once the queen passed, young bucks and buckettes got in front of the drones and sprinted for all they were worth. Reminded me of the running of the bulls in Pamplona back home. Only here it was a little safer. The drones' antenna were too short for goring, but there was still the potential for lots of trampling.

For those not so physically inclined, there was a second option— riding. Not on a drone of course, but animals like the gatwi or a racer that was the local version of an ATV.

The only catch was that they had to start after the drones did, and see if they could cut down a side street to get in front of them, then make it to the end of the course or an escape exit without being knocked down and trampled.

Ever since I was a federal agent on Earth, I make sure to scan any crowd I'm in. Being a Guardsman had only increased my skills and paranoia. One of the racer riders was a purple G'morran in a gray robe.

Looked like Yaton hadn't given up yet. I ran out into the racer crowd, knocked an eight-foot-tall Jante from her vehicle, and joined the chase myself. I know it was mean of me to pick on someone so much taller, and therefore weaker, than myself, but I had to do what I had to do.

I passed a few racers. One thing that was working in my favor was I was sober, unlike many of the other racers. Another was they were all trying to get in front of the drones by using the crossover street. I was just trying to catch Yaton.

Since the route was preplanned, everyone knew where the queen and the drones were heading. It was against the rules for racers to not follow the marked route. The mobs were cheering as the racers sped to get in front of the drones.

Yaton wasn't having any of that, and broke through a barricade to take a shortcut that would put him farther ahead of the racing queen. The crowd booed him. I veered off after him to even louder jeers.

Turns out, I had another advantage. I had commandeered a faster vehicle than the one Yaton was riding, so I was gradually closing the distance.

Even better—with the hood of his robe up, Yaton hadn't noticed I was behind him yet. The only question was: would I get to him before he got to the queen? I still wasn't sure if he was originally just going to hold Vere until after the race or kill her, although my money was on the latter. It seemed the best way for a fanatic to make sure his plan was going to work.

Now he had no choice but to kill the queen. He could run her down with his racer, which would likely injure her. And I had no idea what weapons might be hiding under his robe for him to finish her off with.

I was about a hundred feet behind and closing when the crowd at the end of the street roared. The queen must have turned the corner at the far end of the block.

There wasn't much time to stop Yaton before he got to Vere. I put the business end of my walking stick over the front of what passed for steering-bars, and took aim. My blaster was high-quality, but to keep it hidden from scans, it could only store enough energy for one shot. I had to make it count. I waited as long as I could to close the distance, then fired. I was aiming for his back, but shooting from a moving vehicle is not an easy task. I missed his back, but still managed to take out a rear tire. The racer wobbled, then flipped, throwing Yaton forward so he landed on his stomach and arms. The fanatic looked back to see me racing toward him, so he got up and ran.

The crowd of spectators at the edge of the street were packed too tightly to drive through, so I stopped and went on foot. Yaton was already pushing his way through the race fans, so I followed.

Some of the folks here had been waiting out since yesterday for their spots, and weren't taking kindly to us budging in front of them. I had to block various body parts thrown in my direction.

Yaton was shorter than me, and resorted to crawling. The G'morran made it through the crowd first. When I got to the end, there were a couple of Czarrians—four-armed, wolf-like humanoids—between me and the street. I shoved between them. Yes, that could be dangerous, since they are a race of warriors, but these two weren't. Czarrian warriors sliced off their own tails after their first battle. This couple's tails were intact.

Vere was barely half a block away when Yaton stepped to the middle of the street and waited for the racing queen. He subtly pulled a machete-sized knife from underneath his robe and slipped it in his sleeve, making sure to turn so I could see it. I guess he thought that would be enough to scare me off, because he turned his full attention to the approaching Vere. Thus, my tackle from behind caught him by surprise. We went down in a mass of flailing arms and legs as I struggled to pin his arms. Yaton used his rear leg to kick me back about five feet.

The purple fanatic rose to all three of his legs, and held the blade in front of him so it was pointed at me.

"Infidel! You're interfering with the holy work of G'morra! Stopping this sinful public display of procreation will not only be a public service to all of Liberty, but will ruin Nezzel, traitor to his people."

I didn't think Yaton would be interested in hearing that Nezzel had diversified, and this wouldn't ruin him. I doubt he'd believe me or care. Fanatics and logic are rarely seen hanging out together.

Yaton lunged at me, slicing with much enthusiasm and little skill. I parried his thrusts with my walking stick, and brought my foot up into his groin. Yaton doubled over in pain, and I swung the walking stick, managing to knock the knife from his hand to the pavement just as the queen ran by.

Vere actually waved and blew me a kiss.

From the ground, Yaton raised his arms to the heavens and screamed, "No!" as if everything in his world had been taken away from him. I grabbed the downed blade, then ran toward the wall of spectators. Since

I had the knife, Yaton seemed confused that I'd fled instead of coming to finish him.

Which is when he heard the pounding footsteps of the herd of drones headed his way. Yaton stood and tried to follow after me, but it was too little too late. The drones and some of the recreational runners trampled him. Thur, Lefty, and Stubby had seen my struggle with him, and purposely veered so they could stomp him extra good. The racers hadn't managed to get in front of most of the drones, but were nice enough not to run him over.

Once all the drones all went by, I grabbed a Guardsman, identified myself, then explained what had happened.

Yaton was arrested. The G'morra survived, but had more than half the bones in his body broken. I took my commandeered racer and drove to the block where the new hive building would be. I was there in time to see the big finish. It turned out Stubby was the fastest drone, and got to Vere first. It didn't take long for them to get down to business. I couldn't tell whose screams were louder or happier.

I will say this for the Wornets: it was no wham, bam, thank you, ma'am. They weren't done for hours and then—to Nezzel's surprise— went into the building that Q had arranged for them to own, in order to prepare for the birth of their next generation.

Thur and Lefty spotted me and came over.

"Thank… you," Lefty said.

"You kept our queen safe, and we are in your debt," Thur said. "We will have the remaining comb delivered to your office."

"Appreciate it. So, are you guys happy or sad you lost?"

"Both," Lefty said.

"Is there any rule that says you can't mate with someone other than the queen? Maybe even someone whose nether regions won't clamp onto your dronehood and pull it off?"

Lefty and Thur looked at each other.

"Do… not… know."

"It's something we've never thought to ask," Thur said.

"I think it's high time we brought you gents down to the Empirical House to find out. My treat."

"Can… we… run… there… to… be… ready?" Lefty asked with a leer. I guess that was the drones' version of foreplay.

I nodded in a circle. "Sure. Knock yourselves out."

Dangerous Virgins
David Gerrold

THERE ARE TALES we don't tell, not in public, and rarely in private. And only to people we trust not to repeat them.

Not because these tales are especially good—and not because they're particularly salacious, either. It's because they're just too dumb to be believable.

That's the difference between truth and fiction. Fiction has to make sense. This one doesn't.

I'll start with Milo Twisling. That's not his real name. Milo isn't with us anymore, he's gone to that great convention in the sky—or that other one below, the larger one—so it wouldn't matter if I told you his real name was Goodman Hallmouth or Donald Tinyhands or John Thomas Little. It's just that there are other people involved, and they're still alive, and I don't want to embarrass them unnecessarily.

Milo worked for a porn firm. No, he didn't work in front of the camera. Not even for any of those companies that produced freak porn. He didn't work behind the camera either. He wasn't even a fluffer. One particularly well-endowed male star was known to have said, "I'd rather cut it off and feed it to the dog than let Milo get a liplock on these royal jewels."

No. Milo worked in a dingy little cubbyhole stuck so far back in the files that the air conditioning didn't reach. Milo's job was packaging. Mostly, he packed Betamax tapes and VHS tapes. Later, he packaged DVDs, at least until amateur night on the internet put most of the porn producers out of business.

But as part of his job, Milo was responsible for titles. If you had frequented any big porn store in the latter decades of the 20th Century, you would have seen titles like *You've Got Male, Shaving Ryan's Privates, E.T.: The Extra Testicle, Oklahomo!, Fill Bill, Sorest Rump, Schindler's Lust, Saturday Night Beaver, A Clockwork Orgy, I Love Juicy, My Bare Lady, Driving Miss Daisy Crazy, The Magnificent Seven Inches, Big*

Trouble in Little Vagina, *Pulp Friction*, *Done in 60 Seconds*, and *Free Willy*. None of those were the work of Milo, but they were the standard of greatness he aspired to.

No. Milo's triumph, if you could call it a triumph (and then only by redefining the word beyond the bounds of all rationality), nevertheless, his triumph, such as it was, was his creation of a website of erotic science fiction which he oh-so-cleverly called *Dangerous Virgins*, narrowly avoiding a lawsuit only because no one was courageous enough to show it to the copyright holder of a book series with a somewhat similar title.

Some of the titles Milo authored were *Star Trick*, *Land of the Lust*, *The Man Who Fondled Himself*, *When Harlot Was Won*, *Humping Off the Planet*, *A Master for Me*, *A Gay for Glam Nation*, *A Rape for Revenge*, and *The Trouble with Nipples*.

It turned out that Milo actually had a small talent for erotic fiction. It was a very small talent, but it was large enough to attract enough of a following that he was actually asked for his autograph by three people at an Adult Entertainment Convention in Los Angeles.

Emboldened, he went on to write *Brave Nude World*, *The Handmaid's Tail*, *Stranger with a Strange Gland*, *Time for Enough Love*, *I Sex-Robot*, *Rendezvous with Mama*, *Whore Goes There?*, *The Lust World*, *The Breast from 20,000 Fathoms*, *Whore of the Worlds*, *The Miserable Lay*, *The Man Who Screwed Too Much*, *Been Her*, *A Sale of Two Titties*, *Yankee Doodle's Dandy*, *On Golden Blonde*, *Beast of Eden*, and *The Son Also Rises*.

He skipped *Moby's Dick*. It was too obvious.

When amateur internet porn finally devoured Milo's employer, Pink Taco Videos, his erstwhile employer, feeling that there was no more money to be extracted from Milo's labors, in an act of uncharacteristic generosity (he really didn't give a shit, he'd lost everything to his ex-wife anyway), released the publication rights to Milo, who promptly transferred all of his titles to Amazon's Kindle Unlimited Adult Library, and soon found himself earning three times as much money in royalties every month. Okay, three times what he was previously earning at Pink Taco wasn't all that much, but it was still three times as much. For Milo, it was the difference between eating canned cat food and real tuna. Even dolphin-safe tuna.

So Milo had a career. Sort of. And like all writers, he imagined success was inevitable. All he had to do was build up a fan base. He decided to expand.

Somewhere between *Whoreson Gets a Clue* and *The Cat in the Thong*, he stepped on a cultural landmine. It arrived as a subpoena. A lawsuit. Milo responded by going public, providing the estate the one thing they didn't want—publicity for how inept their lawyers were, that they were unable to recognize that no one is immune to parody, pastiche, homage, or satire.

None of that is especially relevant: the lawsuit died without resolution when the lawyers were fired, but the publicity it gained earned Milo the undying wrath of Randy Fanborg—not his real name, but when he reads this, he'll know who I'm talking about.

Randy was a terminal Trekkie—or Trekker. (Some of these fanborgs take themselves far too seriously.) He had sewn his own command-level costume—not very well. Omar the Tentmaker would have done a better job. His gold velour looked like an unwashed, rumpled bedspread, even worse when Randy put it on. The high point of Randy Fanborg's life was having a photograph taken of him sitting in an inflatable replica of Captain Kirk's Command Chair in a shabby recreation of the bridge set at a local Trek convention. It was the inflatable chair installed in front of a poorly printed backdrop portraying the real bridge of the *Enterprise*. But, it was the high point of Randy Fanborg's life, because for just that fleeting moment, he got to pretend he was Captain Kirk—a swaggering, overbearing, tin-plated dictator with delusions of godhood.

None of this would have been important to this particular narrative, except that Randy Fanborg was an aspiring wannabe troll. He didn't live under a bridge, and he didn't eat goats, but he did still live in his mother's basement, and he mostly survived on Pepsi and the five-dollar pizza special from Little Caesar's. Occasionally, he celebrated Taco Tuesday with a trip to El Pollo Loco.

Oh, and he also had a very small penis. So small, in fact, that when he was born, the doctor assumed he was a girl. Randy Fanborg had indeed been raised as female, until he was fourteen and his voice changed. He failed to menstruate and started developing a mustache instead. After a DNA test revealed him to have XY chromosomes, an endocrinologist prescribed massive doses of testosterone. It worked only to the extent that Randy Fanborg's penis was no longer inverted.

Randy Fanborg's computer was a hand-built assemblage of parts scavenged from the local computer repair shop that had finally bellied up, and a few replacement parts he'd scrounged from eBay. He spent at least fourteen hours a day staring into an HD monitor he'd picked up at a local gaming tournament when no one was looking.

He had a complete collection of every sci-fi movie and TV show that had ever been uploaded to The Pirate Bay. If he wasn't watching the umpteenth repeat of an otherwise forgotten episode, if he wasn't playing the online game, he was checking the various websites and discussion forums where he had fairly earned a reputation as, "Oh, that guy."

Yes. *That* Randy Fanborg.

It didn't matter how much anyone might have liked a particular episode or film, Randy Fanborg was right there to explain why it was not a good episode, not a good film, and why the credentials of everyone involved were suspect. He disdained fan-theories and head canon. He knew better.

Randy Fanborg was The Expert on Canon, diligently pointing out every single contradiction in every episode and film. He was The Expert on Trivia, quickly annotating every jot and tittle of every script he had memorized—which was all of them. Even "Spock's Brain" and "The Alternative Factor." He was The Ultimate Expert.

But Randy Fanborg reserved his greatest enmity for those who wrote poems, parodies, filk songs, and satires of The Mythology of which he'd appointed himself guardian. Randy Fanborg only needed ruby slippers, a white robe, a pointy hat, and a scepter to be recognized as The Holy Protector Of All That's Sacred In The Realm.

So of course, he focused his most aggressive attacks on those who wrote space-porn. Yes, he'd been annoyed by *A Private Little Whore*, *Charlie-SeX*, *The Naked Slime*, *What Big Girls Are Made Of*, *The Groom's Gay Machine*, and *Menage-A-Ree!* But it was *Titty on the Edge of Forever* that finally pushed him over the edge.

In that moment, he became Milo Twisling's mortal enemy.

His first act of cyber-revenge was to visit Amazon and leave a one-star review for every story that Milo had published. "This is crap. Don't buy it. This desecrates a sacred cultural landmark. And the author isn't very nice either." That last sentence was fictitious. Randy Fanborg had never met Milo Twisling, but in his infinite wisdom as a self-appointed online reader of minds and personalities, plus his experience accidentally reading a book on Transactional Analysis, Randy felt he was qualified to make the assertion.

(He hadn't intended to read the book on Transactional Analysis, and he hadn't read much past chapter three, but it was a long bus ride, and he'd finished the paperback novel he'd brought with him. He'd found the book on the floor of the bus where it had fallen out of a bored student's laundry bag. The book smelled of unwashed underwear, something that Randy Fanborg did not notice, it already being a strong component of his own personal odor.)

Anyway...

When Randy Fanborg saw that Milo had not crept off into the woodwork in shame, he decided that stronger measures were necessary. It turned out that Milo Twisling not only had a website, a Facebook page, and a Patreon account, he also had a fan club. Randy Fanborg bit his lip, gritted his teeth, sprained his jaw, and joined.

For a long while—several hours, in fact—Randy did nothing at all He was too bitter. Reading through the slavering fannish adulations of Milo's exuberant readers did nothing to improve his mood at all.

In Milo's favor, his several years of experience crafting fictitious sexual adventures had given him enough experience to distinguish the difference between erotica and porn. Erotica uses euphemisms. While some people believed that Milo Twisling was a skilled practitioner, in truth he was cheating. He had written a simple database program for the creation of euphemisms. It was very much like a game of sexual Mad-Libs™.

The basic sentence was this: "He [verbed] her [adjective] [noun] with his [adjective] [noun]."

Milo would then choose a verb from column A, an adjective from column B, a noun from column C, an adjective from column D, and a final noun from column E.

VERB	ADJECTIVE	NOUN	ADJECTIVE	NOUN
conquered	delicious	abyss	burning	adversary
delighted	delightful	canyon	engorged	advocate
(explored)	dripping	cave	enthusiastic	campaigner
filled	eager	chasm	fleshy	champion
impaled	enthusiastic	gulf	furious	charger
invaded	fresh	honey-pot	hard	crusader
overwhelmed	hot	magic	helmeted	delightful
pushed into	intended	mystery	hot	eagerness
thrust	(inviting)	opening	impatient	enthusiasm

Actually, he didn't choose anything at all. He'd written his database program to randomly create combinations and spit them out by the page-load. The more words he added to each column, the more variations his program would create. Sometimes he varied the sentence structure, but the basic idea remained the same.

Over time, Milo developed other simple programs for creating names of characters, situations, and settings. The stories practically wrote themselves.

Thus did Strong William invade the delightful mystery of Sweet Mary with his upstanding harpoon. And Brave Martin delighted Miss Marlena with his magnificent champion. And of course, Curious George impaled Little Joe with his impatient gladiator. Sometimes it happened in The Victorian Caves. Other times, the scene of sequestration was The Grotesque Cemetery. Once, the setting was The Terrifying Tower.

And this is how Milo Twisling became well-known as an erotic stylist. All he needed was a title, and the rest was easy: *Dr. Yes, From Russia with Lust, Boldfinger, Thunder Balls, You Only Love Twice.* And James Blond thrust his hot eagerness into her open mystery.

Hey—it sold. And it sold well enough for Milo Twisling to upgrade his shopping from the dollar store to K-Mart.

And while fame in the world of erotica is as fleeting as a one-night stand in West Hollywood, Milo had finally earned one of his fifteen minutes. He was invited to be an Author Guest of Honor at the West Coast's most prestigious Adult Entertainment Gathering: The Los Angeles SexCon, held just south of downtown at the Los Angeles Convention Center, 720,000 square feet of convention space, filled with prostheses of all kinds—dildos, silicone vaginas, fleshlights (motorized and self-propelled), sex-dolls, sex-bots, a variety of costumes, lingerie, leather, whips, chains, handcuffs, massagers, vibrators, books and magazines, DVDs and Blu-rays, virtual reality goggles and software (several with bluetooth links to motorized sex-toys), and a variety of booth-babes, porn stars, and various young men and women whose affections were easily negotiable.

Milo, however, was not one of the primary attractions. The Guest of Honor at such an event was primarily a token speaker at a token banquet, a convenient pretense that the convention was actually about something. Nevertheless, the word "honor" was so alien to Milo Twisling's personal experience that he felt he had no choice but to participate. So, he packed his suitcase, loaded his yellow '72 Pinto, and prepared for his long drive to validation.

He intended to speak at some length about how the continuing success of his website, *Dangerous Virgins*, served a specific health need for those whose sexual outlets were of a solitary nature. He was, if you will pardon the immodesty, performing a necessary service. The *Dangerous Virgins* website stroked the imaginations of those who, for lack of a partner, were reduced to stroking themselves.

Upcoming works would include *Sgt. Pepper's Lonely Hearts Club Blonde, Tales of Mystery and Emasculation, The Rocky Whores' Picture Show, A Knight at the Opera, A Gay at the Races, Lest it Bleed, Mommy!, Singin' in the Pain, A Funky Thing Happened on the Way to the Forum,* and his magnum opus, a seven-book trilogy to be called *The Civil Whore.* (A thematic sequel to *Fanny Hell.*)

All of these were already written and scheduled for publication. It was Milo Twisling's goal to have *Dangerous Virgins* become the premiere outlet for those who had no other outlet.

The avalanche of publicity given to Milo Twisling's upcoming appearance in Los Angeles—most of it generated by Milo Twisling—served primarily to attract the ugly attention of Randy Fanborg. By now, Randy Fanborg's hatred of Milo Twisling had evolved into a mortal vendetta that could only be satisfied by a conclusion of Sicilian magnitude.

Unfortunately, Randy Fanborg was neither Silician nor anything else. Randy Fanborg was one cheek shy of being half-assed. There were no candy canes on his Christmas tree. He was not the sharpest cheese in the fridge. To say that Randy Fanborg was stupid would have been a compliment. He approached stupidity only from the far side.

But Randy Fanborg was coherent enough to write a letter. Coherent enough to put a stamp on the envelope. Coherent enough to find a Post Office. And send that letter. To the Los Angeles Police Department—the most feared collection of men (and women) in black since Tommy Lee Jones and Will Smith.

In his letter, Randy Fanborg warned of a devious, depraved, dangerous degenerate who intended to commit dreadful deeds upon the unsuspecting citizens of legendary Metropolis. Randy Fanborg imagined himself a stylist. He also imagined himself the chosen one, and often checked the front porch to see if an owl had arrived from Hogwarts.

But the LAPD is not known for its sense of humor. Or anything else, for that matter. Those red lights in your rear-view mirror almost always signify an unhealthy dent in your gross personal product. Running a city is expensive. The Department of "If you see something, say something," took Randy Fanborg's letter seriously. Quietly, very quietly, an all-points bulletin was issued for any yellow '72 Pinto crossing the border into the state on either I-40 or I-10 or I-15—which is why somewhere south of Barstow, Milo Twisling was pulled over by no fewer than seven flashing, screaming police cruisers. His battered Pinto was immediately surrounded by fourteen armed officers, all pointing their weapons at him. A stern voice on a bullhorn advised him to put his empty hands out the window, then slowly exit the vehicle. Meanwhile, traffic backed up on the I-15 for seventeen miles in both directions, as the onlookers slowed to see what the excitement was about, most of them hoping to see poor Milo shot down like the rabid dog in *To Kill a Mockingbird*. (Milo had not yet figured out a suitable title for that retelling.)

To make a short story even shorter, Milo spent the weekend in the Barstow jail. Because it was Labor Day Weekend, he would not see a judge until late Tuesday afternoon, by which time SexCon would have evaporated into the haze, much like Brigadoon. Milo Twisling wouldn't just be known as the no-show Guest of Honor—he'd be the GoH who stood them up. The backlash was considerable—including a wildcat boycott of *Dangerous Virgins.*

Randy Fanborg would have wet his shorts in glee had he known—had he not accidentally electrocuted himself when he spilled a Pepsi into the second-hand keyboard he had partially dismantled for refurbishing, producing a lot more sparks in his mother's basement than were normally seen on the bridge of the starship *Enterprise,* even after the impact of a Klingon photon torpedo on its rapidly deteriorating starboard shields. ("Oy, Keptin, I kent giff you no more power. The engines are all farpotshket." In Milo's version, *Star Trick,* the chief engineer was Morris, who could repair the engines without all the Scottish kvetching. Plus, he could get replacement parts from Cousin Hermie a lot faster and cheaper than going through those Starfleet momsers.) Never mind that. Randy Fanborg died as he had lived, with one hand on the mouse and the other in his underwear. The mouse was bigger.

Disgraced in the eyes of his colleagues, Milo Twisling had to give up writing porn. Instead, he turned his attentions to science fiction and fantasy, where he became far more successful as the author of—

Never mind. That's a whole other career, and that story will not be repeated here. Milo Twisling has already had one career destroyed by a fanborg. In the current climate of hyper-sensitivity, with various outrage committees roaming the public landscape, nobody, least of all Milo Twisling, wants to be the subject of another internet pile-on.

And what of his unpublished works in the *The Lost Dangerous Virgins* series? They remain unpublished, mere strings of ones and zeroes on his hard drive. His last few desperate fans insisted that they deserved to read what was promised to be his greatest work of all, *Atlas Fugged*—they even created a hashtag.

But no, Milo had left that world behind, and this one as well. (That's the subject of another peripatetic tale for another time. But as his last act, instead of responding to the frenzied demands of his readers, he used their hashtag as the title of an anthology. *#ReleaseTheVirgins.*

Afterword
Thomas Nackid, cover artist

STRANGE THINGS HAPPEN in hotel bars during science fiction conventions. I am not the first to make this observation, and hopefully I will not be the last. I think it is safe to say that more than a few novels, short stories, anthologies, comic books, and paintings have gotten their start in these incubators of creativity and weirdness. The book you hold before you is the product of one such bar at one such science fiction convention.

If there is such a thing as a bucket list item you never knew you wanted until you actually checked it off, then I think unwittingly inspiring a science fiction anthology would count as one for me. (Bonus points if that anthology contains erotica and stories by the likes of David Gerrold and Allen Steele, among others!) Unfortunately, I have to come clean, and admit here and now that this anthology is based on a lie. Well, a mistake, at any rate.

When Hildy Silverman (whose work you can find in these pages) commented on an annoying fruit fly it resulted—in a very round-about way—in me telling the group about a time in college when I was taking a genetics class and the class had to get up in the middle of the night to "release the virgins" from our fruit fly cultures. Since we all had to be up, we decided to turn it into a party. At this point, any competent biologist will realize I misspoke. We actually had to release the mature flies who may have already mated, so the newly pupated virgins left behind could be mated with other pure strains. Ah well.

How did I make such an egregious error? Maybe I was distracted by fellowship and heady conversation. Maybe I experienced a bit of social awkwardness (something not unknown among science fiction fans!). It certainly had nothing to do with growing number of empty gin-and-tonic glasses in my general vicinity. In any case, my faux pas is your gain. This error gives your fearless editor and intrepid publisher the perfect excuse for a follow up anthology! Retain the Virgins? Release the Non-virgins? I'll leave the details up to them.

About the Authors

Matt Bechtel was born just south of Detroit, Michigan (cursing him a Lions fan), into a mostly Irish family of dreamers and writers, as opposed to the pharmaceutical or construction giants that share his surname. As such, he has spent most of his years making questionable life decisions and enjoying the results. Mentored by its late founder Bob Booth, he serves on the Executive Committee of the Northeastern Writers' Convention (a.k.a. Camp Necon). His first collection, *Monochromes and Other Stories*, was published by Haverhill House Publishing in 2017, and he has also sold stories to anthologies published by PS Publishing, ChiZine Publishing, the New England Horror Writers, and Zsenon Publishing. He currently lives in Providence, Rhode Island.

Keith R.A. DeCandido has written five novels and a mess of other short stories featuring Lieutenants Danthres Tresyllione and Torin ban Wyvald, including *Dragon Precinct, Unicorn Precinct, Goblin Precinct, Gryphon Precinct, Tales from Dragon Precinct*, and the recently released *Mermaid Precinct*, with *Phoenix Precinct, Manticore Precinct*, and *More Tales from Dragon Precinct* forthcoming. Beyond the Cliff's End Castle Guard, he's also written fifty-plus novels, a hundred short stories, and a ton of comics and nonfiction in both licensed universes (most recently *Alien: Isolation*, the *Marvel's Tales of Asgard* trilogy, and fiction in the world of the game *Summoner's War*) and milieus of his own creation (the *Super City Cops* novellas, short stories featuring Shirley Holmes & Jack Watson and Cassie Zukav, weirdness magnet, and a new urban fantasy series that started with *A Furnace Sealed*). He also writes about pop culture for Tor.com, is a third-degree black belt in karate, is a professional percussionist, and edits fiction on a freelance basis. Find out less at his cheerfully retro web site at *www.DeCandido.net*.

Ten-time Hugo and Nebula award nominee **David Gerrold** is also a recipient of the Skylark Award for Excellence in Imaginative Fiction, the

Bram Stoker Award for Superior Achievement in Horror, and the Forrest J. Ackerman lifetime achievement award. He was the Guest of Honor at the 2015 World Science Fiction Convention. Gerrold's prolific output includes teleplays, film scripts, stage plays, comic books, more than fifty novels and anthologies, and hundreds of articles, columns, and short stories. He has worked on a dozen different TV series, including *Star Trek*, *Land of the Lost*, *Twilight Zone*, *Star Trek: The Next Generation*, *Babylon 5*, and *Sliders*. He is the author of *Star Trek*'s most popular episode "The Trouble with Tribbles." His most famous novel is *The Man Who Folded Himself.* His semi-autobiographical tale of his son's adoption, *The Martian Child*, won both the Hugo and the Nebula awards, and was the basis for the 2007 movie starring John Cusack and Amanda Peet.

Daniel M. Kimmel is the 2018 recipient of the Skylark Award, given by the New England Science Fiction Association. He was a finalist for a Hugo Award for *Jar Jar Binks Must Die… and other Observations about Science Fiction Movies*, and for the Compton Crook Award for best first novel for *Shh! It's a Secret: a novel about Aliens, Hollywood, and the Bartender's Guide.* In addition to short stories, he is the author of *Time on My Hands: My Misadventures in Time Travel* and the forthcoming *Father of the Bride of Frankenstein.*

Sharon Lee is most often seen writing as half of the blockbuster team of Sharon Lee and Steve Miller, authors of the long-running Liaden Universe® space opera series, as well as other works. Occasionally, however, she sneaks off and writes something on her own, such as the Carousel Trilogy: *Carousel Tides*, *Carousel Sun*, and *Carousel Seas*. You can keep up with Sharon, Lee-and-Miller, and their cats at *www.sharonleewriter.com*.

Shariann Lewitt has been telling stories since she was a little girl. When she discovered that calling them "fiction" meant you could be a writer and not a liar, she knew she had found her calling. She has been a speculative fiction writer ever since. The author of almost twenty novels under five different names, and something between forty and fifty stories, she continues to branch out and explore different forms of the genre.

Among her many short stories, "Fieldwork," originally published in *To Shape the Dark*, edited by Athena Andreadis and published by Gleam Books, was chosen by Gardner Dozois for his 35th Best Science Fiction of the Year anthology published by Tor.

Gordon Linzner is the founder and former publisher of *Space and Time* magazine, and a lifetime member of SFWA. His novels *The Oni*, *The Troupe*, and *The Spy Who Drank Blood* are available from Crossroads Press. Dozens of his short stories have appeared in *The Magazine of Fantasy and Science Fiction*, *Rod Serling's Twilight Zone Magazine*, *Eerie Country*, *Tales by Moonlight*, *Swords Against Darkness*, *100 Wicked Little Witch Stories*, *Bruce Coville's UFOs*, *Museum of Horrors*, *Altered States of the Union*, and *Baker Street Irregulars*, among other magazines and anthologies.

Gail Z. Martin writes urban fantasy, epic fantasy, and steampunk for Solaris Books, Orbit Books, Falstaff Books, SOL Publishing, and Darkwind Press. Urban fantasy series include *Deadly Curiosities* and the *Night Vigil* (*Sons of Darkness*). Epic fantasy series include *Darkhurst*, the *Chronicles of the Necromancer*, the *Fallen Kings Cycle*, the *Ascendant Kingdoms Saga*, and the *Assassins of Landria*. Newest titles include *Tangled Web*, *Vengeance*, *The Dark Road*, and *Assassin's Honor*. As Morgan Brice, she writes urban fantasy MM paranormal romance. Books include *Witchbane* and *Badlands*.

Liaden Universe® coauthor **Steve Miller** writes with Sharon Lee, sharing author Guest of Honor with her at SF cons across North America. First writing for *Amazing* in the late 1970s, Steve is an ebook pioneer and chapbook proponent who operated SRM Publisher for seventeen years. Steve's work with Sharon has been recognized multiple times, including Skylark, Prism, and Reader's Choice Awards. "Command Decision" is the first solo author Liaden story.

Jody Lynn Nye lists her main career activity as "spoiling cats." She lives northwest of Chicago with one of the above and her husband, author and packager Bill Fawcett. She has written over forty-five books, including *The Ship Who Won* with Anne McCaffrey, eight books with

Robert Asprin, a humorous anthology about mothers, *Don't Forget Your Spacesuit, Dear!*, and over 160 short stories. Her latest books are *Rhythm of the Imperium* (Baen Books), *Moon Beam* (with Travis S. Taylor, Baen) and *Myth-Fits* (Ace). Jody also reviews fiction for *Galaxy's Edge* magazine, and teaches the intensive writers' workshop at DragonCon. Her web page is *www.jodynye.net*.

Beth W. Patterson was a full-time musician for over two decades before diving into the world of writing, a process she describes as "fleeing the circus to join the zoo." She is the author of the books *Mongrels and Misfits, The Wild Harmonic*, and a contributing writer to twenty anthologies.

Patterson has performed in eighteen countries across the Americas, Europe, Oceania, and Asia. Her playing appears on over 160 albums, soundtracks, videos, commercials, and voice-overs (including seven solo albums of her own). More than a hundred of her compositions and co-writes have been released. She studied ethnomusicology at University College, Cork, in Ireland, and holds a Bachelor's degree in Music Therapy from Loyola University New Orleans.

Beth has occasionally worn other hats as a body paint model, film extra, minor role actor, recording studio partner, record label owner, producer, and visual artist. She is a lover of exquisitely stupid movies and a shameless fangirl of the band Rush. You can find her at *www.bethpattersonmusic.com*.

Alex Shvartsman is a writer, translator, and anthologist from Brooklyn, New York. Over 100 of his short stories have appeared in *Nature, Analog, Strange Horizons, InterGalactic Medicine Show*, and many other magazines and anthologies. He won the 2014 WSFA Small Press Award for Short Fiction, and was a two-time finalist for the Canopus Award for Excellence in Interstellar Fiction (2015 and 2017). He is the editor of the *Unidentified Funny Objects* annual anthology series of humorous SF/F. His latest collection, *The Golem of Deneb Seven and Other Stories*, was published in 2018. His website is *www.alexshvartsman.com*.

Hildy Silverman is the publisher of *Space and Time*, a nearly five-decade old magazine of fantasy, horror, and science fiction. She is also the author of several works of short fiction, in several anthologies, including *Baker Street Irregulars*, *New Blood*, *Witch Way to the Mall?*, *Fangs for the Mammaries*, *Apocalypse 13*, *With Great Power*, *Sha'Daa Facets*, and *Baker Street Irregulars*. In 2013, she was a finalist for the WSFA Small Press Award for her story, "The Six Million Dollar Mermaid" (*Mermaids 13*).

Allen M. Steele has published twenty-one novels and over one hundred short stories. His work has received numerous awards, including three Hugos and the Robert A. Heinlein Award, and has been translated worldwide. He is a former member of the Board of Advisors for the Space Frontier Foundation and the Board of Directors for the Science Fiction and Fantasy Writers of America. He also belongs to Sigma, a group of SF writers who frequently serve as unpaid consultants on matters regarding technology and security.

Cecilia Tan is an award-winning novelist who writes in many genres, often simultaneously. This story is set in the world of her Magic University books. Her next big project is an urban fantasy series for Tor Books based on sex magick, entitled The Vanished Chronicles. Her Instagram has many cat photos. Find her blog at *http://blog.ceciliatan.com*.

Patrick Thomas is the award-winning author of the beloved *Murphy's Lore* series and the darkly hilarious *Dear Cthulhu* advice empire. His almost forty books include *Fairy with a Gun*, *By Darkness Cursed*, *Lore & Dysorder*, *Dead to Rites*, *Startenders*, *As the Gears Turn*, and *Exile and Entrance*. His is the co-author of the *Mystic Investigators* series and the *Jack Gardner* mysteries. Patrick is the co-editor of *Camelot 13* (with John French), *New Blood* (with Diane Raetz), and *Hear Them Roar* (with CJ Henderson). His Soul for Hire story "Act of Contrition" has been made into a short film. He writes the *Undead Kid Diaries* and the *Babe B. Bear Mysteries* as Patrick T. Fibbs. Visit him online at *www.patthomas.net*.

Brian Trent's speculative fiction appears regularly in *Analog*, *Fantasy & Science Fiction*, *Orson Scott Card's Intergalactic Medicine Show*, *Galaxy's Edge*, *Escape Pod*, *Pseudopod*, *Daily Science Fiction*, and more.

His humorous Lovecraftian story was featured this year in *The Cackle of Cthulhu* from Baen Books, and his novel *Ten Thousand Thunders* has just been released. He lives in New England, and his website is *www.briantrent.com*.

Lawrence Watt-Evans is the author of more than fifty novels and over a hundred and fifty short stories, most of them fantasy, science fiction, or horror, published under at least three pseudonyms. His best-known works are probably the Hugo-winning short story "Why I Left Harry's All-Night Hamburgers," the *Legends of Ethshar* series, and the fantasy novel *Dragon Weather*. His webpage is *www.watt-evans.com*.

About the Editor

Michael A. Ventrella's humorous novels include *Bloodsuckers: A Vampire Runs for President*, *The Axes of Evil*, and *Big Stick*. He has edited the anthologies *Tales of Fortannis* and *Baker Street Irregulars* (with *New York Times* Bestselling Author Jonathan Maberry) and has had his own stories printed in many anthologies, including the *Heroes in Hell* series, *Rum and Runestones*, *Twisted Tails*, and *The Ministry of Peculiar Occurrences Archives*. His web page is *www.MichaelAVentrella.com*.

Kickstarter Supporters

Jonathan Adams
Jax Anders
Lorraine J. Anderson
anon
Anonymous
Anonymous
Anonymous
Anonymous
Cyn Armistead
Bruce Arnold
Samuel and Kit Aronoff
Htet Htet Aung
Tom B.
Sola Balisane
Stephen Ballentine
Jeff Barnes
Charles Barouch
Noah Bast
Thomas Bätzler
Dagmar Baumann
John Bennett
Melinda Berkman
Jenn Bills
Keith Bissett
Deborah Bock
A.J. Bohne
Aaron Bolton
Deb Boyken
Aviva Brandt
Michael A. Burstein
Cathy Caiazzo
Millie Calistri-Yeh
Helen Cameron

Steve Carey
Teresa Carrigan
Dana Carson
T. Chopee
Diana Clayton
Michele Clemente
Jamieson Cobleigh
Lars Colson
Tina & Byron Connell
Sarah Cornell
Cp3o
CR
Mike Crate
Jane Curry
Scott J. Dahlgren
Geoff Dash
Kammi Davis
Randee Dawn
Andy Dent
Carl Dershem
Steve Desmond
V. Hartman DiSanto
Chuck Diters
Tim DuBois
Greykell (werewulf!!) Dutton
Elbowman
elizabeth
Ed Ellis
Jim Emmons
Steven L. Erickson
Eryious
Lukas F.
Diana Fazzari

Mark Featherston
Jerrie the filkferengi
Carl Fink
Deborah Fishburn
Steven Fisk
Q Fortier
Q Fortier
Q Fortier
James B Franks
Fuchsi
Berney Fulcher
Nancy L. Fulton
Andy Funk
Donna Gaudet
June George
Rosanne Girton
Bruce Glassford
Cathy Green
Darrell Z. Grizzle
Carol J. Guess
Anne Guglik
R.J.H.
Jennifer Hancock
Wendy Happek
Pat Hayes
Sheryl R. Hayes
Morgan Hazelwood
Dena Heilik
HELIOsphere/NASF3
Mari Henman
Jenifer L Hicks
John Hicks
Angie Hogencamp
Doug Houseman
Laurie Strock Huddleston
Chris Huning
R. Hunter
Jeanne Hurley
Brent Johnson

Carol Jones
Michael M. Jones
Robin Jurkowski
Susan K
S M Kennedy
Amy Keyes
Geoffrey Kidd
William A. Kilmer
Josh King
K Kisner
D. Kleymeyer
Katie Knaus
Pat Knuth
Tanya Koenig
Linda Kolar
Karen Krah
Jeanne Kramer-Smyth
Leece and Rob
Leigh
Anya Levin
Elizabeth Lobdell
James Lucas
Margaret Lyman
Charisse Lyn
James Lynn
Edward MacGregor
William Martin
Amy Matosky
Debbie Matsuura
Hamish McAndrew McDougal McTavish
Josh Medin
Jeff Metzner
Elaine Morton
Mike Moscoe
Mike Mudgett
Philip Noguchi
Andrew O
Robert Parks
Lisa R Penfold

Dan Persons
eric priehs
David Queen
Scott Raun
Nobilis Reed
Aysha Rehm
Jerry and Cheri Reno
Melissa Rian
Robert
Roland Roberts
Suzanna Rosin
Chuck Rothman
David J. Rowe
Ed Ruffel
L. Runkle
Charlie Russel
S
Jennifer Sandvall
Sasha
Kate Savage
Lawrence M. Schoen
Jenn Scott
Andrea Senchy
Tory Shade
ShadowCub
Wendy Sheridan
Silverjo
Claire Sims
Mike Smith
Scott Smith
Joel Singer
Mary M. Spila
Dianne Stark
Curtis & Maryrita Steinhour
Craig "Stevo" Stephenson

Victor Stringer
Carren & Noel Strock
Victoria L Sullivan
sure
themadcanner
Elizabeth Thorne
Nancy M. Tice
Jörg Tremmel
Micci Trolio
Nathan Turner
Jordana U
Debora VanHeyningen
Russell Ventimeglia
vesta
Geoff Vogel
Sharan Volin
Alessandro Giuseppe A.A. Volta
Rep. Andrew John Volstead
President Fuckface VonClownstick
Captain Miles Naismith Vorkosigan
Elaine Walker
Patricia Washburn
Dick Washington
Zed_WEASEL
Saz Wells
David Wertman
John White
Michael & Paula Whitehouse
Sharon Wood
Mary Alice Wuerz
Marc Yergin
Anne Young
Zeke
Mike Zipser

FIC RELEASE
Release the virgins!

08/12/19

CPSIA information can be obtained
at www.ICGtesting.com
Printed in the USA
LVHW031723280719
625631LV00002B/355

9 781515 423843